Choose your victim: Your first murder is free

Debbie Prince

ISBN:1514359324
ISBN-13:9781514359327

Exodus 21:12-13 Anyone who strikes a man and kills him shall surely be put to death. However, if he does not do it intentionally, but God lets it happen, he is to flee to a place I will designate.

Don't stand idly by when you can save a life (Leviticus 19:16)

Exodus 20:13 - Thou shalt not kill

DEDICATION

To my boyfriend, John Morath Jr. who allowed me to spend hours writing while he kept life around me going. Were it not for him, I would be living in a tough shed instead of a chalet.

To my father, Leonard Prince, who managed to march to the beat of his own drummer but still be successful. Although his pulse no longer goes on, I am inspired by the tempo of his belief in me.

ACKNOWLEDGMENTS

I want to thank The Rainbow Writers Critique group for making the process of writing this novel a piece of cake. Their patience for my bad grammar and experimentation with all things literary is greatly appreciated. Without them, this book would just be lumpy batter.

I want to thank Inge-lise Goss for helping me format this book.

I want to thank Nancy Buford for her tireless persistence in preventing me from making catastrophic spelling and grammar errors.

I want to thank JoAnne Plog for using her wide scope of knowledge to turn my work into something of merit.

And last, but not least, I want to thank Ernie Walwen for not only the constructive criticism he gave to my work but the time he endured sitting with four women without becoming hardened, cold or unresponsive

CHAPTER ONE

The minute Frank saw Lynn through his apartment window, his knees buckled. Down he went, headfirst into his herbed chicken breast sandwich. This was to be his last meal. It had been so carefully and artfully prepared. Now, smeared across his forehead, the finely tuned herb dish was no longer important. What was important, was getting away from Lynn.

Frank hated the idea that stalker Lynn was running him from his home. He loved his apartment. It stood two miles from the Las Vegas Strip, on the nice west side of town, with a view of the Observation Wheel. At night, he could sit on his sofa and see the lights of the glam and glitz of Las Vegas Boulevard. A perfect lair to take a woman, but now threatened by Lynn, his relentless stalker.

But now all he could see out his window was the demonic woman. She stood by her beat-up eight year old Kia Soul, looking down at the ground through her stringy blonde hair.

He had to get out of there. Grabbing his trench coat, he ran to the bedroom, dropped to his knees, and crawled to the French doors. Bent and hunched, he pushed them open, not caring how undignified a position he was in, only that he kept himself hidden from her view.

Lynn was on his stairs, making her way up toward his third floor apartment.

Keeping low, he crawled out onto his balcony and watched her approach his front door. He turned his head toward the neighbor's balcony, ten feet away.

Old man Wright's steely gray eyes met his. "That's your plan, is it?" Roger Wright's gravelly voice carried across the short distance. He sucked in a long slow draw on his cigarette and shrugged. "If you don't take chances, you might as well not be alive."

Frank nodded. He assessed the distance between the two balconies and his chances of making the leap. At six-foot-five he had no lack of length. What he lacked in muscle, he made up for in sheer desperation. This would be easy, right?

Lynn banged on his door. The thin woman appeared frail but she packed a powerful knock.

Frank took one last look at the ugly leach and stepped up on the balcony wall. Hanging on to the side of the wall, he concentrated on his escape, praying that she wouldn't notice his large frame, flying bat-like into the night. He clung to the side of the wall, and slowly straightened his limbs until he stood, upright. Murmuring a short, swift prayer he pushed with all his strength. He had lift off, his open trench coat fluttering behind him. For a brief second, he felt the freedom of a bird.

Then, at that moment, Mrs. Wright, wearing nothing but a too-small, too see-through nightie, appeared at her husband's side. Eyes open, concentrating on his end goal, Frank had seen too much.

And *she* was the one who screamed.

Frank, in midflight, froze, his body suspended in midair for a millennium. Well, really just long enough so that he couldn't quite reach the Wright's balcony with his feet. Panicking, he flexed forward and caught the edge of their wall with his fingertips. His body slammed into the side of the balcony. His fingers dug into the top of the wall.

"Oh dear," Mrs. Wright warbled hysterically, her arthritic digits fluttering helplessly in the night air. "Roger," she screamed, then hid her face in her husband's chest.

Dangling three stories above the ground, Frank knew the old man wouldn't have the strength to pull him up. And then, like a God-given gift, the balcony door just beneath him slid open.

"Fwank!" a childish man's voice called up in confusion and terror.

"Henry!" Frank yelled back, never so happy to hear the large man's voice as he was at that moment.

Henry was all muscle. His brains had stopped working at four years old, but his body had continued to grow. He had the build of a prizefighter, but his face looked like a little boy who had lost his mother. "Why you do dat?" he called up.

"Help," Frank managed, his breath leaving him.

The desperate one word cry galvanized the boy-man. He leaned out, wrapped his meaty arms around Frank's middle and yanked him backward toward his balcony. The two men landed on the floor, Frank sprawled on top of the large man.

"I love you man," Frank said. He wanted to kiss the young man.

"Gross," Henry squealed, reddening to the roots of his curly blonde hair. He scrambled up, dumping Frank to the hard cement floor.

"Get some ice," Mrs. Wright yelled from above them. "You hear me Henry, you get Frank some ice. Oh my! Oh my!"

Frank heard the soft cooing sounds of Mr. Wright. Their door opened. Mrs. Wright had beenushered inside by her protective, loving husband of fifty-nine years. Their door closed.

Henry stared down at Frank. "Do I got to get you ice?" He rubbed the gristle on his chin. Henry lacked a man's influence in his life and his trailer trash mother never thought to teach Henry about grooming.

"No." Frank suddenly remembered Lynn. "Henry, is Lynn . . ? You know her, right? Is she still standing at my door?"

"Yeah, she's just standing there staring." Henry did not try to lower his voice. "You trying to hide from her?"

"Yes. Shh!" Frank's fingers were burning now. He looked down at his long slim fingers and saw blood and lacerated skin. "Oh shit! My fingers. My fingers! What was I thinking? I could have broken my fingers."

Henry took the cry. "You could have broken your hands and your arms and your legs and your-"

"You don't understand. I'm an artist." Frank scrambled to his feet, suddenly furious. "I can't be doing stuff like this. I can't be driven to desperation like this." He leaned over the balconey toward Lynn, hailing a volley of angry words in her direction. "Get out of here," he spat. "Leave me alone. I hate you! Do you get it? I hate you! Get out of my life."

Lynn watched him, her dull cow-eyed look barely changing. The only sign that she had heard his words was a slight coloring in her cheeks. She lifted her huge tote bag up on her shoulder. "I'm tired of being taken for granted by you, Frank Donahue. I'm tired of always pandering to your undeclared love. Not many women would put up with your unexpressed love like I do."

Frank, wordless, gaped at her.

Lynn held up two greasy black hands. "I see I have to be more explicit with you." Without thinking, she rubbed one hand across her forehead. "I changed your car tire. It was flat. I'll be back later, after I get the tire fixed. Your spare is on your car. You can drive it now if you have to go someplace tonight."

Frank opened his mouth, but mere words abandoned him. She had to have a set of keys to his Mercedes to get at the spare. He flexed and unflexed his fingers. Slowly. Testing them.

"You can paint again, Mr. Frank?" Henry asked.

"Yeah." Frank looked at his watch. If he left now, he would only be a half hour late for his church social. All the good women would be taken. But he had to try. He had to get away from this lunatic. Frank, more than anything, wanted to find love in his life. He had to get rid of Lynn. He thought about the new law and then quickly erased it from his mind.

It was the year 2022. President Brad Pitt had allowed a bill to pass that made it legal for each citizen to commit one murder. That law, more than anything, had caused great controversy and uproar, including a divorce in the president's life. There was no way his wife, the great humanitarian Angelina Jolie, would stay with a man that made killing legal.

The President, along with the congress, had deemed the one kill policy necessary. Jails were overrun with shameless people who committed every kind of aberration because they had no morals and they thought they wouldn't get caught. These criminals cost taxpayers hundreds of thousands of dollars to feed and house in jails and then they were released to do more harm anyway. Now with this rule, people thought twice about doing wrong to another person. When the average citizen was allowed one murder, you had given the lambs bigger teeth and claws. And the wolves hesitated now.

There were other reasons, less forgivable, for this rule to have passed. There simply were too many bad people in the world. They were becoming more amoral as time went on. People didn't care about other people. Drivers continued to text and drink and kill people with their cars. Medical personal didn't think enough about the care they delivered. Contractors built structures that collapsed and killed people. The world's population had become lazy about caring for other people. These were the excuses for letting this horrendous law pass.

Frank had been brought up as a Christian. His parents were good decent people. They didn't believe in killing.

"Mom's awake." Henry's words broke into Frank's thoughts and sent blood coursing through his veins. The only other person he hated more than Lynn was Henry's mom, Tanya.

One flight above Frank's head, Mrs. Eva Wright lay stretched out on the divan, a fan in one hand, a glass of wine in the other. Her heart beat wildly, her face flushed. Fast as a hummingbird's wings, her hands fanned her face. "Do you think he saw anything?" she asked her husband for the hundredth time that night. She drew the blanket around her shoulders tighter.

Mr. Wright knew that this was not a safe state for his eighty-three year-old wife to be in. "Drink your wine," he urged. He also did not want to admit that his eighty-five year old eyes had not seen anything either.

The fan stopped fluttering. She took a deep breath and looked deep into his soul. Her sapphire-blue eyes had not faded with time, and neither had other things about her. "I'm cold," she informed him.

Mr. Wright knew that she wanted him to turn up the heat and that she did not mean via the thermostat. Without another word, he lifted her legs up with one arm, sat down and laid her legs gently across his lap.

She smiled at him. She had always loved his strength, even though he was in his eighties.

With a deft flip of his hand, her slippers were off.

And she loved his smoothness.

His fingers began at her toes and worked their way up to her soles. By the time his magical hands arrived at her ankles, she thought that she would have the big one. At her age, that could mean heart attack or the Big O. In her current state, she didn't care.

Kindred spirits locked together, Mr. Wright kept working his way up. His hands worked past her knees and continued their way north.

"You bad boy." Mrs. Wright could barely speak.

Mr. Wright kept taking advantage of her.

"Oh honey, oh honey, oh honey," Mrs. Wright squealed.

Mr. Wright raised his brow. When her eyes opened again they both looked at each other and sighed.

"I'm going to get you."

"See that you do." He took her wine glass out of her hand and took a sip. "See that you do, my dear." Then he reached toward her again. When he drew his hand back, he had the remote in his palm. He switched on the news.

Mrs. Wright took the wine glass out of his hand.

The U.S. President, former actor, Brad Pitt, appeared on the screen. Even at fifty-eight and with the weight of the world on his shoulders, he was handsome.

"There was a time when I really wanted to nail that Dreamboat," Mrs. Wright said.

Mr. Wright narrowed his eyes at her. "But now you wouldn't even want to approach him?"

"How could such a suave handsome hunk like that make up something as barbaric as a law that allowed people to kill each other.

"It is rather an aggressive plan. Is that why you don't wish to nail him anymore?"

Mrs. Wright shot her husband an exasperated look.

He returned her look calmly. "What if there was someone out there who was trying to kill me and the only way you could save me was by killing them? Would you have a change of heart then?"

The couple, married for fifty-nine happy years, stared intently at each other.

"No, my love, I would not have a change of heart. I think the policy of allowing people to take the law into their own hands is deplorable. Even if you are allowed only one murder." She sipped the wine, then looked over the rim of the glass with eyes the color and depth of the Kauai ocean. "But! If I thought someone was trying to hurt you, I would not hesitate to go to war on their behind and then I would string whatever was left up by their underwear."

"I love it when you talk dirty." Mr. Wright patted her knee. He lifted her legs off his lap, stood up, stretched, and casually walked to the window. From their apartment, he had a view of the Tuff Shed. Someone darted back behind the metal building. Mr. Wright closed the drapes.

CHAPTER TWO

Frank never wanted to be able to vanish more than he wanted to right at that moment. But there, blocking his flight path, stood his other nemesis, Henry's mother Tanya.

She was little and scrawny and completely repulsive. She stood in front of him unkempt and braless and not a bit embarrassed. "Well, Frank. You want to explain what you are doing on my porch?"

He did not.

Tanya stood five feet nothing. If she wore every Harley jacket she owned, she still couldn't tip the scale over 100. Yet she brought fear to Frank's knees. This Queen of Tasteless Jokes, this Master of Scorn could make him, a grown man, cry. On the few nights in the past four years that he'd managed to bring a date home, she'd come up with something vulgar and repulsive to say to the women. She'd stand up on the balcony in some cheap tank top two sizes too small, open her mouth and let something come out that would kill his date's desire. The only motive he could think that she had for all this was because she thought it was fun.

"You finally realize that I'm the one you want?"

Frank did not. He took one look at the top of her ratty hair and tried not to wretch.

"Frank has to go somewhere," Henry yelled from the living room. Henry had difficulty modulating his voice. He always took a deep breath and spoke while he was exhaling.

They both jumped, forgetting for a brief moment, that he was there. Henry, despite his size and loud voice could melt into the background.

"Yeah, I got to go."

Tanya stood solid in the doorway, blocking his way.

Alright, he'd have to call her bluff. Steeling himself, he held his breath, protecting his lungs from her garlicky breath, averted his gaze from her missing tooth, tilted his head, closed his eyes and went in for her dry cracked lips.

He'd made a grave tactical error. She was supposed to scream and back away. Instead, she tilted her head up toward him and stretched her lips up as far toward him as she could.

Their mouths almost touched. Frank's lids fluttered open just in the nick of time, saw the dark gap between her teeth moving toward him and screamed.

Her face puckered at the scream. Confused and disoriented, she froze.

He took that moment to squeeze past her. He did not stop running until he was in the car.

"Son of a bitch," Tanya swore.

The man, hiding by the shed, ducked back behind it when Frank jumped into his car.

Lynn sat at the car dealership tapping her feet and looking at her watch. It was eight-thirty and Frank would be at that singles group knee deep in bible-packing floozies.

Mike, the mechanic, came into the waiting room, smiling a greasy smile at her and rubbing his hands to warm them from the frigid air. Even in the dessert, it could get cold. Many people were surprised to learn that occasionally, Las Vegans were told to keep their water running, to avoid frozen pipes. "Whew! It's cold."

"This is Las Vegas, it doesn't get cold," Lynn snapped.

"We live in North Las Vegas. It's colder in the north."

Apparently Lynn did not get his joke. Being insensitive, she could not pick up on his attempt to make human contact. If someone had told her that she was insensitive, and they would have had to outright tell her that she was insensitive, she would have fired back the denial that an insensitive person wouldn't be spending their Saturday night getting their love's tire fixed.

He wished her a Merry Christmas.

She did not return the wish. Instead, she paid him and then just stood and watched while he carried the tire out to her car. He slammed the trunk shut and stared at her for an awkward moment.

"Am I supposed to tip you?" Lynn asked.

The smile dropped from his face.

Lynn prudently turned around and got into her car. Without a second glance to the tired, greasy mechanic she left standing in her fumes, she headed for the mega church where Frank insisted on going to those useless singles nights. The church had a ridiculous name that made it sound like some camp in the dessert, but the campus consisted of two-story modern styled buildings. Contemporary signs adorned the buildings. A huge parking lot enveloped the whole campus. On Sundays it was filled to capacity.

Entering the church lot, she immediately headed for the back row. She took a quick look around, saw nobody, not even the obnoxious security guards. She got out of her car and headed toward the buildings. The minute she stepped up on the sidewalk, she could hear muted laughter coming out of one of the classrooms. The noise got louder the closer she got. Standing in front of the door, she could hear even clearer the staccato beat of their laughter. How could Frank stand this noise? Frank, her beautiful artistic painter. Frank, who didn't even know she was good for him. She put her hand on the door, anticipating Frank's expression when he first saw her walk in the door.

"Hello Lynn."

Lynn whirled around and faced the security guard that had snuck up behind her. Her hand dropped from the door. "Hello John." She craned her neck way up to look at him. How "Big John" could sneak up on her without her knowing was amazing. The mammoth stood seven feet tall and he had a whacked ankle that gave him this dragging, lurching gait.

"What are you doing here, Lynn?" He kept his hard eyes on her and murmured something into the squiggly cord trailing from his ear to under his shirt.

"I'm here to see Frank. What did you say into your mic?"

The huge man did not answer her question. "Lynn, do you remember that we agreed that you would not return here?" He looked over her shoulder at the door behind her. "Besides, the pickings in there are not that great." He snickered at his own joke.

"I didn't come for the pickings, I came for Frank."

John, the giant, looked up at the sky and then back down at her. "Alright, I'm going to have to ask you to leave." He tilted his head down to his neck and spoke into the mic. "I got this guys."

Behind her, a pack of heavy-footed guards retreated back between the classrooms. They had been trying to sneak up on her. She had to execute her mission quickly. She threw open the classroom door, darted in, slammed it shut and leaned against it. When she looked up, a whole classroom of people stared back at her. They were matched in groups of two, some had scooted their chairs so close together that their knees touched.

One man, dateless and ringless to boot, Lynn noted, came toward her wearing the pressed khaki pants and crisp white shirt of a trained professional. He moved slowly and steadily, all the while holding her attention with a serene smile on his face. Behind him, despite his demeanor, some of the people were beginning to look alarmed. Suddenly Big John burst through the door. Lynn darted out of the way. Several women in the room gasped.

The moderator in the white shirt kept the smile on his face and his hands up in the air. "Lynn," he said calmingly.

She scanned the crowd until she found Frank. He had moved away from his table, leaving a gorgyly-eyed blonde with frizzy ends and saggy knee socks. Her tan looked like it had come out of a cheap bottle.

"Lynn," the moderator repeated, trying to keep his voice low. "You are scaring some of these people. Some of them remember what happened last time you were here."

Lynn snorted. "Well, if you were doing such a good job with your little hook-up scene here, none of these people would be back here a second time."

Big John inched toward her. Lynn saw him out of the corner of her eye. She made a quick step toward Frank. "I fixed your tire."

"Thank you. I'll pay you later, okay?"

She did not understand the pained expression on his face. But she liked the fact that he was moving closer to her, only wishing that he would hurry up.

When he was close enough to reach her, he stopped. His voice lowered. "What are you doing here, Lynn?"

Lynn looked back at the blonde with the yellowish brown skin. "Stay away from her Frank. She doesn't look healthy."

Big John made his move. Quietly and neatly, the seven foot tall security guard stepped forward and swooped her up in his arm, tucked her against his side and carted her back out the door.

Frank turned away, back toward the blonde.

She had vanished.

* * *

Mrs. Wright had definitely seen the man dart behind the shed. She was old, but her eyesight was good and the lighting was good. It was a bright and sunny Sunday morning, a typical Las Vegas morning. She shrugged and fluttered about her apartment, getting ready for church. Mr. Wright had left earlier to go and have brunch with his retired casino working cronies. They'd sit around and reminisce about how great it was when the mob ran Las Vegas, a topic she was tired of hearing about.

She hated to be late for church. But still, the sight of someone hiding behind the shed, watching her apartment, kindled the fire in her brain. She crept to the window, looked out and saw the blur of someone's head dart behind the shed. Her heart beat faster. A tangible element of excitement lit up the air. She sat on the sofa, then slid down on her knees and crawled across the floor, keeping her head down. A smile crept across her face. Not bad for an old lady. When she got to the window, she slowly raised her head and surveyed the parking lot. There, on the shed's concrete foundation, a black tennis shoe peaked out.

She snaked a hand out and grabbed her cordless phone.

Tanya answered on the first ring.

"Tanya, I have a man watching me. He's out behind the shed. Can you see him from your place?"

"I see his shoes." Tanya's gum cracked. "You think he's hard?"

Mrs. Wright giggled. "I bet he has well-defined muscles and a sex drive that can't be filled."

"Does your husband know we talk like this?"

Mrs. Wright ignored the question. She did not want to think about her beloved at this exact moment. "That guy out there wants me."

"You be careful girl. Is your husband home?"

"Who?"

"Your husband."

Mrs. Wright bit her lip. Calling Tanya might have been a little hasty. She'd been so excited and Tanya fueled her wild side like a good trashy friend should. Tanya never treated Mrs. Wright like a senile old woman. Tanya treated her like the experienced lustful creature that she was underneath her falling assets. But Tanya could be such a ninny sometimes, asking about Roger while there was a great hunk outside. Mrs. Wright didn't feel guilty about not wanting to think about her husband of fifty-nine years. Although a bit mystified by his wife's friendship with the smoking biker chick, he thought the fueling of his wife's fire beneficial. He left the two women to their devices.

"Eva, are you still there?"

"Yes," Eva Wright answered.

"I'm going to go over there and find out exactly what that pervert is doing behind that shed."

"Don't you dare!"

Tanya ignored her older friend. "Keep a watch. I'm going to get dolled up before I go down there."

"Tanya, I'll hang you up with my Christmas ribbon."

Mrs. Wright was answered by the thud of a phone dropping, two minutes of muffled shuffling and the sound of Tanya's front door opening. Getting "dolled up" for Tanya meant rinsing her mouth with some alcohol.

Tanya made her way down the stairs, phoneless and resolute on her mission.

Mrs. Wright rummaged through her purse and pulled out the little Sony camera her kids had gotten her for her birthday months before. It had a video option. If the little pervert tried anything she'd have his monkey business on video.

She crept out on her balcony, crawled up to the wall and placed the camera on the ledge.

Tanya was thirty feet away from the shed. Through the lens, Mrs. Wright watched her friend walk up to the small metal building.

"Hey," Tanya called.

Fast as a flash, Mrs. Wright saw a blur come out from behind the shed and grab Tanya. The blur and Tanya disappeared behind the metal walls. Mrs. Wright screamed and knocked the camera to the hedge below. She scrambled to her feet and ran for the front door. "Tanya," she screamed. She ran down the stairs. Her heels caught in the stone step sending her pitching forward. Only her deftly placed hand on the rail kept her from plastering her face into the steps. She plucked the camera out of the hedge and, still screaming Tanya's name, charged across the parking lot to the shed. What she saw behind that little metal building froze her solid.

Tanya lay face down, all tied up with packing twine along her body and a duct tape slapped across her mouth. Her hands were fastened behind her back with her fingers clamped to her buttocks. Mrs. Wright had seen roped calves before, but this was even a more secure job.

Mrs. Wright studied her twine-tied friend. "Hey, I can record this with my new camera."

Tanya rolled over, turning purple with the effort. She thrashed and screamed into the tape.

Her kind old friend, taking pity, reached over and gently took the tape off her friend's mouth.

"If you video me like this, I swear I will rip your arms off all the way up to your ears."

Mrs. Wright smiled and removed the ropes. Tanya never treated her like an old lady. This was why the two were friends. Mrs. Wright held up her empty hands to show Tanya that she didn't have the camera. "Let's get you out of here." Before she could begin, she sensed a big shadow come up behind her.

Tanya's eyes grew larger and focused on a point above Mrs. Wright's head. "Ahh, shit."

Behind Mrs. Wright, Henry stood, looking down at his mother. Tears coursed down his face.

CHAPTER THREE

The man ran through the parking lot, heart pounding. He wasn't upset at what he had just done, he was upset about what he hadn't done and what his father would do when he found out. Just how much of his face had the little bitch seen?

Henry, crooning and crying with each step, carried his mom upstairs. Mrs. Wright trailed behind him, assuring him that his mom was not hurt, that she would be okay. Even Henry's dull mind knew that something was wrong. His mother demanded to be put down, but her demands lacked luster and after a few steps, she gave up. The color had already drained out of her face.

Her distraught son practically kicked the door in and brought his mother right to the couch. He laid her down gently.

"Who was that creep?" she asked Mrs. Wright. The minute Henry backed off she sat up. "My whole body has been fouled."

Hearing her words, spoken with almost her normal amount of venom, Henry smiled and plopped in front of the TV.

Tanya ran her hands down her body. "I feel dirty."

Mrs. Wright put on a sympathetic face. "I think the experience enhanced your glow."

Tanya raised her arms, parading them in front of Mrs. Wright's face. A light discoloration had already formed on her wrists. "Do these black marks enhance my glow?"

Mrs. Wright let a little smile play out at the edge of her lips. "Well, my dear, some people think that is very attractive. You know, they might think you like being tied up."

Tanya frowned at her and pushed her bra straps back under the thin straps of her tank top. "There's a stigma to that."

"I told you not to go out there." Mrs. Wright snuck a glance at a slight purple splotch along Tanya's neck.

"How am I supposed to know that there was a calf roper behind the shed? I thought those rodeo guys just stuck to the strip."

Mrs. Wright shrugged. "What can I say? This whole town gets even wilder when the National Finals Rodeo comes here. It's a billion-dollar industry. Those guys are stars and they know it. They win thousands of dollars for roping cattle."

"I'm not a cow."

Mrs. Wright leaned forward. "What did he look like?"

"I can barely tell you. The guy charged me so fast, I didn't get a good look at him. One minute I'm trying to bust him and the next thing I'm looking at the clear blue sky. But not for long. The son of a bitch flips me on my face and jams his knee in my back. Before I can scream, duct tape is slapped around my mouth." She spat tiny shreds of the tape into the carpet. "What kind of people do you and your husband hang out with?"

Mrs. Wright thought about where her husband was at that moment. A frown slipped across her mouth.

Tanya stared intently at her. "You gonna tell your husband what happened?"

"Maybe not."

Tanya hissed at her like a viper. "Why not?"

Mrs. Wright looked away. When she looked back, a sour expression tainted her normally sweet countenance.

"You look like you swallowed some acid. You better tell me what you're hiding."

Mrs. Wright's sharp tone cut the air between the two women. "Maybe it's none of your business."

"I thought we were friends."

Mrs. Wright gave the younger woman a piercing look. "You keep playing around barbed wire, you're going to get punctured."

Henry, oblivious to the darkness descending between the two women, kept playing his video game. A sweet child, he picked up only on positive vibes. In Henry's mind, everything was fine, but in Mrs. Wright's mind everything was just starting.

Unaware of the drama that had just happened in the apartment complex, Lynn climbed the stairs up to Frank's place.

It was ten in the morning and he should be up by now. Men didn't take that long to get ready. They could make the eleven o'clock service. Besides, she'd brought him a steaming cup of Starbuck's to snap him awake. Holding the two mugs in her hand, she had to kick on the door.

Scrambling and giggling could be heard from behind the door. Then, distinctly, Frank swore.

Lynn knew that she'd been seen and she was definitely sure that he had a woman in there. She kicked harder on the door. The door did not open. She unleashed an unchristian strain of invectives and still the stubborn door did not move. Now she was angry. She would have to teach them both a lesson. Obviously they did not understand that the purpose of a church social was not so that you could find some whore and bring her home. What she did next, she did not think of as a breaking and entering, but rather a training lesson. She placed one of the coffee cups on the ledge by the door and slipped her hand into her pocket to grab a set of keys. She had already used his car keys this week, now she would use his apartment keys. Carefully and quietly, she stuck the key in the lock, twisted it slowly, and nudged the door open an inch. She stuck her face up to the crack and peered in.

Her nose met the icy muzzle of a small-caliber Smith and Wesson.

"Show me your hands, bitch." The deep throaty voice of the female whore sounded like she meant business.

Lynn raised her left hand, guiding the woman's eyes away from her right hand. This trick worked for only a second, but that's all Lynn needed. When the blonde's eyes searched for Lynn's other hand, she grabbed the coffee off the ledge and flung the steaming mocha into the floozies's face. Before the woman had time to react, Lynn shoved the door open and followed up with a roundhouse punch to the side of the woman's face. Screaming now, the woman dropped the gun and went down on one knee. Lynn finished her work with a knee slam into the side of the stupid bimbo's head. When the woman toppled to the tile floor, Lynn squatted down and grabbed the weapon. She was holding it on the woman when Frank appeared in the hall doorway, his arms raised.

16

"Frank," Lynn called, waving him over to her side. "Frank, we've got to band together on these evil types. They gang up on good people."

"Set the gun down, Lynn."

Lynn looked down at the prostate woman. She had her hands over her eyes, sobbing into them loudly.

"We need to get her medical attention. Let me call 911." He pointed to his cell phone. It was on the kitchen counter, close to Lynn. "We need to team up and help her, Lynn."

Lynn liked his idea of teaming up together. She lowered the gun. "We're coming together now, aren't we Frank?"

"United, we are." He kept his hands up and his eyes on her. He walked gingerly across the room, as if he was afraid she had hid a land mine.

Lynn giggled. Frank was a large gangly man and the sight of him practically tip-toeing across his living room struck her as funny. "You don't have to keep your hands up. We're an alliance together."

Frank never took his eyes off her. He got to his phone and picked it up. His left arm stayed in the air.

"Here, let me talk to the police." Lynn reached for the phone.

Suddenly, her legs were pulled out from underneath her like a large sucking vortex had suddenly sprung from out of the earth. She went down on her knees, hard. Someone hit her across the nose with their fist, stunning her momentarily. Tears sprung to her eyes and a rage boiled deep within her. She flailed out, catching the bitch in the side of the cheek. Her fingers curled frantically, catching hair and suddenly an earring. Now it was time for this bitch to go down screaming.

She was about to pull earrings and hair but suddenly all light and air was smothered out of her, like being hit with King Kong. Her fingers were pried away, even as her breath left her.

Tanya had dried her tears and gotten rid of Mrs. Wright. Sweat beaded on her forehead. She sat up.

"Why is it so hot in here?"

Mrs. Wright had cranked up the heater on the way out. Tanya had been shaking when Henry had placed his mom on the couch.

Henry, ignoring her, kept playing video games. She liked that about him. He never wasted time by looking stupid and saying he didn't know. Henry had been wrong from birth when the doctors had used forceps to pull him out of her birth canal. His skin was blue and he didn't flinch when they poked him with sharp instruments. Despite this rough start to life, Henry did some things that seemed smarter than what other people would do. For one thing, he never wasted time trying to answer questions that he couldn't. He simply carried on with what he was doing.

The day of Henry's birth the doctors had come into the room, heads down, throats clearing to explain that her darling baby boy had a low APGAR score. APGAR stood for appearance, pulse, grimace, activity and respiration. Henry's was low which wasn't life threatening. But when it remained low thirty minutes after his birth they knew they had serious trouble on their hands. They had to go in and explain to the tough young mother that her baby had cerebral palsy and that he would survive but not with his brain intact. Tanya's boyfriend, Henry's father, left them that night.

Tanya took the abandonment with a shrug. She did everything the experts told her to do for Henry. Enrolled him in an individualized educational plan, went to all the school meetings and took extra time in teaching him things that other children learned naturally. Granted, she might have been better if she'd moved him out of Vegas where schools were terribly underfunded. But the truth was, aside from a miracle, Henry was what he was and taking him to a fancy school with teachers armed with loads of letters after their name wasn't going to change Henry. Besides, living anywhere but Vegas would be tedious and detrimental to her income.

Tanya tended bar at the Horseshoe, a well-established, if not a bit worn Casino on Fremont Street. They were old Vegas without being seedy Vegas. Tourists still went there. Better yet, the management was not afraid of aging. If employees served them well over the years, they kept them. And since Tanya tended bar, she did not have to wear the skimpy little outfits the cocktail waitresses had to wear.

"Mom! I just killed all of the flesh-eating Zombies with a . . ."

Tanya only half-listened to his long drawn-out explanation. How Henry's damaged mind could absorb such detail from the video games and yet not be able to hold down a job went beyond her understanding.

"Boring, dear," she trilled.

Tanya had to admit that her whole life was pretty boring. She worked at the Horseshoe, at the bar by the hotel registration desk. The tourists would check in and then make her bar their next stop. They wanted to start their wild Vegas weekend with a drink. Tanya thought that they were all so uninspired. In her most insipid voice, she would tell them that. She would smile at them and speak a little lower, forcing the men to lean in a little closer. Then, in her sexiest voice, she would tell them if they really wanted a hot time, that they should try doing Sin City sober. They always pulled back, laughing heartily. They tipped her heavily, took their drinks and winked at her. Her boss thought it was part of some made-up comedy/con job of hers to get the tips. He saw them laughing. He saw them tipping. He didn't try to stop her lines.

Suddenly a large thunk sounded above her head, bringing her back to the present. She looked up and tried to imagine what was going on in Frank's apartment.

"Henry, do you know what Frank is doing up there?"

Henry's thumbs worked the controller expertly. "Not supposed to be mean to Frank." The explosions and screams from his Avatars never quit when he spoke. His thumbs never slowed down.

"That is not what I asked you, and you are not supposed to take your eyes off your game," she shot back.

"I didn't."

Tanya stuck her tongue out at him. Smug bastard was right. He could talk and concentrate on the game at the same time.

She walked out of her apartment onto her balcony. Even in December the day was mild. They'd been lucky. Some years it had even snowed on their sin. She craned her neck up toward Frank's apartment. She heard Frank yell, "Put the gun down."

"Holy shit!" Tanya ran back inside. "Stay here! Call 911!"

This time Henry lifted his head from the game, a sign that she had gotten his attention.

She bolted out her front door before her senses could check her. Up the flight of stairs she flew.

She came up behind that crazy Lynn, the one that had the stalking crush on Frank. Lynn stood in the doorway, pointing a gun at a prostrate woman laying at Lynn's feet, crying and grabbing her head. Beyond them, deeper into the apartment, Frank hollered, his hands in the air. Tanya clenched her teeth together with the effort to prevent from crying out.

Frank needed her help. She would have to help him without Lynn knowing that she was behind her.

Lynn was in some kind of psychotic state, babbling about how she and Frank were coming together.

Tanya had to do something. Using all of her 125 pounds, she rammed into Lynn's back. Squeezing her eyes shut and bracing for the shots, Tanya recited the Lord's Prayer, surprised that it had surfaced after years of not going to church. Lynn dropped to one knee like a ton of bricks on impact. For a minute, Tanya feared that the deranged woman would get back up.

Suddenly Frank's bulky form flew across the room in an image that would sketch itself in Tanya's memory for years to come. He looked like a bear with wings, a bulky bear with wings. One that she knew just wouldn't get to the gun in Lynn's hand before the bullets in the gun got to Tanya's face. Tanya's thoughts turned to her son. She hoped that someone would let Henry know that his mother had died a heroine. In the next second, Frank's flying bulk knocked the air out of her lungs, and then blackness descended through Tanya.

Within a few seconds, a rush of life and oxygen flowed back into her lungs. At first, all she saw was darkness and then the shadow moved and Frank's face was an inch from hers. "Call the cops!" he huffed, pulling himself off her. "Now!"

Tanya's head cleared. Frank had rolled off her and onto Lynn. He pinned both of the zealot's arms to her sides and if that wasn't enough, he laid his bulk across her. The gun and the phone had scattered across the room, about three feet from all of them.

Tanya charged for the gun first. Why call for protection when you could be the protection? Tanya had target shot on the farm with her four brothers and their dad. She wasn't afraid of guns. She knew they would protect her. Besides, she wasn't sure if she could talk at the moment. She grabbed the gun and pointed it at Lynn.

Pinned beneath Frank's bulk, Lynn struggled a little and then gave up, quickly losing air.

"Get the phone!" Frank screamed. "Call the cops!"

"One kill law," Tanya said, citing Lynn's brains through the barrel. "I could do this."

"No, no, no," Frank yelled.

"You in love with her?" Tanya asked.

"Kill the bitch!" Frank's date suddenly found her voice. She pulled herself up on an elbow and glared at Tanya. Tanya had almost forgotten about her.

"Mama, no!" Henry clomped up the stairs.

"Shit!" Tanya couldn't do it. She couldn't do it with Henry standing there watching. She reached for the phone.

"Gutless!" the blonde woman screamed and collapsed back down.

She saluted the woman with the gun in one hand while she held the phone to her ear with the other hand.

"You two have been making out with my Frank." Lynn whipped her head back and forth between the two women.

Frank looked up at Tanya. "She recognizes you."

Sirens sounded in the background.

"What are you talking about?" Tanya said. But she knew what he was talking about, she knew what he was doing. He was throwing her under the bus. She looked at Henry. Luckily, for him, his intelligence blindness had shielded him from what his so-called friend was doing to his mother. "Did you forget that I have a gun?"

"Not for an instant," Frank said.

"Whore!" Lynn spat at her.

Tanya held the gun up, displaying it.

"Gutless whore!" the woman on the ground behind them yelled. She was back up on one elbow, in egging position.

"Shut up!" Tanya yelled at them. "I'm not wasting a bullet on any of you." She looked at Frank. "Last time I try to save your neck."

Henry looked on in anguish. He hated it when his mother and Frank yelled at each other.

Three police cars pulled up at the base of the stairs.

"One kill. Killing is legal," the blonde said.

"All of you, hands up! NOW!" A stampede of feet ran up the stairs and before they realized what happened the ants had invaded their picnic. Cops surrounded them, guns drawn.

Tanya dropped the weapon. A swarm of dark uniforms surrounded them. Henry cried out, holding his arms up. She couldn't count the number of officers. They moved and swarmed around her, pushing her arms behind her back, knocking her around. She saw the other players in the drama being pulled to their feet, Henry brushed aside, and the blonde screaming in agony or rage. Tanya could no longer figure things out.

"She's hurt, you don't have to use such force on her," Tanya cried.

The officers answered by dragging Tanya down the stairs and into the police car. She could still hear the screams of the blonde woman. Lynn and Frank quickly joined her, slammed together in the back of the police car, all handcuffed.

Tanya peered up the stairs. She could see Mrs. Wright on the balcony, fluttering her hands. Henry stood next to her, his face in open agony.

"Henry, get Henry!" Tanya yelled through the thick glass. She knew that yelling through unbreakable glass was fruitless but she had to try.

Lynn rammed her elbows into Tanya's side, hard, knocking her into the window. An officer reached back and yanked Tanya back upright.

"Get your hands off me!" Tanya yelled. "I have a son. Someone's got to watch my son." She leaned forward, spewing hatred at Frank. "You got me into this. I thought you were supposed to be Henry's friend."

"Shut up and stay out of my life. Just shut your mouth and stay the hell out of my life," Frank snapped.

"I am the hell out of your life," Tanya said. She turned to Lynn. "I don't make out with him. That's his fantasy."

"All of you shut up." The policeman, a dark angry man, slammed his mass into the driver's seat, barely waiting for his partner, before throwing the car into gear.

On the top floor, between the Wright's and Frank's apartment, Mrs. Wright and Henry stood bunched together. His bulk made her look even smaller than her five and a half foot height. Yet, it was the small woman's strength that Henry needed. He leaned against her, complacently following her into her apartment. "Will they bring my mom back?"

Mrs. Wright handed him the remote. She knew that every man everywhere wanted their mommies and if they couldn't have that, then the remote was the second most important thing. "I'm sure that they will."

Tanya had acted in self-defense and Nevada was still a right-to-carry state. So no crime had been committed.

Mrs. Wright settled Henry in with a plate of cookies and a glass of milk. She wished her problems could be solved so easily. "I'm sorry your day is not going so well."

Henry looked at her quizzically, his teeth noshing on the cookies energetically, eating as if he would never see food again. "I shot twelve zombies today and made it to level eight in the Kingdom of Treadonia."

"Is that where you can never get tired?" She laughed at her own pun. "Get it tread . . . tired? No? Okay, Henry, just keep eating."

Just when she wondered how she was going to get through the afternoon with this serious young man, the sound of her knight in shining silver hair, shuffling up the stairs brought relief. She hated the retired old man's shuffle he'd adopted in later years because when she looked at him, she still saw the solid-shouldered sure-footed man she had married. His lazy sliding gait, with the slippers shifting forward did not jibe with the image she still held of him. But, to keep a marriage going strong for fifty-nine years, you just had to let some things go.

He walked in the door, took one look at Henry's huge figure on his end of his couch and said, "We're not keeping him."

"Don't be so excitable dear, I know we can't keep him."

"Then why did you feed him?"

"Roger, be careful. You are going to hurt his feelings."

Henry continued shoveling cookies in his mouth and staring at the TV.

"It's not like he is oversensitive. In fact, I think Elvis has left the building." Mr. Wright flopped on the other end of the couch and leaned so close to Henry that the boy-man should have smelled the old man's garlicky breath. "He's eating my Little Debbie's."

"Did you want me to give him your beer?"

"The cookies are fine."

Mrs. Wright remained standing in front of her husband. Amongst all the morning's excitement, she had managed to find the time to slip into her red shell dress. Nipped in at the waist, the skirt flared out gracefully, doing justice to her beautiful legs. She kept her gams shapely with weekly line dance lessons at the senior center. Mrs. Wright batted her eyes at her husband and twisted a lock of curly gray hair around her finger.

Mr. Wright felt her shadow loom over him. He heard her expectant breathing, suddenly slower and deeper now. "Uh-oh," he said, taking note of the rise of color in her cheeks. He had already walked a mile this morning, eaten a full and heavy breakfast and argued with the guys. He wanted a nap. "First you are scolding me and now you are trying to seduce me. This erratic behavior is not good for your heart."

"This isn't erratic behavior."

"You are eighty-three years old. This is what passes for erratic behavior."

Mrs. Wright's lips formed into a pout.

Mr. Wright relented. "If I'd wanted a boring easy-going wife, I shouldn't have married a girl on fire."

Mrs. Wright grinned and fell, ever so gently, into his lap. "And I am on fire, my love."

"Sick," Henry commented, scooching away from the old couple.

Mr. Wright chuckled and gently slid her off his lap onto the sofa next to him. "All right, you want to tell me why we have this stray on my couch?"

"The police hauled his mother away."

"Nice. And why?"

"She was holding a gun on someone."

"This story gets better, doesn't it?"

"Well, yeah, I didn't start from the beginning. But I will. There was a man out by the shed watching me."

Mr. Wright did not miss his cue. "Of course he was watching you. You are a very tempting tidbit."

Mrs. Wright smiled. "I know that I'm attractive when I put my mind and my make-up to it, but this man started watching the apartment before I'd gotten a chance to doll up. I was in my bathrobe."

Roger Wright sat up straighter, giving his full attention to his wife. "Go on."

"Do you find the fact that someone was watching your wife rather beguiling?"

Mr. Wright nodded, but inside he did not find it beguiling, he found it frightening. He kept his game face on. "What did you do?"

"I pranced in front of the window wearing nothing but a-"

"Eva, for God's sake." Mr. Wright jerked his head in Henry's direction.

Mrs. Wright allowed herself a giggle before telling her husband the rest of the story. "All right, I'm jerking your chain. I told Tanya that there was a prowler staring at me and, since you weren't here to protect me, she ran down there to see what the guy was up to."

Mr. Wright could not see where this was going. Fifty-nine years of marriage to this woman and he could not always see where she was going.

"The guy behind the shed roped Tanya up like a calf."

Mr. Wright frowned. "I've spent a few minutes with her. I've got to say it's not a bad idea with a woman like that."

Mrs. Wright knew her husband. When his two bushy eyebrows knitted together like that, he was worried about something. "You don't think it's plausible that the guy was just a peeping tom?"

"Given your good looks, it's completely plausible. Still, I'm a little worried."

"Maybe he was looking for you. Roger, if you are in some kind of trouble and you don't tell me so that I can protect you, that would be indefensible."

"No, my dear, what would be indefensible would be if I were in some kind of trouble and I brought it to you." His arm encircled her shoulders.

"Does this have anything to do with the rodeo trying to leave town back in 2013?"

Her husband shifted in his seat, then looked at Henry pointedly. "What happens if we run out of cookies before the police bring his mother back?"

"I take it that's a 'yes', this does have something to do with the rodeo." Mrs. Wright sighed. She knew that getting her husband to spill the beans about his sordid history would be as painful and difficult as running through a hedge backward.

She had her work cut out for her.

CHAPTER FOUR

Big John made his way up to the church's office, where he'd been summoned to see the Chief of Security. Despite the beautiful moonlit December evening, and the elaborate Nativity scene forming in the courtyard, he felt dread in the pit of his stomach. He stopped and stared at the manger. Baby Jesus hadn't gotten there yet.

His job at the church was voluntary. He loved to serve the Lord. He loved to help people. But more than that, he needed a job. The church's Chief of security served on a private security board. Big John felt that if he could impress Stuart, it could lead to a job with Stuart's firm.

Big John came to the meeting with some misgivings. He knew that nobody got summoned to the boss's office to be told that they were doing right. So, with heavy heart he went into the office and sat down and faced the director of security.

"John, you've been a great asset to our team here."

Big John smiled at the well-muscled dork. Stuart had a tiny head on massive shoulders. He had a gap-toothed smile that he tried to hide. John avoided staring at it as the windbag blabbed on, extolling John's praises when he just wanted the little puffed-chest man to get to the point. He thought about Stuart's butt and how it would taste when he would have to kiss it for   infinity.

"So what are your thoughts on this matter?"

Big John, suddenly aware of the expectant pause, jolted to alertness. "This matter, sir?" he said, none too brightly.

"This matter of your sister, Lynn." He picked at the gap between his teeth, waiting for John's response. "Where Lynn is concerned, we think you have a tendency to let things get out of hand."

"Next time, sir, I would just punch her. You know, hard as I could."

"That's not what we want." Now the little man was staring intently at Big John.

As if Big John could easily pull a solution for dealing with Lynn out of his hat. His sister had been sent to experts and hacks alike and nobody had come up with a solution yet. The only coping skill he had left was his sense of humor and a pasted smile. The problem with Big John was that he didn't have a good filter for when to use his sense of humor and when to shut his mouth. There was a fine line between Class Clown and Ass Hound. He crossed the line. Leaning forward he said, "Well sir, there is always the one-kill policy." He winked at Stuart.

"No!" Stuart went red. "Thou shalt not kill. The church does not believe. . ."

"Hey, I'm only kidding."

"This is a very important matter. We have already lost five members of our Saturday night speed dating service. That's very important revenue for the church."

Big John nodded. "I noticed that Jesus wasn't here."

Stuart looked up sharply.

"I meant the Baby Jesus in the Nativity scene."

"Yes, umm, expenses like that." He shuffled some papers on his desk, then raised his head. "Now, I have a tentative job for you in my company if you can demonstrate your ability to handle this complex problem. I don't want to see a recurrence of Saturday night. If that happens again, I'm going to have to take drastic measures. Can't you just talk to your sister?" He stood up abruptly.

"Talk to" Lynn, just "talk to" Lynn? Big John's mind reeled at the naiveté of the solution. Lynn had been "talked to" by teams of psychologists and psychiatrists over her twenty-two years. You could not talk to a bi-polar person. They talked to you. They talked at you. In a conversation, they gave and you took. He felt a shadow hovering over him and realized that Stuart was standing.

"Oh! I see, I guess we're done." Big John stood up, looming over Stuart. That, he couldn't help. He stuck out his hand. "Thanks for your time."

An awkward moment passed. Stuart did not offer his hand. His finger flicked through papers on his desk. "Please close the door on your way out."

Big John walked out. He closed the door gently behind him. When he turned around, Stuart's pretty secretary was gazing at him. She smiled kindly at him.

"He must have had a bad day," Big John said.

She glanced down at her appointment book. "Exploratory rectal exam scheduled for tomorrow. He's nervous." She peeked at him over the rim of her rhinestone glasses. "Don't laugh. If he hears you, it'll be judgement day for you."

Big John saluted her and then made his way out. His ankle bones ached. He knew the weather would be changing. It would get cold soon.

His phone buzzed. He pulled it out, took one look at the screen and shoved it back in his pocket.

He knew he could be a good security guard, but with Lynn shaking things up, how was he going to prove it?

The persistent device rang again. The same caller. He hung up and shoved it back into his pocket. Moving slowly across the grounds on his idiotically messed up ankle, he finally made it to his car. His cell rang again. Irritated and distracted, he forgot to duck and hit his head on the door jam. A curse word slipped out. The call went to voice mail. He shut the door without slamming anything in it. His pocket rang again.

It was Lynn. He knew God was getting him back for cursing on sacred grounds. He answered it. "Hello, Lynn."

"You have to pick me up. These animal cops dragged me down to the station just for the very reason that they could and that they had nothing better to do."

"Hi, Lynn, I'm fine. Thanks for asking."

"You have to give them two hundred and fifty dollars. I'll pay you back."

"How are you going to pay me back?"

"I'll be getting some money for these special nose plugs I'll be selling." She went on to describe her latest invention.

Big John laid his heavy head into his hands. When he spoke, his voice came out timid and beaten. "Why did the police pick you up?"

"Because they were bored. I wasn't the one who brought the gun to Frank's apartment."

Big John lifted his head. "What gun? Lynn, what gun are you talking about?"

"I told you I didn't bring it to Frank's apartment so how would I know anything about the gun?"

"I can't keep bailing you out."

"Then call Mom and she will do it."

Big John suddenly hated his little sister. She was exhausting him. She was exhausting his mother. Their father had escaped this life by dying. His sudden heart attack had whisked him away from the trials of living with a wacky daughter, leaving Big John and his mother to deal with her. They only got a reprieve when Lynn could be persuaded to take her medicine. The problem was, when she took her medicine she thought she wasn't bad so she stopped taking her medicine and then she was bad.

Her whole life she'd been a terror to her family. Late night phone calls always filled her parents with panic. Lynn sneaking out of the house. Lynn doing something to somebody. One night, she'd washed their neighbor's car at three in the morning, loudly yelling at them for leaving the filthy eyesore around. Another night, she'd been caught digging through another neighbor's garbage, scolding them for their unhealthy eating habits and materialistic ways. Growing up, Big John's street was the only place where the neighbors shredded their junk food wrappers along with their bank statements.

Many times, Big John had come home from school to see his mother sitting with the phone to her ear, her brow bent in consternation while a tinny voice on the other end described the atrocities Lynn had done.

Truth be told, his sister gave him the heebie-jeebies. The boogeyman, who other kids feared, lived at his house. The day he turned eighteen, he moved out of from under his mother's roof and away from the demon. Or so he thought. What he didn't understand about mental illness in a family was that it was a determined villain that followed its victims around. Lynn's disease made her rely on her family without any guilt or feelings of culpability. Whatever trouble befell her, it was somebody else's fault and somebody else's job to get her out of it.

"I'm not bailing you out."

"I told you, they weren't being fair. Frank and I were arguing and that bitch pulled out a gun. I got it away from her and they arrested me."

Big John had a hundred questions, none of which she would answer.

"Okay, I'll call Mom. She will have to come down here and bail me out."

Big John was a good boy, even borderline Mama's boy. He wasn't about to let his psycho sister terrorize his mother.

"I'll be right over."

CHAPTER FIVE

Don kicked a boot up on the worn coffee table and opened a beer. The smell of the hops and fertilizer permeated the cheap hotel room he'd taken while competing in the rodeos this week. The best roping he had done so far was lassoing the nosy little hussy who'd come down the stairs to see what he was up to. She had more terror in her eyes than most of the calves he had roped in the last two days.

He took a long swig of the beer and sighed. He hadn't come here to terrorize trailer trash or spy on boring old people. He'd come here to rope some calves, win some prize money and pick up on some lovely heifers in the meantime. That's all he wanted. His father had demanded that he spend a little time bullying his ancient enemy, Old Roger Wright. His father had threatened him, saying he wouldn't have a place to stay anywhere in Texas if he didn't terrorize Wright in some way.

Don lacked a steady income. He lived in his dad's house in a run-down suburb of Dallas. The dingy little shack was crowded with things that belonged in a ranch house like they used to live in when he was a kid. His father just wouldn't let go of things.

Don had no desire to settle a score between two old fogies.

Reluctantly, he set his beer down and pulled his cell phone out of his pocket. He dialed his old man's number.

His father's voice, deep and gruff, came on. "Hello."

"Hi, Dad."

"Well, did you see him?"

Don wished his father would get with the twenty-first century and

31

text. It wasn't likely that father and son would have a warm heartfelt conversation, or that Don would get to hear pride and joy in his father's voice when he heard about his son's rodeo feats. That wasn't going to happen. Ever. "Yeah, I saw the old guy. We had a lovely conversation. I asked him what was the matter with him and he described his fecal habits and how he could no longer get the damn thing up anymore. I told him I didn't give a shit. He said he couldn't give a shit. Then he laughed and told me not to make him laugh too hard because the laundry was down two flights of stairs and the old lady couldn't climb stairs too good anymore. So could I . . .? And then he lost his train of thought. Oh wait, I think that was the conversation I had with Granddad the other day, and the day before that."

"You'll get old someday and then you won't be such a smartass."

"Yeah, but you won't be around to see that."

His father's breathing came across the phone angry and fast. "Do I have to remind you that that man ruined your life?"

His father often referred to "Asshole" Wright as the reason for anything bad happening in their lives. Don just never felt that he had a bad childhood.

"That man kept the rodeo from coming to Texas back in '13. I had invested our whole family's savings on that. Because of him, we fell to the poverty level. The stress caused your mother to have a stroke."

Nine years had passed since she'd had the stroke, yet tears still welled up in Don's eyes at the mention of his mother. He remembered the day that his father had come back from the hospital, alone. Despite Don's resolve to remain tough, his father could dreg up memories that made him cry. The man could extract a tooth from a tense tiger's mouth. "Dad, I'm sorry."

"That's okay, Son." The old man's voice softened and Don knew he was in trouble. "There is something I want you to do to Wright the next time you're down there."

Textbook Dad. Always in there to rip something out of your hands when you started to lose your grip. His old man had written the handbook on wrangling bad things out of people. Don felt a tightening across his forehead. "What dad? What do you want me to do? You want me to strip his car down to the primer and write obscenities that he'll never understand or be able to read? You want me to break into his house and steal his Geritol or his little blue pills?"

What his father wanted him to do was far, far, worse.

"Take me home," Lynn demanded. She lobbed her huge purse into the backseat of her brother's car without a second glance or thought as to the damage the designer bomb could wreak.

A pink box lay crushed under the mammoth bag.

"That's okay, I can go and get another cake for Mom," her brother, Big John said.

"You can take me home first. I have stuff to do." She did not bother to turn around and see what her brother was talking about.

Big John had actually entertained the thought that someday his crazy sister would thank him. "Wouldn't you like to come to the house and express a happy birthday wish to dear old Mom?"

"No, you can do it." She turned and looked out the window. Rows of earth-colored houses passed her line of sight. "I've got some big plans for next week."

"This is the one day of the year when you could show your appreciation to Mom."

"There's Mother's day next year and Christmas coming up next week."

A small plane flew overhead. The piper's shadow darkened the inside of John's pick-up, casting the two siblings into darkness.

"One of these days, those things are going to kill us," John said, looking up.

Lynn turned toward her brother and her face brightened up. John had seen that same shining look on her face when she spotted Frank. But she didn't mention him. "That's my invention."

"What's your invention?" Often times talking with his sister felt like he'd been dropped into a conversation already going on and he had to catch up.

"It's what I was doing my thesis on in college."

John frowned. He and his mother had speculated that Lynn had gone to college just to husband-hunt. When they found out that she had actually enrolled in some classes and was planning to stay in school, they quickly despaired. School cost money and Lynn could be in school forever without a degree. They assumed that she would find a good man who would take care of her and take her off their hands. She could then drop out of school and make her trust fund last. There wasn't enough money in there to sustain a twenty-two-year-old in a life of leisure.

Lynn took just enough classes to put a decent dent in her trust fund, and then dropped out. No job. No man. Just a shrinking trust fund. She was twenty-two years old. Mental illness was a tough disease. It limited your ability to fend for yourself without having the consideration of shortening your life.

John rounded the corner and the lights of two huge casinos vied for his attention, their bright neon signs glaring into his glasses. "I don't remember that you had a thesis in college."

"There was some speculation that I had cheated and copied somebody else's." Lynn rolled her eyes.

"There was more than speculation, there was a suspension."

"I was never charged."

The system had found her mentally ill and dumped her back on her family. "So, what is your money-making scheme?"

"It's not a scheme. I've invented nose plugs that keep you from getting sick. When you board a plane with a hundred other hacking, drooling people you won't inhale their diseases."

John turned right and drove along the small North Las Vegas Airport. "Really?"

Lynn nodded. "I'm going to L.A. tomorrow to get some investors."

Big John's foot came off the gas. "Did somebody invite you to L.A.?"

"Yes, that's why I'm going."

Big John's heart thumped rapidly in his chest. He was glad for the dim light on this stretch of the road. "Lynn, you didn't somehow steal somebody's phone number, and call them up, say, more than five hundred times to ask them for money?"

"No, I found an invitation to bring business ideas to this TV show where you come on and present your business ideas to a panel of multi-millionaires."

"Wait! What? You're talking about *Shark Tank*. Where did you steal the invitation for that?"

"I didn't steal the invitation I found one printed in a newspaper."

"You never buy newspapers."

"I took it out of some guy's back pocket."

"There's the stealing part."

Lynn sighed. "A little pickpocketing. He wasn't reading it, he was asleep. Do you want to hear about *Shark Tank* or not?"

"I wouldn't miss it for the world."

"I told the booker at *Shark Tank* about how I had found this semi-permeable material"-

"Yeah, yeah. They liked the material and invited you on the show." John pulled into her apartment complex as the sun set. Lynn could motor mouth all night if you let her run on.

"Yes, that's why I'm going on the show. Have you not been listening to me?"

Big John resisted the urge to turn off his headlights to sneak into her apartment complex. Half of her neighbors had called the police on her and the other half hovered in silent fear. Lynn lived in an envelope that protected her from reality. Her infractions were anything from yelling at someone for eating too loudly to sneaking up on people and starting some off-the-wall conversation with them while they were just trying to get their laundry done. "I've been listening to you, Lynn. That's great news." The nachos he'd eaten earlier refused to settle. He swore they were gnawing on his insides.

Nothing ever turned out good for Lynn. Did the show call her because they figured that the little psycho would make good television when they laughed her off the show? What if she flipped out and tore up the set? Well, even better.

"Aren't you happy for me?"

The way that she looked at him made him think of when she was twelve years old. Innocent and so full of promise. His heart softened. She was still his baby sister. "I'm ecstatic for you." He stopped in front of her place. A thousand things crossed his mind. Things that he wanted to say to her. Warnings. Encouragement. Instead, he watched her gather her stuff. Clutching her unwieldy tote bag and purse to her chest, she clambered out of the car, then slammed his door and jogged across the beam cast by his headlights. Instead of continuing to her front door, she headed towards his driver's door. What now?

"Thanks for the lift." She leaned into the window briefly. Her baby fine hair brushed across his face along with a flicker of the scent of cherry Lifesavers. His vulnerable baby sister then turned and headed up the stairs.

Something was definitely off. He rubbed his roiling belly and wondered what an ulcer felt like.

.

CHAPTER SIX

Brad Pitt, President of the United States, four time Oscar nominee actor, Nominee-awarded director and father of eight leaned back in his seat and smiled out at the ethereal view outside his window. He would never get over the wonder and thrill of being on Air Force One. But, the consummate actor and distinguished leader of the most powerful nation on earth managed to resist the urge to jump up and down like a schoolgirl. Instead, he sipped his Vodka and tonic, kicked his feet up on the Ottoman and opened a folder. He pretended to read it, but inside his brain, a little voice kept singing, "It's your birthday, it's your birthday." He was going to Vegas, baby.

The only thing dampening his joy was that his wife was not coming with him.

Tanya sat on the metal chairs in the Detention Center for what felt like hours. A powerful thirst had thickened her tongue and she had to go to the bathroom. A woman twice the size of the state of Vermont eyed her with desire. The deputy that kept poking her face into the room to check on the inmates looked more like she was looking for a clear shot rather than a distressed prisoner. Tanya stayed quiet.

Finally, the deputy spoke when she poked her nose in the door. "Tanya Newer."

In her charge for the door, Tanya stumbled over a woman with "Fuck Mom" tattooed on her arm. Tanya barreled on, arms stretched out, reaching for something to grab should she fall and need to pull herself out of the muck of stinking humanity in the room. She did not breathe until the deputy slammed the door shut safely behind her.

"Your boss has come to get you."

Tanya almost asked if she could get back in the jail cell. Sal would be mad. He would breathe fire and garlic into her face and make her take the week day shifts. She'd have to deal with senior citizens who figured their tips on 10% of what a drink cost in 1947. She was in big trouble.

"Cheer up. You're not in trouble with the law."

"Are you sure you can't think of something to get me back in that cell?" Tanya asked the deputy. Sal when angry sweated a lot and stood too close.

"No, your story checks out. Wrong place at the wrong time. The gun was registered to another woman on the scene."

"That crazy woman?"

"Lynn will never get a gun as long as I live. No, the other blonde."

Tanya marveled that the deputy seemed to know Lynn personally. She followed the large woman in the starched uniform down a long corridor. They came out to a cold grey room where the night sky could be seen out the window.

And then a garlic-flavored shadow blocked her view. "Hi kid," Sal boomed. "Hey, you hungry?"

Tanya stiffened. She sniffed the air and smelled sweat. She could eat an elephant but she had to play cool. "No, I don't want a knuckle sandwich."

Tanya nearly choked on her tongue when Sal threw back his head and laughed, filling the room with the aroma of spices from the Old World. He put his beefy arm across Tanya's shoulders. "This girl is a rip, ain't she? The salad bar around the corner is still open. We'll get you something there."

Salad? What the hell happened to her Boss? If the food didn't stop the heart, he didn't eat it. She could tell him to stuff his salad back in the hole in the ground and get her a steak but she was afraid to stir him up. What happened to the Sal she knew? This cheerful version of her cranky old boss was unnerving. She played it cool and smiled at him.

The deputy watched the exchange, then took a large manila

envelope containing Tanya's worldly possessions and dumped them on the table.

Sal observed the contents of her purse. A corkscrew and a picture of her son on a keychain floated among the usual things in a woman's purse. Her boss picked up Henry's picture and studied it. In the picture, Henry was five years old. The kid had a yellow duckie clutched in his hand. "Your kid's going to be real proud of you someday."

"Alright Sal. Lay it on me. Did my mother die? Did Harley stop making motorcycles? What's going on?"

"I'm not going to tell you." The big Italian guy looked like he was going to burst.

Tanya rolled her eyes and yawned into her hand. "Is the President coming to see me?"

Sal looked like he'd been smacked sideways with a big bag of cement. "Who told you?"

"Sal stop it. I'm hungry. Really hungry. Can we go?" Tanya slung her purse over her shoulder and headed out the door. After a few steps she realized that he wasn't following her.

"My god. Somebody has already found out and gotten to you."

Lynn pulled out her tablet and ran through her multi-million dollar Power Point presentation. She tapped on the screen and the picture of the specially designed osmotic semi-permeable membrane appeared. She swiped her finger across the screen and it streaked away. Quickly she moved through all the images. Her presentation was in order.

She just knew Frank couldn't wait to view it with her. She looked at her watch and wondered where he was. She had called him nearly six hours ago to tell him that he needed to take her to the airport. That would be his part.

The doorbell finally rang. Her heart rate sped up and she nearly tripped over her own feet running to get to Frank. She yanked on the knob, hitting herself in the face with the door in her haste. She almost flung herself into . . . an old lady's arms? "Where is Frank?"

"Working," the spiky-haired octogenarian shot back.

"He doesn't work. He's an artist." Lynn folded her arms across her chest and stared down at the woman.

"Don't argue with me, Chicky. I have a barbed tongue and a husband who was in the mafia." Mrs. Wright elbowed her way sharply into Lynn's apartment. "Now stop acting so tough and get me a drink."

"It's eight in the morning and you have to drive."

"Frank didn't tell me you'd be so troublesome. Stop worrying. It's five o'clock somewhere and I've got one of those self-driving cars."

Lynn uncrossed her arms. "You are the first one I know to have one of those. But you do have to drive to the self-drive lane."

Mrs. Wright waved a hand. "I could do that in my sleep."

"Yeah, so, I don't think I'll be getting you that drink. I hear in a few more years all cars will be self-drive from door to door."

The old lady shrugged. "I won't see that. I'm so old I could drop dead at any time. Just help me find my keys and we can go."

"They're in your hand. Why can't Frank take me?"

Mrs. Wright studied the young woman's face. The wrinkles around her heart-shaped face crinkled. "You know, Frank told me why and I could try to give you his excuse but I'm eighty-three years old and the whole thing would come out convoluted and confusing as hell, so let's just leave it at, because he can't stand you."

Lynn stared, her eyebrows creased. "I don't understand."

"Oh dear, my explanation came out confusing anyway. Well, let me try again. Frank doesn't want you. He's involved with that woman who pulled a gun on you. They go to church together. Isn't that sweet? Now get your things and let's go."

Lynn felt her cheeks burning in anger. She inhaled deeply, trying to cool her rising temper. The tears fell, angry and hot, streaming down her cheeks. Resolutely, she picked up her suitcase and followed the old lady out to her car, an old Prius. Faded, but still readable, was the word "Google" on the side of the car. Lynn swallowed hard. "You bought the old Google car. This was one of the first self-driving cars they made."

Mrs. Wright shrugged and smiled. "Google's probably moved on to inventing yoga mats that float to the gyms by themselves. They gave me a good deal." She kicked her tiny foot under the back license plate and the trunk flew open. "This little gadget is more useful than most husbands."

Lynn smiled at her, a terse polite smile. She placed her luggage into the trunk and would have stomped away had it not been for Mrs.

Wright clamping a surprisingly strong grip on her arm. "Listen, young lady. I still have my faculties of reasoning around me. I know you are mad and you are hurt. You are probably thinking that I'm some senile old woman that let the beans spill out of the bag. You couldn't be more wrong. I didn't spill any beans, I poured the hot mess out, right into your lap." Mrs. Wright abruptly slammed the trunk down.

Lynn jerked her fingers back. She'd felt the scrape of metal on her skin as the jaws of the trunk glazed over her knuckles. If she'd been a little slower, she would have been fingerless. "You have all of your faculties?"

"Maybe I'm missing a few marbles, but I have something better than a few missing marbles."

Lynn raised her eyebrows.

"I have your suitcase."

"Lynn put her hands on her hip. "I could get the keys from you."

Mrs. Wright stared back, planting her sensible shoes on the sidewalk. "You could. But I'm counting on the fact that you would have the consideration not to attack an arthritic old lady."

"I'm mentally ill. I'm not accountable for my actions. Being bi-polar is like a Get-out-of-Jail free card." Lynn allowed herself a small hair flip of victory.

Born at the tail-end of the depression, Mrs. Wright came from a family of fighters. "I like your line of thinking but here's the bottom line. I'm packing." She patted her little pink beaded purse. "I could blow a hole right down your line of thinking and into your ass. I have a very good aim."

Lynn quickly came to the conclusion that the old lady was crazier than herself. She jumped into the car.

Mrs. Wright followed suit and started the car. She checked all of the mirrors, and then pulled out slowly in front of a flying UPS truck. She did not speed up, even when the truck's screaming tires sounded like a woman in labor. The old lady's expression remained serene. "Do you want my opinion, dear?"

Lynn said nothing.

Mrs. Wright giggled. "Oh I forgot. I've got the gun. You're in no position to disagree. So here's my opinion. You don't stand a chance with Frank. He doesn't like all the lunatic attention you've been bestowing on him."

Lynn regarded the older woman carefully. "Not that it's any

concern of yours, but I am bipolar, a disease that messes with my emotions, not my brains."

"You are a lunatic, my dear. I call you that with all kindness."

"What would you call me without any kindness?"

"An asshole."

Mrs. Wright turned her attention to the road. They were just entering the Interstate 15 on-ramp and would need to merge across three lanes to get in the self-drive lane.

Lynn ducked and hunched slightly in case of bullets. She saw hand gestures from the car Mrs. Wright had cut off that Lynn was sure the Catholic Church had banned. She didn't breathe again until she heard the magnets in the self-drive lane engage the car.

Mrs. Wright shut the engine off. "Ahhh, we're living the dream." The lane carried the car along at an even fifty-five miles per hour, self-adjusting to let cars merge in. "McCarran Airport," she said into the voice box next to the steering wheel.

"Prepare to exit in eighteen minutes," the disembodied voice intoned from the speaker.

Mrs. Wright turned to her passenger. "I'm sorry if I was a little harsh back there. It's just that my husband and I are very fond of Frank. We saw him nearly kill himself trying to get away from you. Does that not tell you something?"

Lynn stared out the window. "I love Frank. Why can't I make him see that?"

Mrs. Wright sighed. "I guess your answer to my question is no. I know what would help you understand. A good horse-whipping. In my day, and where I'm from in the South, we didn't believe in all this namby-pamby psycho babble. Grandma would rap you over the head with her cane and that would be that."

"Nobody spanks their children anymore." Lynn's face showed her horror. "It's barbaric."

"But it's perfectly civilized to let kids run around like wild animals in public places. I say a good wallop up side the head would save the police a lot more work later."

"Did your mother ever have any kids that lived? I suppose you think this one-kill law is acceptable."

Mrs. Wright swiveled in her seat. Lynn thought that the old woman might lunge for her throat. "You say anything like that again and you will be vanished from this car right now. That one-kill law defeats the whole semblance of a civilized society."

"I'm sorry. I just can't stop thinking about Frank. Didn't you ever have a crush on somebody?"

Mrs. Wright smiled. "Yes. On Mr. Wright. The first time I saw that hunk my tongue fell out of my mouth and you could have wiped up the floor with it."

Lynn shuddered. The image of the current Mr. Wright, gray and stooped, would not leave her head. "Mr. Wright was a hunk?"

"Oh, yes! The first time we made love was like an octopus and molten metal meeting. Limbs were all over the place and heat and steam smoked up the room."

Lynn knew she would be tossing and turning all night to get that image out of her mind.

"Oh, I could tell you stuff that would make you squirm." The old lady beamed at her.

"PREPARE TO EXIT IN SIXTY SECONDS." The electronic voice intoned suddenly and loudly.

"Technology saved my life," Lynn muttered under her breath.

Mrs. Wright swiveled in her seat. The turn signal had automatically been activated. She checked the rear-view mirror, loving the power she felt when the other cars obediently dropped back to let her merge. Although the auto-drive technology had only been out for a year now, people knew that when a car in the auto-drive lane signaled, it meant that it *was* coming over. Now.

Mrs. Wright found being thrown out into the fast lane thrilling. She gripped the steering wheel and placed her foot on the accelerator, ready to take over the driving, once auto-drive tossed the car out onto the freeway. She counted with the electronic voice.

"Get ready in 5 . . . 4 . . . 3 . . . 2 . . . 1 and go!"

Lynn braced herself. The self-driving mechanism changed lanes like a teenage driver bent on showing his friends how cool he was.

Mrs. Wright let out a "Yee-haw" and then giggled hysterically.

In a second, the Prius had completed the lane change and Mrs. Wright had control of the car. "Sorry," she said, slightly out of breath. "I have to get my Adrenalin rush when I can. My daily life consists of going to the doctor with my husband. That doesn't exactly replace the heart-throbbing sex that we used to have." She suddenly changed lanes, mirroring the auto drive's technique of a sudden dodge to the right.

A Smart Car braked violently to avoid being side-swiped.

Lynn's hand trembled. The old lady changed lanes again, this time without mishap. Maybe the other cars had seen the way she drove. They had about a half mile to spare before the airport exit.

"Well, that got my heart fluttering," Mrs. Wright said. She placed a hand on her chest, as if feeling for a pulse.

Lynn found this more alarming than their hair-raising lane changes. "Are you okay? Is something wrong with your heart?"

Between the seats, Mrs. Wright's cell phone rang insistently.

"Don't answer that now," Lynn urged.

"It's probably my husband. Every time I drive he worries that I will have a heart attack." She scooped up the phone before Lynn could grab it. Holding it to her ear, her face froze.

Lynn watched the old woman's complexion go from peachy to red to white, all while they were hurtling down the road at 53mph and coming up on a line of slowed cars at the Tropicana exit. "Mrs. Wright?"

Mrs. Wright came to. She dropped the phone and then braked expertly, avoiding the rear end of a small car with two children romping around the back seat. "Never a dull moment," she said.

"What happened? Did somebody die?"

"No," Mrs. Wright assured her, color flooding back into her cheeks. "Just another threatening phone call. Mr. Wright was involved in the Mafia back in the day. I get so many threatening phone calls that they are becoming monotonous."

"Then why did your face turn the color of a beached whale? What did this person say?"

"He wished us good luck with catching our flight."

Lynn swallowed. "He knows that we are going to the airport."

"Relax. It's not the Mafia. It's this punk that we had a run in with the other day." Mrs. Wright told her about the thug who had lassoed Tanya.

"What else did the caller say?"

"He reminded me of how good he was with a rope."

Lynn's stomach churned and she checked her rear-view mirror. "So you know what he looks like."

"Yeah, hunky kid with spiky blond hair. He looked like a real-life Bart Simpson, except this guy had bulging muscles. Not much taller than you. A real cutie. Really dear. There are a lot of people around at the airport. He can't get you. And besides, he's after *me*."

"Then why did he rope Tanya?" Lynn checked the side view mirror. Two young black men sitting on her right side in an older, lowered Mercedes beat their heads to loud rap music.

To Mrs. Wright's left, a young businessman in a Lexus looked at his watch anxiously. She let him get in front of them.

Mrs. Wright shrugged. "She got in the way."

Lynn let that one go. "Why are so many people threatening your husband?"

"Nine years ago, my husband was pivotal in getting the rodeo to remain in Vegas."

"I thought that was a good thing."

"It was, but they think my husband got a big chunk of bribe money. The Mafia wants their share."

"I thought the Mafia left Las Vegas before the eighties."

"That's what everyone thinks."

"*Did* your husband get a big chunk of money?" Lynn asked boldly.

Mrs. Wright smiled. "Let's put it this way, we are two senior citizens who won't be eating dog food anytime soon."

"Why are you so calm about this?" Lynn looked around. The one that had attacked Tanya knew they were going to the airport.

Mrs. Wright drove past the beautiful hotels along Tropicana. On one corner alone they had the New York skyline, competing with a medieval castle on the other corner. They crossed the Strip, driving under the pedestrian bridge and saw the MGM on one side and the elegant, remodeled Tropicana Hotel on the other side.

"It wasn't the Mafia that called. It was that little two-bit cowboy that trussed Tanya up like next week's meat special." Mrs. Wright shot Lynn a look, daring her to make a snide remark.

"Well, Tanya is a bit of a hoodlum. She butted in last night, almost getting me killed."

"She stopped you from becoming a murderer."

"I'm no killer. I prevented that crazy woman that Frank brought home from killing us all. Why are we even talking about this?"

They continued along Tropicana, past a row of cheap motels and gated construction areas.

"Do you think he's following us?"

"Why don't you call him back and ask him?" Mrs. Wright held her phone out to Lynn.

Lynn stared at the phone so long that the older woman had to rest her arm on the seat.

"This guy that is calling is the son of a man in Texas who lost his life's savings when the rodeo didn't come to Dallas. He was so sure that the rodeo would be coming to Dallas that he took his kid's inheritance and spent it on a huge arena that just sits there empty."

"So now, after nine years, this guy is after your husband?"

"His kid's after us."

Lynn developed a nervous tic at the corner of her mouth.

"Call him," Mrs. Wright urged. "Just go to calls received-"

"I know how to call him," Lynn snapped. She grabbed the cell phone.

"Well, do it," the old lady urged.

Lynn brought up the last number, glanced at Mrs. Wright and dialed.

"Hello?" A voice, cautious and slow, answered.

"What do you want with us?" Lynn barked into the phone.

"Who? Oh shit-" The connection broke suddenly.

Mrs. Wright laughed. "The little chicken."

"He hung up on me, the coward hung up on me."

Mrs. Wright was still chuckling when she pulled into the departing flights lane. "We're here." She maneuvered around two cars that appeared to be more abandoned than parked and cut right up to the curb. "Hey, how about something from the till to cover my gas?" Mrs. Wright tilted her blue-tinted 'do toward Lynn's bag.

"That's a purse, not a cash drawer," Lynn snapped.

"Oh, I get it. Your bipolar disease prevents you from thinking about anybody else."

"Nope, I'm just an asshole." Lynn snapped up her purse and jumped out of the car, slamming the door shut.

"Watch your back," Mrs. Wright muttered to the slammed door. She pulled away from the curb, her mind musing about what she could do today. It was a beautiful day and she had nowhere she needed to be. She felt healthy. Craig Regional Park had miles of walkways lined with a lush but rare plant in Vegas that other cities and places took for granted. They were called trees. Yes, today would be perfect to get out and walk.

She took her time moving over to the fast lane. She was in no hurry, and it would be all right if she didn't make it to the auto-drive lane. Finally, a truck in the fast lane yielded to her but when she moved over, it suddenly sped up. The medium-sized pick-up clipped her on the right back panel, spinning her around. The last thing she remembered was how ill-timed this accident was. It was just such a beautiful day and she-

Everything went dark.

CHAPTER SEVEN

Early Monday morning and Big John had been called to Stuart's downtown security office. Stuart was head of security at Canyon Ridge Church but he also owned his own security business and this summons was to his fancy office headquarters in downtown Las Vegas. Nervous and excited, Big John had spiffed up his shoes and pressed his best shirt, shining among the homeless population that loitered around the glass office building. John felt he was closer to them than the polished people who worked behind the glass towers looming above him.

Stuart's bovine middle-aged secretary ushered him into the office and pointed him to a chair, letting the door slam behind her.

"No, thanks, I don't need coffee," he said to the back of the door.

Suddenly a door behind the desk opened. Stuart entered the room, surrounded by the sounds of a toilet flushing and toxic fumes. He stopped abruptly, turned slightly, and quickly zipped up his fly. "You're early. Edith didn't tell me you were here."

"Probably because she was so busy talking to me. I don't know how you get any work done with that chatterbox around."

Stuart gave him a strange look and then realized it was a joke. He forced a brief smile to touch his lips and then, without wasting another moment on pleasenteries, the little man launched into the reason he had called Big John in. "We need you on our team, Mr. Buttoni."

Big John exhaled the breath he didn't realize he'd been holding. "Thank you, sir. Thank you." He tried not to gush but a year of unemployment with only dim lights at the end of the tunnel made one gush. John had been so nervous. Suddenly his cell phone rang, interrupting Stuart's next comment.

"Sorry, sir. Sorry." John fumbled for the thing, stuck deep in his back pocket. Finally his large fingers curbed around it. He pulled the screaming electrical device out of his pocket and, just before squelching it, saw who had called him.

His sister. She was supposed to be on the plane.

"An emergency?"

"No, sir." John nearly let the little thing fly out of his paw. "Please go on, it's dead now. It can't hurt you."

Stuart did not like jokes. "I was going to say that it is pure desperation that made us bring you here."

"My mother said the same thing." Big John gave his knee a triple drum beat. "Be-dum-pum."

"You'll be on a strict trial probation for the next ninety days. Do you understand?"

Big John nodded. He glanced down at his cell phone. His sister made him nervous. And when he was nervous he made stupid jokes.

Stuart stood and held his arm out.

The two men shook hands.

"You will take care of your sister, won't you?"

"Yeah." Was the man psychic? John wasn't quite sure what the man meant by take care of, but he had to keep his sister under wraps.

Stuart stared at him until Big John got the hint.

Big John gathered his big feet underneath him, scooted out of the hole he was sitting in and took a deep breath. Mustering all his strength, he pushed himself out of the short stuffy little chair Stuart had laid in the room for him like a trap. When he lifted his head, the little man was gone.

He hobbled past Stuart's spinster secretary. Her back remained toward him and he said a short thank you prayer to God for sparing him a gander at her ugly mug. He was not a vicious man, but sometimes, things like the shitty attitude Stuart and his typing cow had shown to him just got under his craw. That and whatever little surprise his sister had in store for him.

He finally made it to his car, got in and rolled his windows up so no one could eavesdrop on his call. Looking around, he pulled the cell out of his pocket and dialed his sister's number. The back of his neck trembled. The more her phone rang, the more his hand shook.

"'Bout time you called me back." Lynn's accusatory voice prickled his last nerve.

His lips quivered. "Why aren't you on a plane?" He hated the tremor in his voice.

"Just listen," she started, as if that was something different. His whole life, his mom and he had been forced into listening to Lynn. "I want you to check on Mrs. Wright. She's that old lady who lives next door to Frank."

Big John knew exactly where Frank and the old lady lived. Many times he'd been dragged to the apartment complex on silly off-the-wall errands because Lynn thought that she would need her big brother with her. They had to check to make sure Frank's car was alright. They had to check his mailbox to make sure no one had pried into it the night before and the worst one was when they'd had to sit in the complex for hours for a glimpse of Frank because Lynn had seen an image in her head of him limping. When the bastard finally did decide to emerge to take out the trash can, she'd yelled at her brother to scrunch down in the car. A seven-foot man does not scrunch down in a little car.

Big John ground his teeth, forcing his voice to be normal. "What am I supposed to check on her about?"

"Just see if she's alive. I think some guy was going to kill her."

Big John massaged his temples. If he screamed, his future employees could hear him and take him for a lunatic. "Is this something that the police should be involved in?"

"You're kind of like the police. You're a security guard. Just go over to her apartment and see if she's alive."

"You mean kick her tires, take her pulse?"

Lynn did not react. "I have to turn off my cell phone now. We're boarding the plane."

"Wait-" The line went dead. Big John tried not to curse. If he let loose with all the things he wanted to say, he'd be washing his mouth out with soap and rinsing it with a power hose. Typical Lynn. Dump a load of crying babies on his lap without telling him what they needed. He knew he would not be able to rest until he checked on the old lady. He looked at his face in the mirror. His color was not good. He took a few whiffs of his Albuterol and threw the car into reverse.

He saw the little shit jump, almost a second too late. Big John slammed on the brakes, causing a lightning rod of pain to shoot from his foot to his face. Before he could stop himself, the f-bomb flew out of his mouth.

Stuart regained his balance and some of his dignity. Slowly, he approached the passenger window.

Big John's cell phone lay on the seat face up. He quickly grabbed it before Stuart stuck his shiny bald head in the window.

Big John looked into his future supervisor's and said, "Two number one's, leave off the onions and super-size me, please."

"I don't find you funny. I find you very fatiguing."

"Yeah, I guess dashing out from under a speeding vehicle can be exhausting." Big John couldn't stop himself. "Sorry, sir, very sorry. How about if I just stay here and wait until you are safely inside your vehicle."

"That would be a good idea. Thank you, Mr. Buttoni." He pulled his head out of the car and stalked off on his way.

Big John watched and waited until the little guy placed himself in one of those little stuck-up Rolls Royces that were mass produced for the masses. Big John considered himself a good church-going man, but right at that moment, the One-Kill Law popped into his head. He allowed himself a second to fantasize about the pleasure of snuffing that smug little bastard's self-important expression off his face, then quickly chased the image away. Killing was wrong. What was the world coming to? What was he coming to?

Taking a deep breath, he did his best to calm himself down. This time, he took a good look around and pulled out of the parking space and out of the lot. He would just go over to the apartment complex and check on Mrs. Wright.

It was Monday morning and thankfully the streets were clear of traffic. He skipped the 15 and took Decatur instead. Decatur paralleled the Strip but it was two miles and a world away from the famous glittering boulevard. Aside from one casino for the locals, no glittering lights lined Decatur. Shabby apartments gave way to mediocre ones. Strip malls ruled the spaces in between. A few questionable individuals ambled up and down the streets.

He found Frank's apartment complex on the right, just past Flamingo Drive. Big John drove past the abandoned guard shack and pulled into one of the visitor parking stalls near the Wright's apartment. When he got out of his SUV and turned to look up at the Wright's apartment, an old man appeared on the balcony. He stood smoking and peering down on John.

Slightly unnerved by the elderly man with the hard stare, Big John struggled up the stairs. When he got on the landing with the Wright's balcony, he turned and faced the man.

Mr. Wright focused his steadfast gaze on the younger man. "Good morning, son."

"Good morning, sir." *Is your wife alive* did not seem like a good opening line. "Umm, sir, is your wife home?"

This aroused the old man's hackles. He threw down his cigarette. "Who wants to know?"

The only thing Big John knew about old people was that the slightest bit of stimulation could set off a heart attack. He worried about how he was going to answer that question, and then decided that maybe he should just tell the truth. "I'm Lynn's brother. Your wife took Lynn to the airport this morning."

The old man squinted. "Is your sister the one who thinks that fat boy next door is a turn-on?"

Big John nodded.

"My wife ain't back yet."

Beads of perspiration dotted Big John's forehead. "Sir, I think you should call her. I think you should call her now."

Mr. Wright reached into his pocket. Even from the distance, Big John could see his arthritic hands tremble as they pulled out the cell phone. Big John watched the terrible scene unfold before him. Mr. Wright's grim face listened to whoever had answered the phone, then dissolved into fine lines. His mouth shouted questions into the phone until he had run out or been run down by the person on the other end. Now he nodded humbly. He gently pushed the button, ending the call.

"My wife's in a coma."

"I'll take you to the hospital," Big John offered.

The old man disappeared inside the apartment and came out the front door, holding a sweater and a cane. He didn't seem to know what to do with either one of them.

Big John made it up the stairs. He stood at Mr. Wright's side and gently took the sweater and held it out to him.

Mr. Wright slipped his arms into the sweater, nodded his thanks and took the cane in his right hand. "My wife makes friends with everyone, she is so tolerant."

Big John nodded. He stepped alongside the old man, holding his arm out slightly so that Mr. Wright could take it if he needed to.

"My wife thinks your sister is a complete lunatic, no offense."

"No offense taken. I do think we should hurry, sir."

Mr. Wright nodded his understanding. Gripping his cane in his thick knobby knuckles, he proceeded down the stairs. "This is mighty charitable of you to give me a ride. Are you being so indulgent because you think your sister had something to do with this?"

"No, sir. I don't think Lynn had anything to do with your wife's condition." Big John realized that he actually believed his words. They made it to the bottom of the stairs. Big John steered Mr. Wright towards his SUV.

"Good. Because I won't be this easygoing if I find out you or Lynn had anything to do with what happened to my wife. She's the tolerant one, not me."

"I understand, sir. You would tar and feather me."

"No, I'm narrow-minded and short on time and energy. I'd just kill you."

CHAPTER EIGHT

Frank sat in his studio, dejected. Sunlight streamed in through the large windows, blinding him with the reflection on the blank canvas. The paint brush in his hand would not put anything on the board. His mind wasn't helping things either. It kept running back to last night's disaster. He'd been stuck in jail until almost ten p.m. The woman whom he'd thought could be the one he'd been searching for, wouldn't talk to him. In fact, the police probably took her away to a very nice place with soft padded walls.

He forced his attention back to the canvas. He stared hard at his hand, hoping it would just spring to life and do something, draw anything. This was to be the painting he planned to donate to the Tablet Computer Fund for Underprivileged Kids. Draw, hand. Heart and mind, feed hand. Please, work for this good cause.

Miraculously his hand dipped the brush into the dark brown paint. He slashed a long horizontal line and then some short vertical lines. Then, he squinted at the canvas, trying to figure out what he had done. He'd just drawn a coffin. He shrugged and tried to relax. He let his hand do what it wanted with the brush. Swish. Swish. A heart appeared in the coffin. He knew it was his heart. He had to find a woman before his heart died. He had to find a woman before he kept talking to himself and he had to find a woman before he got too old.

He removed the canvas and placed a blank one in its place. But his hand stayed flat in his lap.

Two women stood in the way of his finding love. Crazy Lynn and Tanya, the whore. Between Lynn's stalking and Tanya's lewd talking, they were killing his hopeful love life. They were killing his career. A painter, an artist, such as himself, needed love and romance in his life to feed his muse. If he couldn't feed his muse, he couldn't feed his face.

He turned toward the doorway, half expecting Lynn to be standing there. In fact, he should have driven her to the airport himself. That way, he could watch her get on a plane and know that she'd be gone for a little while.

That's when the idea hit him. Crazy insane idea but therapeutic. He would paint Lynn. He would put her thin-haired bony face on canvas so that he could have her right where he wanted her. He could chase her out of his mind and right onto the canvas.

Oddly enough, he had a five-by-seven photograph of her. One day she'd stuck the picture on his windshield. Not wanting to litter, he'd thrown the photo in the back seat and forgotten about it. And then, for some unknown reason he'd put the photo in his briefcase.

He pulled the picture out now and propped up her smiling face on the table next to the blank canvas. Lynn stared at him from a heavily made-up face. She carried a flaming torch dangerously close to her teased and hair-sprayed hair.

Now he would put her on canvas exactly as he wanted her. The idea stimulated his artist's juices. He cranked on the old stereo he kept in the corner. The music filled the room, its steady beat like a constant shot of adrenaline in his arm. His fingers dabbed at the canvas, then they swished, stroked and dabbed again until Lynn's face appeared, make-upless and slightly frightened. Such a picker-upper to have your enemy before you, helpless. The power of the brush. You could humiliate, torture or wipe them off the face of the canvas with a simple brushstroke or two.

Robin Thicke's voice filled the room singing, "I know you want me." The next thing Frank knew he was singing along and dancing about the room, taunting the helpless Lynn. He completely forgot about his depression, his lethargy. He completely forgot that his mechanic would be dropping off his car. "You're an animal," he sang to the painting. Laughing, he turned and pirouetted about the room, spinning 180 degrees until he saw Mike the mechanic standing there open-jawed, the keys to Frank's Mercedes in his greasy fingers.

"I know that girl." Mike pointed to the painting.

Flustered and red with embarrassment, Frank stumbled a bit.

"Yeah, I know her, too." He followed Mike's gaze to Lynn's face, staring at them from the huge canvas.

Mike's eyes went from the painting to Frank. "She's going to be in the news someday."

Frank nodded. He agreed wholeheartedly. He punched the power button and shut Robin Thicke up.

"Is she your girlfriend?" Mike asked.

"No," Frank practically shouted. He cleared his throat. "No," he said, softer.

Mike's face registered something. Frank thought it might be anger. The mechanic pointed at the photo. "That photo is outdated. She doesn't have teased hair anymore. It's straight now." The mechanic's fists tightened, making the cords on his sinewy arms stand out.

Frank nodded. "It sounds like you really know this girl."

"Yeah, I know Lynn. I do her car."

Frank decided not to make any off-color remarks about his phraseology.

An awkward silence followed in which the two men stared at each other. Frank could feel anger emanating from the mechanic.

Frank swallowed hard. "Do you like Lynn?"

Mike's chest rose and fell. He licked his lips. "If I could have only one party in my whole life, it would be with her." He turned his attention to Frank. "Sir, I'm as American as apple pie and I know this sounds very undemocratic of me, but if that woman told me to put my cammis on inside-out and parachute into Kabul waving an American flag, I'd paint a target on my backside and do it."

Frank laid his brush down slowly. "You'd be perfect for her."

"She has absolute power over me."

"Has our fair-haired Fascist ever asked you to parachute anywhere?"

"She doesn't even know I'm alive."

"Well, let's change that." Frank put a tentative hand on the smaller man's shoulder. "You need to tell her how you feel."

"Whenever I think about telling her how I feel, my sphincter just closes up and shuts off my emotions. Besides, you're the one she likes."

Frank nodded.

"Well, I can see why she likes you. You're as tall as a basketball player and you drive a Mercedes. And you don't have to work."

Frank glanced around at the dozens of paintings lying around the room in various stages of completion. Half of them were on a commission basis and had deadlines, the other half were for a show he had to do in three weeks' time. He looked at his paint-dabbled hands, the fingers soft and cushy. He looked at Mike the mechanic's scratched-up greasy fingers.

"I wouldn't touch Lynn with a ten-foot pole." Frank stepped close to the mechanic. "I cringe at the thought of coming into contact with her. The two of us converging is like liver and onions converging. It makes a completely repulsive dish."

"I like liver and onions."

"I hate liver and onions." Frank tapped out each word lightly on Mike's chest.

Mike stepped back. "I can't believe you feel that way about Lynn. I would give anything to just hold her."

"And I would give anything to just hold her head under water."

Mike moved across the room, away from Frank.

Frank realized he was frightening the smaller man. He took a deep breath and lowered his voice. "Anything you could do to interfere with her obsession of me would be appreciated."

"I could ask her out for a drink."

"Make an impression on her."

"Influence her with a nice dinner." Mike looked to Frank for approval.

"Yes, but do not upset her in any way."

Mike's eyes widened. "How would I upset her?"

Frank wanted to say 'breathe' but he held his tongue. "Just be a good listener. Give her sympathy when she tells you about her terrible family, laugh at her jokes and praise her when she tells you about her grandiose ideas. That kind of stuff." Lynn never made jokes and she never paid attention to anyone else's reactions.

Mike's eyes lit up. "Yeah, her great ideas. I sure want to be around her when her invention hits it big."

"What are you talking about?"

"Her nose plug company. Didn't she tell you about it? It's going to be as big as the Bionic Eye."

"Nose plugs are going to be the biggest invention since the Bionic Eye? The guy that invented the Bionic Eye is in a league with Jesus. The Bionic Eye is making blind men see. There's no way nose plugs are going to rival that."

"Lynn's nose plugs are preventing people from getting the common cold."

"Just get her out of my hair." But now Frank's voice lacked the conviction he felt earlier. "What did she say about these nose plugs?"

Mike shrugged. "Just that they were great and I believe her. Dude, do you mind if I have that painting?"

"Give me a free oil change."

Mike patted his wallet. "If I'm going to take Lynn off your hands I'm going to need a lot of money for wining and dining."

"Let me just add the finishing touches." Frank reached for a can of varnish.

"This won't take long will it? Lynn's going to be on TV tonight, and I don't want to miss that."

Frank began spraying the painting.

"Lynn's going to be a millionaire."

Frank caught a whiff of the gaseous spray at the same time that Mike threw that tidbit out. He started to cough. With the dexterity of a seasoned painter, he finished the painting with one hand while holding a tissue to his face with the other hand.

Mike watched. "Awesome, man."

"How is Lynn going to be a millionaire?" Frank popped the top on the spray can.

Mike filled him in on the "Shark Tank" details, then reached for the painting.

Frank kept his grip on the canvas.

"Dude, the painting. You said I could have it."

"You left out some details before I said you could have it." Frank showed off his adeptness by wrangling the canvas out of the mechanic's hands. "I might be interested in Lynn's business. Maybe I should be the one to be around when her business takes off the ground."

Mike shrugged and turned to go. Then, slick as a weasel, he darted back, snagged the painting and placed his skinny body between the artwork and Frank. "She needs someone with better management skills." He looked up at Frank defiantly.

Frank closed his eyes, bent his head and went in for Mike's lips.

The mechanic flared back, releasing the painting and Frank grabbed it.

"Maybe she prefers my method." Frank held the canvas tightly and grinned down at the shorter man. "Answer me this. Do you really like Lynn?"

The mechanic whirled on his feet, stomped out the door and slammed it, leaving Frank with the painting, a free oil change and a smug smile on his face. The smile stayed until he realized he never got his car keys back.

.

CHAPTER NINE

Big John left the hospital feeling like he'd been trampled on by forty aging showgirls in stilettos. He thought his morning couldn't get any worse after a crappy interview, then nearly squashing his future boss under his SUV. If he had any spirit left in him the depressing trip to the hospital with the cranky old man completely flattened him. And then his cell phone rang.

When was he going to learn to disregard his phone at times like this? But the ring of a cell phone is like the demanding bellow of an ape, he was drawn to it, he couldn't ignore it. He flipped the phone over to see the screen. Lynn. He should never say that things can't get any worse.

"Hello, Sis. How can you encroach on my happiness today?"

"I want you to go over to Mike the Mechanic's and get my car."

"Sure, Lynn. I'll just leave my car at your apartment and march over to the mechanic's and grab your car. Or maybe I can infringe on Mr. Wright, who's got nothing better to do than stare at his unmoving wife. Thanks for asking."

Lynn at least had the decency to have a moment of silent shock. "She's in the hospital?"

"Yes, somebody ran her car off the road."

"Is she okay?"

"She's great. She's staying there for the awesome food and the comfy bed. No, she's not okay. She's in a coma."

"Oh, God."

"Yeah. Oh, God."

"I should call Mr. Wright."

"I think you might be overstepping your welcome. He might be a little bitter."

"You're right. I don't want to overstep my welcome. Can you go and get my car? The shop is just across the street from my apartment. You can walk across Decatur. Your ankle won't break."

"No Lynn, it won't break, it just hurts. It's painful to put weight on that ankle."

"I suppose you're still mad at me for that. I was ten- years old when I went out skating on that lake. I didn't know it was dangerous."

"I know, Lynn, you can do no wrong. Even though Mom told you a hundred times not to skate out there."

"Every child misbehaves. I was ten. It was a little lapse in judgment. Let the one who has never sinned throw the first stone."

Big John just wanted to smack her. She hadn't progressed much from the bratty child who had sneaked out of their grandfather's house to skate on the neighbor's pond. Soon as his mother saw Lynn skating on that ice, she'd sent Big John out to get his sister.

Lynn had been oblivious to the cold, the danger of thin ice and her brother's calls. He'd been forced to skate out onto the ice, his nose and fingers almost frozen by the Wisconsin winter. How he wrangled his angry, rebellious sister back to the solid shore, he had no idea. They made it, literally skating on thin ice, even with Big John's weight. At fifteen, he weighed a hefty two hundred pounds and was already six foot five inches tall. Soon as she'd hit shore, she'd dug her ice skates into solid ground, screaming loudly and ran back to the house.

Big John didn't have the energy to chase her. The artic atmosphere numbed and lugged him down and he couldn't move well in ice skates.

That's when his grandpa's angry self-righteous neighbor came out of the house with a rifle, yelling something about how he was going to get the dirty pervert. It took Big John a second to realize *he* was the dirty pervert. You cannot argue with an angry man brandishing a loaded rifle. John got up and ran as fast as he could toward the house, trying to keep his ass from being loaded up with buckshot. Fifteen feet from his grandfather's property he fell, twisting his ankle violently in the process. Rolling over on his back, he'd decided to face his attacker head on. There was nobody there.

Big John's ankle still hurt to this day. It hurt when it was about to rain. It hurt when he walked on it too much. And sometimes he thought the thing just hurt to spite him.

"John?" His sister's voice, now grown up, brought him back to the present.

"I'll do it."

"Thank you. I'll pay you back."

"I appreciate that, but I don't know how you'd pay me back. I don't need any errands done."

"No, I'll pay you back for the bill. I haven't paid the mechanic yet." The phone went dead.

"Well, I guess we've exchanged enough pleasantries," he said to the dead phone.

Dutifully, he headed toward the repair shop across the street from his sister's apartment. It sat in a strip mall, the last shop on the end. John pulled up at one of the empty bays.

At the back of the shop, a wiry man in greasy overalls poked his head out from behind a hood, hollered something and dipped back under the hood. A few minutes later, he resurfaced and ambled over to John's SUV. "How you doin' today?" His teeth looked perfect and gleaming underneath the grease on his face.

"I'd switch places with a man on death row right now, but otherwise I'm hunky-dory."

The man regarded him kindly. He had soft blue eyes and, in spite of the smudge, could probably lead a desperate woman astray. "Want to put your day in reverse and try it again?"

"I'd love to but I came to pick up my sister's car."

"You must be Big John."

"I guess Lynn already told you I'd be down to pick it up."

Mike nodded. "Hey, I'm about done here. Want me to drive it across the street for you?"

"That'd be great." Big John could have kissed the man. "I think I owe you some money."

"Nah, I'll get the money from Lynn later."

Now Big John wanted to go deeper than a kiss. He wanted to buy this guy a beer. Slowly, something dawned on Big John. The mechanic knew where she lived. He wanted to collect his bill later, probably to have an excuse to see Lynn. "Do you like my sister?"

The man laughed and looked at his hands. "Is it that obvious?"

CHAPTER TEN

Swearing, Frank walked out of the apartment complex and out onto Decatur. He had to take a bus, a flippin' bus. He, who had enough talent as a painter to afford a Mercedes, was now hobbling to the bus stop. His transverse vertebral processes hurt from being hunched over a canvas for long periods of time. His doctor had told him that, and he'd looked it up. As a painter who painted nudes, among other things, Frank had an intent interest in the human body.

He had now walked a half mile from his studio door to the corner of Decatur and Flamingo. Up Flamingo, he could see the grand casinos, playgrounds for the rich and crazy alike. Up Decatur, he could see strip malls, real life for the working class. His route took him up Decatur.

Despite the mild December temperature, sweat gathered under the collar of his corduroy blazer. He didn't consider himself a germ phobic, but the thought of taking an eight-mile ride on a public conveyance packed with diseased and open-wound victims, bothered him. Hopefully, Mike the Mechanic would have cooled his jets by now, and Frank could get the keys and be on his way. Frank made sure his wallet was loaded with plenty of cash.

Miraculously, he did not have to stand at the bus stop balanced between wads of gum and garbage for very long. Not two minutes later, the bus drove up. He shoved two dollars into the slot and made his way to the back of the vehicle.

The only seat available was next to a friendly-looking middle-aged man. The ride would take twenty minutes. Frank took the seat. As he sat down, the man smiled at him. His teeth, the ones that he had left, were bad, very bad and whatever had killed them was still dying in his throat. Frank could smell it.

"Hello," the rotted mouth breathed. "I'm a tourist."

Too late for Frank to run. "Hello," he said, reluctantly taking the man's hand. "I'm a passenger."

The man laughed, the toxic fumes wilting the hairs on the back of Frank's neck. "Your Mercedes is in the shop, right?" He followed the remark with another hearty laugh.

"Yes," Frank said, staring hard at the man.

"I hate it when that happens." He laughed some more. "Well, buddy, my globetrotting ends here." He slapped Frank heartily on the back, then yanked the cord, signaling for the driver to stop. He excused himself and stepped over Frank's legs. "Hey buddy," he said. "When you get your Mercedes out of the shop, go see the President, I hear he's in town." The bus screeched to a stop. The man grabbed the pole and swung himself out the door.

"Your Mercedes is in the shop?" A small dark Hispanic man snarled, taking up the conversation. "Every day that man say that to someone. Every day, he laugh like eetz the funniest joke in the world." The man crossed his skinny legs and spat in the aisle.

Frank looked up, saw the North Las Vegas Airport. He reached his hand up and pulled the stop cord. When the bus rolled to a stop, he stepped over the pool of spittle and climbed off, relieved to be out in the fresh air. At Decatur and Cheyenne, he crossed the street to the little strip mall where Mike's Shop stood at the very end.

He wandered up to the far end of the strip mall, and made his way across the store fronts to the end, gathering his courage. When he got closer, he could see that the bays were closed, the windows dark. He considered just giving up and going home again, but he had come this far.

He stepped up to the shop's large window and scrutinized the interior of the office. Dark and without any signs of life, his prospects were dim. But just for fun, he tried the door. It opened.

"Hello?" he called into the office.

No one answered.

He stepped into the waiting room. "Hello?" he called again. He tried the door leading to the back office. It opened into a small hallway. Looking back and glancing out the window, he couldn't see anybody around out in the strip mall. He stepped into the hallway, now at the point of no return, but what the heck he thought. He kept moving down the hallway. Late afternoon light from an office window directly in front of him dimly lit his path.

Standing in the office doorway, he called again. Boldly, he switched on the light. Blinking in the sudden blaze of brightness, he managed to focus. His eyes scanned the office walls. He blinked again, rubbed his eyes and took another look.

The walls were a shrine to Lynn. Her homely thin face with the mopey chin covered every inch of the free wall. Some were hastily scrawled images, some were amateurish oil paintings, but the scariest were the photographs. Most were grainy and blurry, obviously shot quickly before the photographer could be caught. Frank couldn't take his eyes off the images, they were so invasive.

One near the bottom caught his eye. He realized it was because the background was the apartment complex across the street. Lynn was walking down the stairs, her hair flopping in her eyes, arms loaded down with two large tote bags. It suddenly occurred to him that he'd had no idea where she'd lived or what she did.

But this stalker did.

Frank had read about stalkers. If they caught someone violating their precious lair, things got treacherous. He could just see Mike's reaction if he caught Frank in here. Frank decided he better just find his keys and get the heck out of there.

He opened the drawer, and there they were. So far, so good. Keys in hand, he felt better already. But he'd feel better if he could get out of here before Psycho-Mike-Oh! returned.

He hurried down the hall, reaching into his pocket for the $100 bill. That should easily cover the repair bill. He laid it across the counter in the front office, near the register. His hand was on the exit door, when he heard the sound of heavy boots shuffling up the walk. This was not a good time to be six-three. The office did not have a single place for a man of his stature to hide. Maybe whoever was out there would just walk on by.

No such luck. The door opened.

Frank froze in the dark, facing a man almost as big as he was.

"The shop's closed," the man stated obviously. He had the slow drawn out speech of a Southern preacher.

"I know, I left some money."

The man glanced at the bill. "I'll let Mike know."

"Great," Frank said.

The man still did not move to let him pass. "Do I need to say it in any other language, the shop is closed."

"I can't get by you."

The man obliged, stepping out into the late afternoon light, giving Frank just enough room to pass, if he held his elbows in. Frank felt the air, icier now than when he'd first entered.

"Wait," the man commanded.

Frank waited.

The man reached into his pocket. He withdrew his hand and gave Frank a business card. "I own the language school in the complex. If you want to learn any language, we got teachers. We'll get you talking to Chinks, Beaners, Japs and even deaf and dumb people. Whatever. We can learn you to speak so good you can tell your mail-order bride in her own language that you been monkeying around with someone else and that she has to go. Pretty cool, huh?"

Frank tried to smile. He took the card.

"I also know body language. Like you wandering around some dark office. It looks a little deceitful. You want to be careful not to anger Mike."

Frank nodded.

"If you do, he'll dump you. You'll be stuck with some moronic mechanic who won't deliver your car to you."

"That would be perilous."

"What is perilous?"

"Aren't you the language man?"

"Yeah, but I don't teach foreign languages myself. Just plain English."

Frank felt a strong urge to get away from this dicey character. He'd gotten his car keys. The icy air chilled him and sundown was on its way. He did not want to ride the bus back when the creepier creatures of the night came out. Walking down the aisle of a RTC City Bus at night was like walking the slippery line between the sane and axe-murderers. He patted his pocket, feeling the keys to his good, beautiful car. Nodding to the guy and mumbling something about having to go, Frank jogged to the bus stop and was lucky enough to get picked up fairly quickly. He made his way to the back of the bus and sat down, crammed between a weary-looking businessman and a prostitute. The whole ride home, the businessman kept sighing, depressingly, and the prostitute kept rubbing against him, seductively. By the time the bus dropped him off near his apartment, he was ready for a drink. He didn't even go up to his apartment, just made his way to his car, and jumped in. His baby crooned to life. Mike was a good mechanic. Frank let the car warm up while he thought about where to go. And then he remembered the man on the bus telling him that the President would be downtown. Tanya worked downtown at the Horseshoe. He felt mischievous and ready to kick up some dirt. Downtown it would be.

In his powder blue 280 SL, he felt young and debonair. He headed for Fremont Street, the heart of downtown, ready for a drink and a little action.

He found free parking easily enough. He walked the two short blocks to Fremont Street into a world of difference. Dark parking structures gave way to lighted neon ceilings, loud music and drunk boisterous people parading around with long brightly colored drinks in their hands. Maybe President Pitt was here. He elbowed his way through the crowds. From one establishment, a showgirl beckoned him and from another a man invited him to come in and have a deep-fried Oreo cookie.

But Frank could really use a drink. He was going to have that drink at the Horseshoe.

Finally, he stood in front of the great green striped building. In contrast to its brilliant flashiness outside, inside it was dark and sedate and not very crowded. He added his fingerprints to the already smeared glass doors and entered. The darkness slowed him down, but he found the bar. And a cute redhead who smiled at him. And then Tanya appeared.

She stopped dead in her tracks when she saw him. "What are you doing here?"

"My neighbor," he explained to the redhead. He turned to Tanya. "I brought you your medication."

She came right up to him, the top of her head barely higher than his. "You better get out of here before you need first aid."

Just as quietly, he answered back. "Are you on drugs? Threatening me at your workplace?"

"You're going to need something by the time I'm done with you," she hissed.

Frank raised his voice so the redhead could hear him. "Just get me and . . .?"

"Ruth," she supplied.

"Just get me and Ruth a drink."

Tanya smiled. "Sure, what'll you have?"

Ruth ordered a glass of red wine. Frank beamed at her. "The same. And a visit with the President."

"What???" Tanya asked.

"I heard the President was here and I'd like to see him."

The redhead giggled.

Tanya glanced around. "Keep your voice down."

Frank followed her gaze. A man in dark glasses stood at the end of the bar watching them intently. Tanya moved like a nervous rag doll being jerked around by an amateur puppeteer. "My God, he is here."

"All right!" the tipsy redhead said. He hadn't seen her drinking when he walked in.

"Listen, let's make a deal. If I get you in to see the President, you will behave," Tanya hissed.

"The Redhead comes too."

"I can't do that."

"Pledge to me that you'll try," Frank demanded.

"Listen, this isn't some convention that you can walk in off the street and join." Tanya lowered her voice so that Frank and Ruth had to move in close to hear. "He wanted to spend some time with local people so Sal, my boss, submitted a list of his friends and business associates. Everyone in the private room with the President has had a thorough background check. You I know, her, I don't."

"I come in here every week." The redhead pouted.

Tanya sighed. She went down to the end of the bar, spoke briefly to the guy in dark glasses and pointed back at the redhead and Frank.

"He's coming over," Frank whispered to the redhead.

The man put his hand to his ear. "Come with me, sir." He abruptly turned, forcing Frank to hustle. Frank marched after the guy. A little excited, Frank didn't notice that the cute redhead had not made the walk with him until they reached the solid door separating him from the President.

"Where's the girl?" Frank asked, dismayed and rattled.

"We sent her back out on the range sir." His answer was as

straight and sharp as his crew cut.

Frank cursed, once again thwarted in love by Tanya.

"We can't let just anybody traipse in to see the President, sir." The large man stood at the door, waiting for Frank's reply.

"This is a trip. I'm not passing it up." Still so excited over getting to meet the President, Frank was ready to march over the big guy and barge into the room.

"Not so fast. There are rules, sir."

"No talking politics?" Frank giggled.

The guard glared him down. "Do not offer him anything. Food, cards, candy, nothing." He turned and muttered something into his earpiece.

"Why, will he follow me home?" Frank was cracking himself up.

"No, we will have to shoot you if we see you reaching into your pocket for anything. The second you reach into your pocket, you'll be full of bullets. Understand?"

Frank gulped, slightly sobered. He nodded.

"Do not touch him. The minute you reach over to shake his-"

"I'll be full of bullets," Frank interrupted. His voice quivered, a mixture of fear and excitement.

"Remember, there are at least two people in the room watching the President's every move. They have very twitchy fingers."

Frank's heart beat so hard that his whole chest vibrated. The warnings had rattled his cage, but still . . . Damn! This was the President.

The guard continued to stare down Frank, but his expression softened. "Well, Mr. Frank Donahue, Social Security number 411-63-1277, 3250 S. Decatur, Apt. 366, loyal son of Mabel and Don Donahue, are you a little afraid?"

Stunned, Frank could only manage the merest tilt of his chin.

"Good. Be really worried. And follow me."

The guard finally flung open the door. The two men entered into a softly lit room. Plush leather couches filled the spaces and a bar with a deep mahogany shine lined one wall. People sat comfortably, relaxed, sipping drinks and munching on peanuts. It seemed so oddly normal that Frank had to blink and pinch himself. Suddenly, the huge guard stopped and stepped aside.

And there sat Brad Pitt, forty-sixth President of the United States, smiling warmly up at Frank, as if they were college roommates, one arm slung casually along the back of the couch, the other arm holding a beer. One knee was drawn up, the heel of a scruffy tennis shoe resting on the couch. He wore a plain blue oxford shirt and sharply creased khaki pants. He looked like he should have had a baseball hat on backward, but instead, his hair was combed neatly, a little long, but perfectly trimmed.

"Come on, Frank. Have a seat. You're not trespassing. Waiter, get this guy a beer." The command was said in a jovial tone, to be answered in such by the waiter.

"Right away, sir."

The President pulled his leg down, sat up straight, giving Frank room to sit down. "Forgive me for not shaking your hand but I cannot stray from the straight and narrow." He gestured around the room.

Frank sat down, then looked around the room. An older woman in a dark suit with a severe bun raised her eyebrows. She stared without wavering. She was as scary as his high school principal. There, in the other corner, stood the pretty little redhead. She winked at him, and gave him a come-on smile. Then she lifted up her jacket and patted her hip. There it was, unmistakable. A weapon. A big one. He swallowed.

The President was blithely rattling on about the baseball games on TV.

Frank could barely focus or grasp what the President was talking about. Being a sports atheist, he had no idea how to comport himself in the world of manly athletic banter.

The President suddenly stopped talking. Mistaken Frank's silence for brooding, he became serious. "I know what you want to talk about. You want to talk about how I could allow the One-Kill Deal to pass, a law that breaks one of the Ten Commandments."

Startled that the president had called the law by its' street nickname, Frank could only nod.

The President sighed. In that moment, he became just a guy, trying to survive. "It's hard to even begin to explain how I could allow such a law."

"Yeah," Frank said, his voice barely above a whisper. He cleared his throat. "I mean, wasn't your wife awarded numerous humanitarian awards?"

Brad Pitt put his beer down. "She left me because of that law."

For a moment, he stared at Frank, displaying pain. "It really hurt her. This is a woman who's visited third world countries and gotten in there and helped them to survive and have a good life. She earned all of those humanitarian awards. On one trip she brought me a pair of shoes made by some women in a small village. They refused her money because they said that I was a good man and that they'd be proud to have such a righteous person walk miles in their shoes." He snickered a little. "But our world here in America was becoming a horrible out-of-control place. I don't care how good a man I am, I wasn't able to do anything to stop it. Nobody cares about anybody but themselves."

Frank glanced around. The two female sharpshooters had not moved, both overtly stared at him. Still, with the president's candid talk, he felt emboldened to ask his next question. "Sir, who would you like to kill?"

The President laughed, shaking off the somber mood. "The guy who invented coffee. Who would you off?"

"The waitress, Tanya. Do you know she's my big-mouth neighbor? She's run off more women than my stinky feet. But man, now I find out that that cute little redhead over there, whom I thought I had in my back pocket, is just a government plant."

"Her name is Ruth and let me tell you, she's been a real trial to us. As an undercover person, she's excellent. Pretty and tempting, better than fish bait. Only problem is, she'll shoot you at the drop of a hat. Want to know anything else?"

"No, I think the pursuit stops here."

Brad Pitt smiled. "Good call. Our administration doesn't want to be bothered with a legal investigation of still another Ruthless shooting."

"Cute pun." Frank licked his lips.

"She's been on probation more than any other agent in history."

Frank wanted to ask the President more questions but he checked himself. Suddenly his phone rang. Without thinking, he reached toward his pocket.

The old lady and Ruth had their guns drawn before his fingernails came close to touching his phone. A collective gasp filled the room. For a moment, time froze.

The President snapped too and raised his hands cautiously. "No attempt," he commanded. His voice, strong and sharp, cut across the chatter from the television sets.

Frank's heart had stopped.

"Guns down." The President's voice filled with annoyance.

The guns withdrew.

"Everything's fine," Brad Pitt called out. Then, lowering his voice, he spoke to Frank. "Such an irritation."

Frank's phone continued to ring. He cursed. "Such a pain in the neck."

"Pick up, buddy, or it will continue to plague you." The President held up his arms. "Don't worry. I won't let them shoot you."

Sweating and shaking, Frank hesitated. He didn't want to blow his time with the President.

"It's okay. See who it is."

Frank slowly did as he was told and raised the phone out of his pocket. He looked at the Caller I.D. "It's my neighbor. He's going through a bit of an ordeal right now."

The man who allowed murder gestured impatiently and said, "Then you must talk to him and be there for him when he is in distress."

Frank nodded. He steeled himself to deal with Mr. Wright's misery. Sure that Mrs. Wright had passed away, his mind fumbled with inanities to utter to the grieving man. "Hello," he said.

"Frank, you fat son of a bitch, you get your woman-chasing ass over here."

Frank pulled his ear away from the phone. "Sir, I'm with the president right now."

Mr. Wright didn't miss a beat. "Well, then you tell him to get the Air Force One pilot to fly you over here." The old man was shouting so loudly that the president heard it. "Eva's awake."

"Hallelujah!" Frank shouted. "That's great." To the president he said, "His wife's come out of a coma."

Brad Pitt raised a victory fist. "You better go, buddy."

"I'm sorry. The old man doesn't have a car right now and he really needs me to drive him over to the hospital to see his wife."

"Go buddy, go!" Brad Pitt grinned from ear to ear, genuinely happy.

Frank leapt to his feet. "Can we take the jet?"

"Highly unlikely." The President saluted him. "Better take your car."

Frank's special night with the President ended.

Oddly enough, the next thought in his head wasn't about what more he could have discussed with the President. It wasn't about still another failed romance with the ruthless redhead. It wasn't even about the miracle of Mrs. Wright coming out of a coma.

That thought was about Lynn. He wasn't going to get a chance to watch her on *Shark Tank*.

CHAPTER ELEVEN

Frank and Mr. Wright entered the glass doors of Spring Valley Hospital as if they were entering a hot new night club. The old man, slightly behind Frank, teemed with excitement, pushing on Frank's heels as if he held Mr. Wright from joining the party. When they got to Mrs. Wright's door, Frank wisely stepped aside, enjoying the stumbling happy gait as the old man reached for his wife's hand.

At his touch, she opened her eyes, looked at him and smiled. "Fool," she pronounced. Her eyes closed with the effort.

The door opened and a white-coated doctor walked in. He smiled. "Ahh, the family has arrived."

"Not the whole clan. We have four daughters coming from California. This young man here is my neighbor, Frank." Mr. Wright kept his large knobby knuckles clutched around the pale tiny one of his wife's.

"Well, let me explain some things before the party begins. You are going to notice a number of different behaviors about your wife. Number one, she will be more forgetful. At first it will be a lot of stuff, then, as the brain heals, it will be fewer incidences."

"We are in our eighties, doctor. This is not news to us."

The doctor carried on in his professional and brusque manner. "The second thing is that she will have difficulty making decisions. The injured brain cannot weigh all the pros and cons of a decision. You may have to make the decisions for a little while."

Mr. Wright's eyes brightened. "This is good. This woman has been bossing me around for fifty-seven years."

"The last thing is, Mrs. Wright may lose her inhibitions. She may blurt out embarrassing and inappropriate sentences."

Mr. Wright shrugged. "That's normal for her. Tell me, doctor, what will happen to her sex drive?"

Frank had finally found a fissure in the doctor's professional veneer. Redness seeped from his neck to his face. He looked like he was passing a kidney stone. "Well, when the inhibitions are gone, the fears and fences we normally put up or down can leave nothing in the way to regulate us as to what is, or are, our normal mores and likes and comforts."

The old man looked from the doctor to Frank. "What did he say?"

"He said your wife will spurt out horniness like a gushing geyser."

The doctor looked at his cell phone. It stayed stonily silent in his hand. He hazarded a glance up at the old man and nodded.

"Well. I'm gonna need some heart medication for when the old girl comes home," Mr. Wright said.

For Don, getting to the old lady to finish the job proved more difficult than trying to catch a mad cow in a cornfield maze. Her old man kept a constant vigil over her and, although he slept like a stone, there was always the awkward chance that he could wake up while Don was smothering the life out of her. Being a bull rider, Don's strength only lasted eight seconds. He hoped the old girl would take less than that.

Killing was legal, but only one massacre per person. Don resented his old man for making Don use his one shot on this old lady. What if someone came along in Don's life later that he really wanted to kill? Then he'd be screwed.

He could hit the old man over the head and then do the old lady, but if a nurse came in and caught him with two dead bodies, things could get ticklish.

The old man snorted in his sleep, a sound as painful to the ears as a paper cut was to the skin.

Don watched Mr. Wright for a few minutes, knowing that he needed to get out of there, but he had to make sure the old man was truly asleep. Old people were deceptive. They looked the same whether they were awake, asleep or dead.

The young man stared at the old couple for a few minutes more, thinking. He could snuff both of them now and when the nurse came in he could just say, "Shh! I just got them both to fall asleep."

Could he pull it off with his devilish mug? He looked too much like Bart Simpson to play an innocent well. He picked up a pillow.

Suddenly the door opened and a nurse came in. She started when she saw his dark figure standing close to the bed. "What are you doing here?" She did not whisper or try to lower her voice.

"I'm visiting."

"Sir, visiting hours have long since been over. It is ten o'clock at night."

"I know. Sorry. I just got in from Texas and I just had to see them." He gripped the pillow. Why did he have to blurt out where he was from?

She looked at him suspiciously. "How did you get in here so late?"

"My sister works in laundry. She let me in the back way."

"Your sister is going to be in big trouble. She's really not supposed to be . . ."

Don didn't hear the rest of the loud-mouthed nurse's lecture. She didn't seem to understand that two old people were trying to sleep. Why was this nurse such an agitator?

The old man shifted in his bedside chair. He muttered in his sleep.

If the old fart woke up, he could identify Don. People said Don bore a striking resemblance to his father.

"Young man?" The nurse's voice burned into him like a firebrand. "Did you hear anything I said?"

He whipped his attention back to her. "No!" And then his eyes went back to the bed.

In the dim city lights coming through the window, he saw the clearest pair of blue eyes looking at him. "Hello," Eva Wright said.

The nurse turned to her. "You have a visitor," she said.

Don's heart nearly beat its way out of his chest.

Mrs. Wright looked at him calmly. "That's the rabble rouser who ran me off the road."

When the nurse looked up, Don was gone.

Don's heart beat as quickly as his legs beat a hasty retreat down the hall. He had to get out of there. He needed a drink. He had to get to his car.

He slipped down the stairs taking the steps three at a time, any moment expecting to hear the scream of the alarms, or the yelling of a pack of security guards, guns drawn. But nothing. If he had known or been around nurses, he would have taken his time. Most nurses were too tired and too immune to things going wrong to even care beyond the fact that the intruder had left. Besides, Mrs. Wright had just come out of a coma. Mrs. Wright was old. They expected her to say crazy things. Crisis over. Next case.

He made it to his car in a cold pointless sweat. Not until he had driven out of the garage did he realize that there were no guards or dogs after him. He relaxed and turned on the radio. He caught the end of deejay chatter about the rumor that the president was in town hanging around some old joint known as the Horseshoe Hotel on the famous Fremont Street. "That'll do." He plugged the name into the GPS and he was on his way.

He parked in the dingy but free parking structure and made his way to the hotel, not really expecting to see the President. The gloomy lobby was so dark it'd be a wonder if he could see anybody in there. The place was surprisingly uncrowded. Apparently, nobody had their radios on at eleven o'clock on a Monday night.

"You!" a female voice shrieked at him from the bar on the far wall. "You get the hell out of here!"

Don turned toward the bar and the voice. There, behind the counter, stood that Harley whore that he'd roped and tied.

He held up his hand. "I don't blame you for not wanting me in your bar." Damn! Pegged twice in one night.

She pointed a finger at him. "You caught me unsuspecting, otherwise I would have kicked your ass."

"Hey!" A voice, gruff and reeking of old world Italian came up behind her. "What is this? You talking to my customers like this?" The middle-aged man's white wife-beater tank stood out in the gloomy darkness.

"This is the guy who tied me up like a little cow," Tanya spat at her boss. "I'm going to kick his ass."

Sal's face went from surprise to credulous. He turned toward Don. "She could, you know. But you are customer so I tell her not to. You are customer, no?"

"Yeah, definitely."

Tanya slammed down her rag and stomped around the corner.

Sal looked after her and shrugged. He turned back to Don. "Tanya is innocent girl with bad temper. I like father to her. What you want for drink?"

"Any beer on tap. And don't let Tanya pour it. Even 'innocent' girls spit in drinks."

Sal got the beer. He slid it across the bar. "You not here to hurt my Tanya, no?"

"No," Don said quickly. "Listen, what I did to her was pretty stupid. She thought I was a prowler, she came down the stairs to confront me, got all in my face and I freaked out and hog-tied her."

Sal laughed. "That is very funny." Sal's smile drained from his face. He turned very slowly and nearly bumped into Tanya who stood behind him, her head barely reaching his chest.

"I guess not to Tanya," Don said. He took a long swig of his beer.

Tanya glared, then walked away.

"For the rest of the night, better you order the drinks from me."

CHAPTER TWELVE

Back at Lynn's apartment, Mike the Mechanic handed Lynn's keys to Big John. But he didn't turn to go. John took the keys and waited, his large frame blocking the entryway to his sister's home.

"I got to be honest with you Big Guy, I really like your sister."

"Well, you can't be Frank."

"I am being perfectly frank with you," Mike protested. "I really like your sister."

"No, I'm saying you can't be Frank. Frank Donahue. That's the guy she's got a crush on. It ain't right, but that's the way it is."

Mike frowned. "She's got to learn that I'm exactly right for her."

Big John smiled. He didn't know what to say.

"I got to be even more honest with you."

Big John tensed. "Sometimes lying is okay."

Mike put his hand on his heart. "I would never be dishonest with you. So here goes. My television's broken and Lynn is about to go on *Shark Tank* right now. I would love to just go in there and watch her on TV. Would you mind? We could kick back and drink a Dr. Pepper Ten and I'd be on my way."

"That's exactly what my sister drinks."

"Yeah, I know."

Big John shifted his feet. "Did she tell you that?"

"Yeah, probably. Let's go inside, man. We are going to miss the show."

Big John had to admit that he wanted to see the show too, but he was filled with a sense of dread. People could be cruel. If his sister had a mental meltdown on national TV, that would kick up their ratings, but the more he thought about his sister showing off her invention, the more curious he became. "Alright, but the apartment's a bit dilapidated."

Understatement of the year, that was. His sister shopped at dumpsters for furniture that a family of fourteen had used, abused and dumped. For someone who had invented a way to keep people from catching a cold, she had no germ phobias herself. The most amazing thing was how she coerced people into dragging the dumpster items up a flight of stairs. Then she'd spend a day scrubbing them down, but the way Big John saw it was that you can't frost a pig and get Miss Piggy. Some of the pieces were just too far gone.

"I don't care how it looks." Mike danced on his heels in excitement.

Big John looked at him. He was probably the one that she had coerced to drag the stuff up there. He shrugged and unlocked the door, then stood back to allow Mike to take a peek. It would give him a chance to change his mind.

Instead of peeking in, Mike charged into the place without hesitation. He made a beeline for the disintegrating recliner John's sister favored. The mechanic bent down behind the decrepit chair, pulled out the remote and turned the television on. Then, turning to the coffee table that looked like it'd been excavated from some ancient trailer park ruins, he fished out the remote that worked the sound from a pile of remotes.

Teetering between the point of disbelief and suspicion, Big John stared down at the little greasy man, now sprawled in the recliner. "You figured that out awfully quickly."

"Show's on." Mike patted the sofa next to him.

Slowly, Big John eased himself onto the stain-colored sofa. He was always afraid that it would collapse under his great weight, releasing a band of bugs on him and he would look like Jonathan Swift in Gulliver's Travels.

Questions formed in Big John's head, but the opening credits were on and soon the announcer was going through teasers of tonight's guests. When Lynn's face flashed across the screen, Mike yelled, "There she is, there she is!"

John hardly recognized his sister. Her lips were painted a bright hot pink that matched her shirt. Her normally flat hair was slicked back into a super-chic French roll.

Before they could see Lynn, they had to watch two housewives hawking specialized gift packages for spoiled snobby two-year olds and then a frat boy peddling organic yogurt that he had literally peddled with his bicycle's yogurt-making crank.

Finally they got to Lynn. She came out poised and confident. "Good evening, Sharks." She nodded to each of the panel of five billionaires or millionaires. Most returned her greetings with stiff nods. Non-plussed, she started her presentation. "Have you ever started a vacation sick because somebody on the plane coughed all over you? Have you ever missed a fine spring day's activities because your allergies kicked up, trapping you indoors? Then you need Manhole Covers. Manhole Covers are a simple product that you just place in each nostril." And with perfectly manicured hands, she took a little plug and shoved it up her nose. "I'm asking for two million dollars for fifteen percent of the profits."

The panel stared her down. The guy on the end, a bald middle-aged man, leaned back. He tossed his pen down. "I don't know anything about this product, I'm out."

Lynn's eyes flicked over him and never looked back.

"Oh, she is so done with him," Big John said.

The rest of the panel looked at her. Deep thinkers. John could not read their stern expressions.

"So you just take one of these things and shove it up your nose?" Mark Cuban asked. He was a billionaire who made his first million funding skateboard parts.

The other billionaires or millionaires laughed.

Lynn's face remained impassive. She nodded.

"What do you think your gross revenue will be?" Barbara the female billionaire asked.

Here it comes, thought Big John. This is where they tear her apart for the sake of ratings.

"I think that it will be about twenty-five million in the first three years."

More laughing from the panel.

"What is your current volume of business?" one of them asked with a smirk to the others on the panel.

"Online, in six months, I've made $36,000. I have three major chains that want to order 40,000 units each, but I don't have the capital to manufacture that much."

The laughter stopped. "Do you have the sales figures for us?"

"I expect this product to have a lot of reorders. You can only use them once and a package of two is under five dollars."

"I'll give you a million dollars for a quarter of the profits," Mark Cuban offered.

The man next to Mark raised his eyes to Lynn, taking another good long look at her. "So you expect a high replacement demand?"

"Yes. Once people discover how effective they are, they will stock up on them. We've had clinical trials run by an independent research company that concluded that 90% of the people who used these were asymptomatic ten days after they left their flight."

"I'll give you 2.2 million dollars for 50% control of the business."

Mike dropped the remote.

"No. I still want more control than that."

A strangled cry came out of Big John's throat.

Startled, the billionaires looked at her.

"Maybe these people would have gotten sick anyway," one of them said

Lynn shook her head. "In standardized test, 70% of people flying came up with one or more symptoms of a cold within ten days of getting off the plane."

"Four million, but I want 25% of the company," Mark said.

Lynn shook her head.

"I'll give you five million dollars and we split the profits 50%, but you get full say in the company," Barbara said.

The cameras focused on Lynn's face, sullen and rock hard. This unreasonable stubbornness typified Lynn. She was the bull personified. Big John sat and watched helplessly while she screwed up a chance that life had handed her.

"Is she waiting for the sum to go up?" Mike asked.

The cameras watched Lynn. This was a record-breaking offer. Then, almost imperceptibly, Lynn's chin jerked down, indicating that she would take the deal.

"Hot damn!" Mike yelled, illustrating his enthusiasm with a spray of Dr. Pepper. He did his hot damn dance for a couple of rounds around the apartment until the can had emptied.

Big John, on the other hand, sat frozen in his multi-millionaire sister's shitty sofa. He thought maybe his whole nervous system had gone into shock. He couldn't move.

The show had finished, followed by a teaser for the ten o'clock news. They were going to interview Lynn. She had snagged the most money ever invested on *Shark Tank* history. When the news came on, Big John found his voice.

"Shut up," he yelled. "I want to hear what she says."

Mike shushed up. He sat down.

The interviewer asked her what she would like to do with the money.

Lynn, very serious and matter-of-factly stated that she would like to invest her profits in green housing. "The amount of people putting such a draw on the planet is unacceptable. I especially want to help poor people living in unsuitable homes find nice solar-powered homes."

"That's very noble. Anything for yourself?" the newscaster asked archly.

"Yes, there is a young man I love, but he finds me intolerable. I think, with money, he would find me less undesirable."

"How distastefully honest my sister is." Big John watched Mike's face. "She's already learned that if you have a lot of money you can get away with saying improper things."

"I think she's wonderful."

Big John winced at the star-struck glassy-eyed mechanic's comments.

"You do know that she's not talking about you."

"I know who she's talking about. He won't be getting in my way."

Big John had a sinking feeling.

The next day, Tuesday, the hospital transferred Mrs. Wright to the rehab floor. It took almost an hour for the staff to convince Mr. Wright that this was better than bringing Mrs. Wright home.

Mrs. Wright came out of the coma with an unassailable resolve to get better. When she hurt, she asked for more pain meds, and when she was tired, she asked for more rest time. But she did everything her nurses and therapists asked her to do. "I am invincible," she would warble. "It's Helen Reddy's latest song. Haven't you heard it?"

Her therapists, all under thirty, did not know who Helen Reddy was.

There were other problems. She wouldn't wait for the staff to help her out of bed. They would often find her hanging half over the bed rail like some East German scouting the wall. The more serious problem was that she did not feel secure. She felt somebody was after her. The staff assured Mr. Wright that because of her head injury, this was not uncommon, but he knew there was some truth to the matter. The nurse on the acute floor had asked him about the man in the room that night.

To the hospital's credit, they had put her on a security alert. Visitors had to sign in and they had to be on a checked list, approved by Mr. Wright. While Mr. Wright felt that their protectiveness was unquestionable, they were merely medical personnel, not the secret service.

After a week, Mrs. Wright's progress was irrefutable. She could get out of bed with only one person's help. She could walk ten feet with a walker and she had stopped telling her physical therapist exactly what she thought the young professional woman smelled and looked like. Mr. Wright told her doctor that this brutal honesty was normal behavior for his wife. "She once told me she thought I looked like a drunken Indian had scalped me. That was the first and last designer haircut I ever had. So, Doc, can she come home now?"

The doctor smiled. "Absolutely not. Unless you think you can carry her up two flights of stairs."

Mr. Wright's face fell. "Who told you where we lived?"

"You did," she answered cheekily. "Remember all those questions my team asked you the day she arrived here? They're so we can use your answers against you. You told us you have 34 steps up to your apartment, no elevator. So no, she can't go home yet." She smiled and patted his hand. "You are a very lucky man. Your wife came out of a coma relatively intact. She's working hard. Her therapists have been giving her good reports."

"Her therapist, Sara, told me that my wife told her she dressed like some immigrant from a third world country."

The doctor shrugged.

"And that she smelled like she had ridden here on a donkey."

"Ouch." The good doctor winced.

Mr. Wright clasped and unclasped his meaty hands. "The house is so quiet, it's like being unmarried."

"Your family is coming, right?"

"Yeah, but now I'll have all my daughters around me, and no Eva. I'll be like some unwed father."

The doctor bit back a smile. "You will not be wifeless for long. Mrs. Wright will be discharged from this place in a couple of weeks. Her therapists think that's all the time they'll need to get her in tiptop stair-climbing condition. Unless you think you are going to move."

"We're too old to move. Besides, we have to take care of that punk, Frank, who lives next door and my wife is pretty close to another neighbor. That one's a real floozy with a retard for a son."

The doctor frowned.

"Oh, Henry's a great person, he's just a retard. He can't help the way he's born."

"No, I suppose not. Well, until your wife gets home, enjoy your bachelorhood. You can live footloose and fancy free."

"At my age that means drinking an entire can of beer without one single thought about how far away the bathroom is." Mr. Wright winked at her and got up to leave, ending the meeting.

CHAPTER THIRTEEN

Tuesday morning found Mike the Mechanic elbow deep in grease. He had just finished a tune-up on a car that needed an oil change and was now starting an oil change on a car that needed a tune-up.

The phone rang. Mike lost his grip on the bolt and it fell into the murky pan of dirty oil. He ran to answer the phone.

"Can you come pick me up or should I just get one of those buses?"

"Hi, Lynn." Mike fumbled with the phone in his excitement. The oil slicked around his fingers did not help. "No, no, I'll pick you up. We can't have the princess coming into town unescorted."

"Princess? What are you talking about?"

Mike wondered what she meant by 'What are you talking about?' but if that is the way she wanted to play it. "I meant after. . ."

"I'm an independent businesswoman, not a princess."

Mike did not understand bipolar people. He did not realize that they ran on a self-governing track of things that were important to them, and that their train of thought did not jump the track to run by things that other people thought important. So while Mike saw her as newly rich and powerful, she saw herself simply as a self-ruling businesswoman. "Yeah, I'll pick you up."

"Good, 'cause my plane is sitting on the tarmac now." She gave him her flight info and hung up.

Mike slapped the phone back in its holder, grabbed a rag and bolted into the sales office. He told his assistant to finish the car he was working on.

"But that car needs a tune-up."

"Just finish the oil change. The car will run better and the customer will be none the wiser." He ran out the door, stripping off his greasy coveralls as he headed for his car.

The drive to McCarran took him a little over a half hour. He would have been there sooner but as he passed the small North Las Vegas airport, a Cessna flew low over Rancho. The little plane distracted the drivers and slowed the traffic down considerably. Ten years ago, there had been a rash of plane crashes in this area, so when people could read the numbers on the side of the plane, they got nervous.

Farther up the road, an old man caused traffic to slow down again. The elderly man's wheelchair batteries had died and he was pushing the heavy chair across six lanes of traffic. People just sat in their cars, staring sullenly out at the old man.

Mike finally made it to the southbound 15, but a pile-up threatened to slow him down again. He avoided the clump of trashed cars by driving on the shoulder. The accident was probably caused by some moron desperately trying to get in the self-drive lane so that he could be free to sit there and roust his snake while his car drove itself. Instead of hitting the self-drive lane, the nincompoop had hit the side of a bakery truck, knocking the poor delivery driver's buns all over the highway.

When Mike got to Tropicana Boulevard he decided to take that exit and cut across the Strip.

Normally he liked crossing the Strip. Tropicana and Las Vegas Boulevard had to be the most dynamic corner in the world. New York, New York Casino had the face of the city, complete with a tugboat moving around the harbor. Across the street, the luminescent green of MGM brightened the whole corner, although Mike missed the lion that used to guard the entrance. Those had been gone eighteen years now. Someone had found out that Chinese people believed that a lion brought bad luck. Mike could not wait for the day when he'd have so much money that buildings would change because of his beliefs.

Today he was intent on getting to Lynn.

When he finally reached the airport his heart beat in anticipation. She'd flown in on Southwest, an airline that catered to budget-minded middle-class people. There they were, dragging their plain black suitcases behind them. Many of them juggled a menagerie of plastic bags adorned with the name of the tourist trap the sitting ducks had been drawn to. Probably filled with plastic copies of the places they'd seen from their tour buses. The next time he and Lynn traveled together it would be on an airline where the customers all had matching luggage sets and other people to handle them.

He watched, one by one, as each of the jeans and t-shirt clad passengers were picked up by smiling suburbanites in sensible sedans. They all drove away, smiling.

Mike scanned the crowds for Lynn but all he saw was a woman with a plain black suitcase and leather pants. His eyes rested on her derriere for just a minute too long.

She starred back at him boldly and marched up to his car, her jaw set in a determined hard line.

Where was airport security when he needed them?

She yanked open the car door.

He couldn't decide whether he should just yell at her or apologize quickly.

"You never told me what kind of car you drove."

"Lynn? You never told me what kind of pants you would be wearing." He giggled nervously. "In my unbiased opinion, you look great."

Her face remained neutral. "The producers wanted to take me out to a club in LA. They said I couldn't go out in elastic pants, that I should wear these." She stood on the curb, not moving to get in.

"Oh, your luggage." Mike jumped out of the car and grabbed her bags. "So did you go out with them? Wearing those pants?"

"Yes." She got into the car and Mike ran around and threw himself in the driver's seat. "They all drive foreign cars there."

"This is a foreign car. It's a Traubbie, an East German car. Popular before the wall was torn down. I've completely restored it."

She nodded. "They all drove BMWs and Mercedes."

Mike wanted to steer the conversation away from the subject of the producers. "So how was it, being on the show and going up in front of those guys?"

Lynn gave a disinterested wave of her hand.

Mike, open-minded and eager as a puppy, tried another channel to get to her. "Okay, I understand. You are probably tired. I just wanted to hear all about your experiences."

"I'm not tired. I already talked about it enough. Didn't you see any of my interviews?"

"Yeah," Mike lied. "I just wanted to hear about it from your point of view. Maybe there's things that you would like to only tell me."

Lynn shook her head. "I want to see Mrs. Wright."

"Mrs. Wright?"

"She's the old lady who took me to the airport. Somebody ran her off the road. She's Frank's neighbor. I'm sure he's really mad at me. I better go see her."

Something rank and vile twisted deep in Mike's guts at the mention of Frank's name. His grip tightened on the steering wheel. He forced cheerfulness into his voice. "Fine. No problem. I'll take you to see her. I have some cars back at the shop that I have to finish up by morning but . . ."

"Can you take me now?" Lynn was unconcerned about his work responsibilities.

"Yes." Mike couldn't wait for the day when mundane concerns such as job duties left him unruffled. "Then afterward, can I take you to dinner?" He forced nonchalance into his voice.

"I ate on the plane," she answered blithely.

Mike's insides churned. How was he going to make Lynn see that he was there? He glanced at her. She sat serenely in the passenger seat, clueless to Mike's desperation. "Can I go in with you to visit her?"

"That would be very nice." For the first time since he had picked her up, Lynn turned to him and smiled warmly. "It's a little rehabilitation place on Flamingo. We won't have to stay long."

Encouraged by her smile, he felt generous. "We'll stay as long as you like."

"Really? Because I don't think Mrs. Wright will like you very much."

Mike swallowed. He almost reached over to pat Lynn's knee but restrained himself. "I'll charm the pants off the sweet little old lady."

Lynn simply laughed and gave him the directions.

CHAPTER FOURTEEN

Mike's first visit to an old folks' rehab hospital was different from his other forays into the rehab world. His friends had all been into some kind of rehab.

Those places were normal compared to what the old folks could come up with.

The first step he took into Shady Acres was over a huge snoring dog.

"That's our therapy dog," the chirpy receptionist called out. "She's a little lazy."

"I'm a little irregular," a well-dressed lady in an electric wheelchair volunteered. "That's why I need to keep this chair. In case I have to get to the bathroom quickly."

"They're just visitors, Jenny. They're not here to take your chair away."

Ms. Jenny smiled and zipped away.

"I bet she's relieved," Mike said nervously.

"She is now." The receptionist waved a hand in front of her nose. "I'm sorry. It's not uncommon for the residents to talk about their toilet troubles. Please sign the guest book."

Mike bent down to sign. "It is a little out of the ordinary for us."

The receptionist nodded her understanding. "Who are you visiting?"

"Mrs. Eva Wright," Lynn said.

"Oh, you ain't heard nothing yet."

"She's definitely a little different." Lynn bent down to sign the guest book.

"Umm-hmm." The receptionist quickly gave them directions before Lynn could say anything more.

They followed her directions, walking shoulder against shoulder as if they had to fortify each other. One looked left and another looked right. When they rounded the corner, they headed into the second room on the right.

And immediately exited so quickly that they almost tripped over each other.

"Was she nude?" A nurse asked striding up to them.

Both nodded, unable to find words.

"I'm not sure what I saw," Mike said.

"She's a nonconformist," the nurse said. "I'll go fix her up. She can't help it. She's a vegetarian. They're a little strange to begin with. Add her old age peppered with a few strokes and you get some freakish behavior." The nurse disappeared inside the room.

"Talk about being out in left field," Lynn said.

"That was about ten miles outside of left field." Mike shuddered. "I don't know if I can face her."

"That's not Mrs. Wright. That's her roommate."

"You mean there is more behind curtain number two?"

Lynn nodded.

"Okay, she's covered," the nurse announced. "Still, I'd avert my eyes if I was you."

"I'd like to just stab mine out," Mike said.

"Mrs. Wright?" Lynn called out.

"Come in." The voice was bright and cheery.

Mike let his guard down a little. He followed Lynn behind the curtain.

A cherry-cheeked woman in a blue gingham robe smiled at them. White perfect little curls adorned her face.

I got this, Mike thought.

"Sorry about the coarse welcome you got."

Mrs. Wright's roommate suddenly burst out in peals of laughter. "You should have seen their faces."

Mrs. Wright's perfectly cherubic face crinkled in mirth. "You are so uncivilized, Molly."

"You owe me ten bucks," Molly called.

"You pay Molly to flash your visitors?" Lynn asked. "Gross."

"I'm a total whore," Molly called proudly.

Mrs. Wright wiped a tear of laughter from her eye. "Oh, you'll have to forgive us. Our act is a bit unpolished but it cracks the shit out of us."

"You're not thinking of something else, are you?" Lynn asked.

Mrs. Wright ignored the question. "Why don't you and your

oafish young man take a seat?"

"Oafish?" Lynn asked. "Mrs. Wright, why are you being so rude?"

"I don't mean to be so bad-mannered, but the way you two nearly fell over each other running out of here, I about peed my pants." Mrs. Wright shifted in the bed. "No, I guess I really did."

"Her head injury makes her vulgar," Molly shouted.

Molly the whore was calling Mrs. Wright vulgar. Mike didn't know if he should laugh.

"Show's over, Molly. Shut up and let me visit," Mrs. Wright called.

"Over and out," Molly called back.

"Very sophisticated," Mike said. He felt good about Lynn sticking up for him.

Mrs. Wright turned her piercing blue eyes on him. The laughter had left her eyes and she looked all business. "Where's Frank?"

"I don't know," Lynn said. "I called but he doesn't answer his phone."

"He's got a block on you." Mrs. Wright patted Lynn's hand.

"Oh, yeah," Lynn said. "My mom and my brother don't answer their phones either. I ended up having to call my mechanic."

Mrs. Wright turned her evil eyes on Mike and voiced what he'd heard. "She called you last. And you don't even have a name. Why are you here?"

"She called me and I came for her." Mike's face reddened. He glanced up at Lynn. She made no move to apologize or defend him. In fact, she didn't even seem to realize she had slighted him.

"We have to go." Lynn stood up.

"Alright," Mrs. Wright said, but when Mike stood up the old lady grabbed his wrist. "Lynn, I'm going to talk to your young man for a second."

"He's not my young man." Lynn strode out the door without a second glance.

Mike wanted to wrench his arm out of the old lady's grasp, but he made himself man up and stay still.

"Don't underestimate me young man." Mrs. Wright's nails dug into his wrists. "If you think you are just going to waltz into Lynn's life, sweep her and her millions off her feet, then you have seriously misjudged me."

Mike was losing his hold on his cool. "I set little store by a senile old lady who pays her roommate to flash me."

"And Lynn sets little store by you. In fact, I'm sure she'll be back tomorrow belittling you and your greasy fingers. And don't look down on me. I can influence that girl. I'll make sure she knows exactly what you're up to."

Mike jerked his wrist free. He resisted the urge to spit on her. "Old people depreciate faster than old cars. I'll tell you what I'd do with an old clunker like you. I'd just leave it out in a field somewhere." He turned and stalked out of the room. No old lady was going to get between him and Lynn. He didn't think his day could go any worse until he made it out to the parking lot and saw the worst possible thing he could have seen.

Frank, tall, large, and clean stood next to his car talking to Lynn. His hands were on her shoulders and he was gently leaning down to her, his face coming close to Lynn's. Her eyes were locked into his.

Mike was not going to let this happen. But even as he vowed that, Lynn saw him approaching, gave him an inpatient flip of her hand and turned her back on him. She lowered herself into Frank's Mercedes.

"Dude," Frank yelled to him as if Mike stunk too bad to come closer. "We're gonna need that suitcase out of your car."

Mike experienced the most intense anger he had ever felt in his life. He dug his nails into his fists, hard, in an effort to help him get a grip on his emotions. He walked over to Frank, reached into his pocket and held out his keys.

But Frank had already turned his back. A chirp came from his hand and his trunk opened. He looked at Mike patiently, waiting for the mechanic to schlepp Lynn's suitcase over to his car.

Mike grabbed the suitcase. "I see you got your keys," he said.

"Yep. That's not all I got."

Not only had Mike lost Lynn, he was being subjected to the servant's treatment by this thug that didn't even love Lynn until she made money. Mike could not endure this. He wasn't going to put up with anyone getting between him and Lynn. His thoughts were interrupted by the slam of the car door. The Mercedes sped out, as if escaping a monster.

They hadn't even said good-bye.

Furious, Mike opened up the back of his trunk and found a hammer in his tool case. Not caring who was watching, he brought the hammer down on an old flashlight, smashing it again and again until nothing was left but dust. Scooping the particles up, he went back into the hospital, heading straight to the cafeteria. He bought the nicest and biggest piece of chocolate cake he could find. A quick stop in the bathroom and he was on his way to Mrs. Wright's room.

He knocked. The topless old roommate was asleep.

It was like Mrs. Wright expected his return. Her blue eyes meant his expectantly when he entered the room.

"Lynn made me buy you this cake. She said I was supposed to apologize to you for making you so angry."

The old lady smiled and held out her hands for the cake.

Mike placed the dessert gently in her hands. "I really do love Lynn. I won't take her money. I'll just take care of her."

Mrs. Wright nodded. "Good. And don't think I still won't be watching you."

"Yes, ma'am."

"So we have an understanding?"

"Yes, ma'am."

"You don't have to bring me cake, I'm supposed to be eating healthily."

"Oh, I'm sorry. I'll take it back." Mike reached for the cake, but Mrs. Wright kept a strong grasp on the plate.

"Our little secret?" she asked.

"Our little secret." He smiled.

Three hours later, Tanya went to visit Mrs. Wright. When she walked into the room, she screamed.

The scream brought an army of staff, running.

Tanya rubbed at her eyes. Her perception must be off. Her view must be clouded by the stress of the last few days, working around the president, having that thug come into her bar.

The army of staff burst into the door like a herd of buffalo being chased by Native Americans. They slammed past her, jostling her from side to side until she started feeling sick to her stomach.

"What happened? What else did you see?" a nurse shouted into her face.

Tanya's brain scrambled. Her gray matter had trouble assembling what was in front of her. Her friend lay unmoving in a pool of blood.

A gurney rolled in, knocked Tanya aside and pulled up to the bedside. The throng of medical personnel formed a perfect circle around the old woman in the bed and the gurney, closing Tanya out. "One, two, three!" a voice counted and they flipped her friend up and off the bed and over onto to the gurney. The crowd of white lab coats and blue scrubs once again closed ranks around her friend. Running and shouting things that were incomprehensible to Tanya, the group pushed the gurney back out the door. The pounding footsteps and barked orders receded down the hall until all Tanya could hear were the blinds rattling against the wall where they had been knocked in the scuffle.

In the ensuing silence, Tanya thought she was alone.

"Hello, are you all right?" This voice had compassion and gentleness.

Tanya looked up and saw a young Asian woman dressed in a lacy white blouse and pleated skirt. She held a clipboard in her hand and waited patiently for Tanya to answer.

"What happened?" Tanya asked.

"We were hoping you could tell us."

Tanya started to cry. "I don't know. I just came into the room and she was . . ."

"Why don't you sit down?"

Tanya looked at the blood-soaked bed. "Is she . . . ?"

"We don't know yet." The Asian woman's eyes went to the blood-soaked bed. In her gaze, Tanya saw that Mrs. Wright was dead.

Tanya studied the young woman, so full of life. If she whipped off the blazer and let her hair down she'd be ready for a wild night on the town. How could this woman have been entrusted with a job that helped people deal with death? What could she possibly know? Suddenly Tanya came up with an idea. "You know I'm not the next of kin, I'm not the one you should be talking to." In her muddled mind, Tanya figured that this information would be enough to stop the nightmare.

The young woman shrugged indifferently. "Sorry, my misunderstanding. I'll look in the chart for her next of kin." She asked Tanya a few questions about what she had witnessed, then swept out of the room. Tanya was not the person she was paid to be compassionate to and she had to move on.

Abandoned with the empty bloody bed, Tanya came to her senses. "Wait!" she called.

The young woman stopped and came back toward her.

"This is kind of sensitive. Do you mind if I call her husband?"

The woman waited patiently. "Okay, but will you promise to do it, like now? Because we're supposed to call the family any time something like this happens. If the husband should show up and see that bed and nobody has called him, let's just say they will not be lenient on me." She clattered off to grim-reap somewhere else.

Tanya watched her walk away, afraid that Mr. Wright would indeed come around the corner and witness this grisly scene. She tried to think of words to say when she didn't really know anything yet. Maybe she should hang around and see if Mrs. Wright would come back. Death was not something announced without certainty.

One hour later, a phone call interrupted Henry's video game. At first he ignored it, but after twenty-four rings he decided that he should pick up, that it must be something really urgent for the caller to let it ring that long. He picked it up and held the phone to his ear.

His mother's voice, he was pretty sure, stumbled out in a flow of sobs and blubbering sounds. Henry's mind started to race. He couldn't understand what she was saying, but maybe he'd done something terrible to get his mother so upset. Maybe he'd left his breakfast dishes out, maybe they stunk real bad. Maybe they'd made bugs come. Maybe the bugs had bitten his mother. He started to cry. He loved his mother.

Something about his sobs reigned hers in. She got ahold of herself and then calmed him down. In the end, she resorted to a stern voice. "Henry! You did nothing wrong but I need you to do something for me. I need you to go over to Mr. Wright's house and give him a hug."

Why would she ask him to do something so unpleasant? "He's a nasty old man and he hates me." The old man smelled foul, too.

"Henry! Now is not the time to be obnoxious. Just do it."

Henry did not know what obnoxious meant, probably when you told your mother that you did not like one of the neighbors. "All right." He put the phone down and went next door to complete the distasteful task.

The old man was already stepping out his door. When he saw Henry, he threw his arms around the man-child first and sobbed. Henry just stood there, trying to be stable for the old man leaning against him. They stayed like that, one man bracing himself, the other crying loudly until Frank came out of his apartment to see what was happening.

"My Eva's dead," Mr. Wright wailed. "My baby, my bride."

Shocked, Frank stumbled back. He looked behind him.

Lynn stood there, her face stoic. "I know who did it."

Tanya didn't remember driving to work. She barely acknowledged Sal's greeting. Robotically, she went to the back and started washing dishes. But the more she worked, the more the tears flowed and the more the anger built up. She just knew that her friend was murdered. Probably one of the unsavory people Mr. Wright hung out with or that creep who had roped and tied her. She slammed a pot in the sink. And then, because it felt so good, she continued to slam pots until Sal came running in, eyes wild. It was only three in the afternoon and already a trickle of sweat ran down the front of his shirt.

"What!!!" he screamed. He didn't really want an answer. He wanted peace.

Tanya was in no mood to give it to him. "Somebody murdered my friend and they will probably get away with it because of that man in there." Her hands pointed wildly to the private room. "I'd like to tell him what I think of his stupid rule, I'd-"

"So tell me."

Tanya whirled around.

Standing in the doorway, stood their president, Mr. Brad Pitt. He looked ordinary and tired, not like the president or even like a famous actor, he just looked like a working-class man in a blue polo shirt. Aside from the fact that there was a Secret Service agent standing behind him ready to shoot them, he looked like an everyday office worker.

"I tried to tell you he was still here," Sal said.

"I'm running a study on the working woes of everyday Americans." The President smiled, instantly changing him into the boyishly handsome man she recognized from the screen.

"I'm about as run-of-the-mill as you can get," Tanya said, feeling her face go red. "But, I'm really, really angry right now."

"Angry or no, I need to listen to you. Please." He held out his arm, pointing to the private dining room that had become his lair this week.

Tanya followed. The Secret Service agent stared at her openly.

The President breezed by him as if an armed man staring at his guest was as unremarkable as the family dog begging for food. "Ah, he's nothing special," the President said. "He couldn't hit a sumo wrestler from two feet away. They always put the people who are nothing to write home about near me."

Tanya did not think it wise to laugh at the joke. The man was armed and probably highly skilled. "At least *he'll* have something to write home about."

The president laughed.

Tanya couldn't believe she was making jokes with the noble leader of the free world.

They stepped inside the room. Brad Pitt resolutely shut the door, barring the Secret Service agent from entering. When Tanya's eyes adjusted to the dim light, she saw Ruth in the far corner. "Hey, she's . . ."

Ruth did not look up.

"I'm never alone." President Pitt sat on a couch, patting the one next to him. "Please sit down. Tell me about your friend."

"She was an innocent old lady. Somebody killed her because they could. Your law allowed this to happen." Tanya remained standing.

He looked up at her, his unequivocal gaze filled with concern, his clear blue eyes searching her soul. Up this close, he didn't seem like a plain middle-aged man; he seemed special.

Tanya sank down on the couch next to him.

"Maybe I was wrong to pass that law."

Tanya couldn't think of a thing to say. His direct statement startled her and his gaze drilled into her, unnerving her.

"I'm always straightforward, blunt, my enemies say. My advisors hate it. They think that I should always be positive, even if it takes me hours to think of something positive to say." He took her hand. "If you are certain that your friend died because of my law, then I will repeal it immediately."

Stunned again, Tanya's mind raced.

Brad Pitt released her hands. He leaned back, rubbing the bridge of his nose with one hand. "I've gone over this law a thousand times in my head."

"Then why, if you had any doubts, would you make this law?"

"To reign bad people in. They're going wild, cutting each other off in traffic, lying to get ahead, going after the big buck. Our prisons are filled, but worse yet, the scourge of society is still out there: the ones who are getting away with their crimes. Bad people who just haven't been caught.

"But something did happen when I made my law. People suddenly became more helpful, drivers friendlier, neighbors more considerate. Don't tell me you haven't noticed. Don't tell me that overall you can't see a change in the world."

Tanya nodded.

"This law is teaching people to be more sensitive."

Tanya looked at him quizzically. "How is allowing someone to kill teaching them to be more sensitive?"

"Remember the case down in Georgia where a pack of high school kids ganged up on that mentally-challenged man. They didn't hit him, they didn't threaten him, but they somehow figured out how to make him cry without doing anything illegal. They were minors, he was an adult. They couldn't be punished. But every day that man was punished. His mother was punished by watching her loved one become more and more withdrawn. The parents of the high schoolers? Their attitude was 'Boys will be boys'. They even laughed a little bit at their children's cruelties."

Tears filled Tanya's eyes. This man could see into her soul. This was Henry and her story this man had just told her. She recalled the helplessness she and her boy suffered while the others got a good laugh. "How . . . ?" She couldn't finish the sentence.

The president patted her hand, but didn't answer her question. "Maybe they'd think more about what they were doing, if they had to look down the barrel of a shotgun."

Tanya swallowed and looked into this man's baby blues. Such candidness was unheard of in a president. "I don't know if I could have killed those boys," she said. She knew in her heart that he knew that he'd been talking about her and Henry.

"A good person's evilness is packed down deep in some undiscovered place in their soul. It's packed there by their precious parents, pushed down harder by the lessons we learned from our virtuous teachers, and nearly sealed by our love and fear of God's lessons. Most of us go through life playing by the rules, holding ourselves as good upright citizens, even when we're wronged. We will probably never find the nameless evil that lurks down inside of us. Criminals, on the other hand, being exceptionally observant, know this. They'll find extraordinary ways to destroy us, sometimes because they can and not because they gain by it. Remember that family in Minnesota? Two criminals took the whole family hostage. They made the mother go down to the bank, withdraw the family's life savings, the kids' college funds, the money they would need in their old age. They took everything. They drove her home and, in unrivaled savagery, they slaughtered the whole family anyway. People said it was unbelievable." Here the President smashed his hand on the table.

It wasn't until then that Tanya realized that the President was angry, that he had a rage building up in him that she hadn't noticed when she first walked into the room.

"I call it inconceivable that free-range evil running around a band of sheep doesn't strike more often."

Tanya studied the famous man before her. An actor and now President of the United States. Was it possible that he could have secrets? "Did something happen to you?"

For a minute, she thought President Pitt would answer her, then she saw his eyes flicker up to Ruth, her nose still stuck in her laptop. His eyes returned to Tanya, staying on her for just a minute.

There was real pain there.

CHAPTER FIFTEEN

.

Earlier that evening, Don went to the Rehab Hospital to check on Mrs. Eva Wright. He signed in. When he filled in Mrs. Wright's name under the person he was to visit, the receptionist gasped. She looked like she had swallowed a golf ball.

"Ya alright?" Don asked. Despite her gargoyle-like expression, he thought her quite pretty.

"Ummmm," she managed. Now she also sounded like she'd swallowed a golf ball.

"Ummmmm."

"You said that already." He smiled at her. "Has Mrs. Wright up and died?"

His unreserved manner snapped her out of her catatonic state along with the golf ball. An unconstrained river of words flowed out of her neon pink lips. "They found her in a pool of blood and hauled her out of the room but when they got her as far as the nurses' station they realized she really was dead and they just stopped because they didn't really know where they were going with her blood-flooded body in the first place."

During this nervous geyser of words flowing out from the pony-tailed receptionist a distinguished silver-haired lady in an electric wheelchair had glided up. "A little free and easy with the information, aren't we?"

Don hadn't even heard her roll up.

"I'm sorry, Ms. Jenny," the distraught young receptionist said to the lady in the chair. She turned to Don. "I'm sorry sir."

"It's okay, I never really liked her. My dad made me visit her."

"Come with me young man," Miss Jenny commanded from her electric wheelchair throne. She smiled up at him invitingly and rolled away from the receptionist desk. "That is, if you want the unrepressed version of what happened here this afternoon? I'm unconstrained by Hippa bullshit. I'm also capable of unbridled love."

Despite the last scary statement, Don followed Miss Jenny to her private room where she told him about the words Mrs. Wright and a young man had had and how he came back to the room not an hour after his girlfriend had left. According to the nosey old lady, the young man had stayed a few minutes and then was gone.

"Next thing I know, this hard-looking whore in a Harley shirt comes in and starts screaming like someone had taken her TV remote control away from her."

"Could she have killed Mrs. Wright?"

"No." Miss Jenny shook her silver-lined head firmly back and forth. She scowled up at him.

"What makes you so sure?"

"She wouldn't have had time. She walked in, wailed, and ran out. The whole unit of staff ran into that room. No, someone poisoned Mrs. Wright. I know what happened."

"What?" Don wanted to shake her.

"You'll have to kiss me first."

"Where?" Don couldn't believe he had asked when any normal male would have run out of the room.

"On my part." To his relief, she dipped her head nobly, indicating the part on her head. To his surprise, he bent down and kissed her. She smelt of lavender and reminded him of his mother.

"Thank you, young man." Her eyes beamed as if the kiss had also brought her back to some happy moment in her past. "I'm sorry you can't kiss me on the lips. Only my dearly-departed husband got that right."

"That's okay," he said and really meant it. "You were saying . . ."

"Back to business, are we?" Her eyes twinkled. "As I was saying, after screaming and crying, the Harley whore left. That's when I went in. There wasn't blood everywhere like that dimwit said, only on the bed. So that tells me that there was no struggle, only a little old lady, quietly bleeding out."

Miss Jenny kind of reminded Don of the time when he was a child and the sweet little story lady at the library had binged on some bourbon right before story time. The tale that she told had the younger kids crying and the older kids yelling "Badass" until the other staff members got wind of the party and hauled her out of the room. He brought himself back to the present. "What made her do that?"

"I'm getting to that point. So I go into the room, root around and find a portion of the cake that he had brought to her. I pick it up and the cake sparkles, it's really very pretty. But very deadly."

"What was it?"

"Ground up batteries. They looked like the silver shivers that they put in wedding cakes. The residual acid will eat through your inners in ten minutes flat."

Dan rubbed at his stomach. "Who are you?"

"I wasn't always some hot item in an electric wheelchair. I was a homicide detective. I still have a measure of intelligence left."

"Did you tell anybody what you told me?"

She shrugged. "Doesn't really matter, if the murder was legal. Glad I retired before that law went into effect, the One-Kill Deal would have cut into my business."

"No, that law wouldn't have cut into your business, it would have improved it. They still have to investigate every murder because each person is allowed only one and now that it's legal, there will be more murders."

Ms. Jenny cocked her head. "You're right. How else would they know whether you'd had your one murder? It could be your tenth. Business for the detectives is going to boom. I'd be rich if I was still working. Shit. Always a day short and a dollar spent."

Don did not dare to correct her.

Agitated, she knocked the steering knob on her wheelchair. The motorized conveyance banged back and forth in the narrow space between the bed and the wall, leaving what looked like a deer track in the linoleum.

Don had to step back.

"Dammit! Why did I have to go and get old when murder becomes lucrative?" Her voice steadily rose.

"Ms. Jenny?" a nurse called out.

"You better go." Miss Jenny said, fervently.

"I better."

Miss Jenny leaned over in her wheelchair and gave Don a fist bump. "United we stand."

"Divided we fall." Don watched the old lady extricate her wheelchair and leave.

He called his father.

To get Mr. Wright to sit down in his chair took the concentrated effort of Henry, Frank and Lynn. In a collective movement, the three walked him back into his apartment and lowered him into his chair. Bewildered, he looked at the basket of yarn and knitting needles and the indentation of where his wife used to sit.

Henry wandered over to the kitchen. He sat watching the three of them from his corner.

Mr. Wright looked up into Frank and Lynn's faces, still leaning over him. "You two in unison now?"

Lynn nodded.

"You said you knew who killed my Eva."

Lynn nodded.

Mr. Wright turned to Frank. "And you, you of the same opinion?"

"Frank and I are like-minded," Lynn piped in. "I told him that Mike and I were the last to visit your wife, that I left and he was still at the hospital, and that Mrs. Wright didn't approve of him too much. She let him know it."

Mr. Wright met this confession with a hard stare. "You ever lose anybody you love?"

Lynn shook her head.

"It feels like shit. Makes you angry. Inside, I'm screaming, Why? Why? Why? My question to you is why did you leave him loose around my Eva if you knew that she made him mad?" His voice was quiet, but hit her like a drill.

Lynn stepped back a step. "Mr. Wright, I didn't leave him loose around Mrs. Wright. I was-"

"You left her," the old man yelled so fiercely that even Frank jumped. "You knew Eva didn't like him. You knew that he knew that."

"I didn't think that he would kill her." Tears formed in Lynn's eyes.

"And you?" The old man's head swiveled around to Frank. "Now that she's got money, you have unlimited love for her? Last week when you saw her coming up to your place you flew over that balcony faster than an unrestrained passenger."

"Mr. Wright, I don't see what all this is going to help," Frank said. He tugged at his collar, as if it had crept up to choke him. The old man's words hit too close to home, some of it was true. But Lynn was different now. She'd also been back on her meds, bringing out a different Lynn.

The old man could read his mind.

"I'm trying to show you that you think you are going to use her for your money. She will use you up first. She uses her mental health as an issue to get away with murder. Well, maybe she is mentally ill. You know what I am? I'm totally pissed. And I'm a totally pissed person with boundless resources."

Frank swallowed hard. His mafia neighbor was now angry and making veiled threats.

"My power in this town is immeasurable," the old man said, finally sinking back in his chair.

Behind them, Henry watched quietly from the kitchen chair, his face incalculable. The man-child looked bewildered over what was happening. "Mr. Wright, shall I pour you a glass of milk?"

Mr. Wright looked up quickly, startled by Henry's presence. "Yes, thank you. Your kindness is endless." He smiled at the man-child, then turned back around to Lynn, his expression instantly hardening. "You're going to know what it's like to lose someone you love. You careless, inconsiderate girl. Now, get out of my house." He barely looked at Frank.

Which made Frank very nervous.

It was Wednesday morning and Lynn had still not gotten around to calling her brother. Big John knew, now that she had money, she would not need him anymore. He pushed back in his chair, closed his eyes and wondered how he felt about that.

The phone rang, waking him up.

"John!" Stuart barked into the phone. "We need you to get down here right away. You know why?"

"There's an unwed pregnant woman down in the parking lot claiming I'm the father."

To Big John's surprise, Stuart laughed heartily, a quick staccato chortle that was so like Stuart, in a hurry to be done so he could get on with the next task. "No buddy. We know you are completely partnerless and not a soul in the world would sleep with you."

Affronted, John cleared his throat. "I'm a bachelor, yes."

"I didn't call you here to discuss your wifeless state. I called you here because we need you to work."

"Did you just call me Buddy?"

"Yes, I did, Buddy." Again with the chortle. "Business is great. You're great. And you are going to make a lot of money."

"Okay." Big John pinched himself. "You are not high, are you?"

"Ho, ho, ho. You are so funny, Big Guy."

Big John took that as a yes.

"We just got a large contract opening up and life is looking good."

"For me too." Big John couldn't help but think that this had something to do with his sister. The idea wasn't sitting too well with him. At this point, he figured he didn't have anything to lose, so he would just flat out ask. So he did.

"Well, of course it has something to do with your sister. Isn't that as plain as the nose on your face?"

And just like that Big John's good optimistic feelings dissolved. He was now being hired by this little monkey because his sister had jerked the chains on Stuart's simian arms. He would take the job because he had no choice, but his anger was palpable in the way he thrust himself out of the chair, like a torpedo on a direct course for Stuart's nuts.

"Let's do this," Big John said. "Let's fill out the paperwork and let's get this started." He would deal with his sister later. Obviously she was going to need some boundaries defined.

CHAPTER SIXTEEN

Don could hardly wait to tell his father the good news. The witch was dead. He could come home. No more skulking around. He held the phone up to his ear, counting the rings, picturing his old man's bowed out legs making his way across his small dark living room. Finally, on the fourteenth ring, the old man answered the phone.

"Don Senior." Don would know the gruff voice anywhere. His father had spoken to him in that voice since he was a child. In fact, it was the only voice he could remember hearing coming from the old man.

"Hi Dad." Don forced his voice to be calm. He never knew who could be listening in.

"Why are you calling so late? Don't you know I'm retiring for the night?"

His rebuff was like a fire hose quashing the flames of Don's excitement. In the instant it took for his father's harsh words to come out, Don had been reduced from a swaggering champion roper to an unassertive piece of milquetoast. His voice, subdued now, came out barely audible. "It's done," he said.

"What's done? Speak up."

Don tried to be inconspicuous as he crouched down in the rental car. He now wished his bright yellow hair was not so spiked up. "That thing you asked me to do," he hissed into the phone.

His father finally caught on. "Well, I'll be dammed. How'd you do it, boy?"

"I didn't do it," Don corrected him firmly. "Somebody else did."

"What? Somebody beat you to it?"

Don nodded. "Yeah, Dad. Somebody beat me to it."

"You still got one left."

"Yes, yes I do." Don looked around the parking lot. Five cars down a large Hispanic family tried to cram their last five generations and one old lady into a Chevrolet Impala. "I don't think it has to be a goal for me in life to fulfill that option. I don't think that's the idea behind that law. You should have a good reason to . . . you know."

"I get it. You want to save it for an unplanned incident, like when some damn teenager cuts you off in traffic."

"Dad, I think you might have unintentionally smoked something stronger than a normal cigarette. I'm not saving my allowance so that I can indulge in random axing."

"You never were much for spur-of-the-moment fun," the old man grumbled. "Oh well, I've got somebody else that I want you to take care of. Another person that's responsible for us losing the ranch and living like sardines in a track tin can house."

Don sighed. "Really? And who is it?" "Who do you think has been responsible for stripping me of my hard-earned money so that he can build "green houses" that won't kill the earth?"

"Off the cuff, I'd say the president." No sooner had Don had it out of his mouth then he knew that his nutcase father really did mean for him to go after the president.

"With Pitt gone, George Clooney can step in and run the country. He'd get the illegals out and he'd reduce our taxes."

"They all say that." Don rubbed his forehead.

"If you don't help me with this I'll go over to Kathleen Rae's daddy and have a talk with him about his daughter and the man she is going to marry."

"Stay out of my love life."

The old man snickered and hung up the phone.

Kathleen Rae meant more to him than life itself. "Shit!"

Mike the mechanic was a simple man. After he fed the battery-acid cake to the old lady he went home to freshen up. He put on a plain, but clean brown t-shirt and some khaki pants. He looked respectable. A clean cut guy looked back at him from his bathroom mirror. A face that would make Lynn love him. Why shouldn't she? Smart. Owned his own business, yet unimposing. The fact that he had just murdered a defenseless elderly woman with a cruel method never crossed his mind. What filled his thoughts as he left his apartment was how much Lynn should love him because he wasn't Fat Frank. Mike's auto shop provided him with a modest means of support, but with Lynn's money, they could move up into a bigger house in Summerlin. They could get one with a pool and central air.

He had to be honest. Lynn's money did make her more attractive.

Crossing Decatur, a small plane flew over, heading for the nearby North Las Vegas Airport. Mike looked up and smiled. Lynn's money would buy him one of those. He could learn to pilot and fix it. He had their whole life worked out before he reached the other side of the street. Jogging back to her apartment, he pictured her thrilled face when he told her his plans for them.

But Lynn wasn't home.

Five o'clock on a Tuesday and she wasn't home, yet. She must have left with Frank and they were still together. Mike felt his blood boiling. He raced back through the apartment complex, barely seeing cars or small children scramble out of his way. He did not hear their mothers' epithet and he was lucky he was fast enough to get across the six lane street before fathers could be summoned. Mike heard nothing. He saw his customer's Jaguar parked in front of the shop, just waiting for the owner to come and get it. Mike had the keys in his pocket. That's all he needed.

He loved Jaguars. He'd done a good job with this one. The engine roared to life. The car jumped forward, flying out of the parking lot. An angry truck driver layed on his horn. Unrepentant and furious with Frank and the world, Mike stuck his middle finger out the window and kept his foot on the gas. He sideswiped a tiny M.G., but kept going. Shameless, he even flipped the guy off for daring to be in his way. In the wake of his fury, his morals were completely abandoned. His mother always said that he drove with half the IQ of a complete idiot. Cars around him scattered. Like wild animals, they sensed something dangerous and predatory behind them. Mike just knew that he was going to kill Frank and take Lynn.

The intersection of Charleston and Decatur had other plans for him. Regardless of his needs, the light stayed red and the cars dutifully and peacefully waiting for the green light did not scatter for him. He forced himself to be calm, to pull up behind them. And wait.

He saw the truck barreling down on him in his rearview mirror almost too late. Actually, it was the grill of the truck in his rear-view mirror. Without a moment's more of hesitation, he turned the wheel sharply to the right. The powerful luxury car jumped the curb like a tick on a fat dog. Once on the curb, Mike slammed on the brakes and narrowly missed plowing through a line of migrant workers lined up at the taco stand.

The people at the light did not fare so well. He heard the scream of metal and bystanders as the truck slammed into rows of stopped cars. Already, plumes of smoke rose up from the hoods and an altruistic man ran among the carnage banging on roofs and yelling for people to get out.

Appalled, Mike couldn't move. But one vehicle among the squashed cars could move. With a generous push on the gas pedal, the huge truck pulled out backward. Burnt rubber filled the air.

The truck slammed into drive, making a beeline right for Mike.

Mike stomped on the gas. The Jaguar was still running but the jump to the curb had crippled the car's front alignment. The car jittered across the parking lot, the truck in hot pursuit.

Mike just had to live. Even with the truck's grill just inches from his bumper, Mike knew he had to live. He had charitable plans for Lynn's money. He did two things he thought he would never do again. The first was praying. The second was pissing his pants.

The massive truck clipped his bumper sending him into a dizzying tailspin that flipped him nearly 180 degrees until he was nearly windshield to windshield with the angry driver. He stared at the truck driver, a young woman with a mournful basset hound at her side. Her mouth worked furiously at him. He couldn't understand a word she was saying but he got the jest. She was going to kill him.

His engine was still running. He had a chance.

CHAPTER SEVENTEEN

Frank sat in his bachelor pad, feeling very unsophisticated. Lynn had just left. She'd been explaining to him, or trying to explain, her need to go: her business took some time. There were blog posts to write, store managers to call and chemists to contact. The more she explained P.R. and product development, the more simple-minded he felt. She had a hundred balls in the air. He drew pictures for a living.

A knock on the door interrupted his thoughts. Henry, Tanya's child-like son from the apartment beneath Frank, loomed in the doorway. "Mr. Frank, I think you better come see the old man."

Frank's blood ran cold. This was it, his summons from the old mafia man.

Henry's guileless green eyes held no menace. "He is coughing up big green wads of stuff and hanging on to furniture when he does it."

Frank immediately motioned for Henry to lead the way next door. As they walked across the landing, Frank couldn't help but hear Mrs. Wright's voice in his ear saying, "Oh, Henry, how gauche."

Henry pushed his way into the Wright's apartment. For the past three days, he'd been going over there after his mother left for work in the afternoon. Frank followed closely, his nose wrinkling slightly when they entered the place. Mr. Wright had done some basic housekeeping, but a stale odor that had not been there before Mrs. Wright's death, hovered in the air.

Henry continued into the bedroom. When he opened the door and the two men saw the old man lying on the bed, sprawled there as if he'd been thrown, Henry let out a primitive cry of anguish.

Mr. Wright coughed and sat up. When he saw Frank, fire burned in his rheumy eyes. "Your new girlfriend is going to be sorry she let my Eva die. Sorry. You hear me? Straightforward enough for you?"

Henry ran out of the room, leaving Frank with the angry old man. The front door slammed.

Frank swallowed, frightened to be alone with Mr. Wright. "Some nurse, eh?"

"He's not very specialized." The elderly man looked up at Frank and his eyes softened. "He's been here for me." To Frank's alarm, tears rolled down Mr. Wright's tough leathery face. His large bulbous nose turned redder.

Now Frank really didn't know what to do, aside from wishing desperately that Henry would come back.

"I miss her so much. Why would your stupid girlfriend leave my Eva alone with that guy if she saw that they weren't getting along?"

At that moment, Frank remembered why Lynn had left her date or ride, or whatever that guy was to her. She'd left the monster to be with him, Frank.

"She's not suitable for you," Mr. Wright continued. "It's unfitting that now that she has money, you go after her like a dog in heat. I guess money is the grease that makes incompatible people compatible."

The old man's apartment suddenly felt very hot. Here Frank had come over to help his neighbor and now he had to defend his love life.

Mr. Wright chuckled. "You think it unseemly that you're sitting here discussing your love life with an old man. Let me tell you something, young man. Have your life's rug yanked out from underneath you, you really don't worry about what's improper or not. You just try to get back on your feet."

"What are you going to do?" Frank asked.

"Well, first of all, I gave that monster's name to the police."

A trickle of sweat ran down Frank's back.

"They have to investigate a crime, unless he out and out confesses to what he did. Despite the fact that murder is legal, only one murder is legal. They have to mark it down on his record so that he knows, and they know, that he can't kill again." The old man's voice cracked at the end of the sentence. He had to keep his head tilted down, trying to compose himself. When his head lifted, his eyes were clear.

Frank wasn't sure if he should ask the next question, but he had to know the answer. "Mr. Wright, what are you going to do to Lynn?"

The old man looked up, his expression guarded and hesitant. He seemed undecided about what he was going to say. "To Lynn? Absolutely nothing."

The ambivalent words reeked with threats.

"You don't seem convinced," Mr. Wright said. "Don't look so skeptical. If I tell you I won't touch Lynn, I won't touch her."

Suspicious, Frank backed up. "Are you okay now?"

"I'm just great."

"Henry said you were coughing up big green things."

"Yeah, well, sorry that I can't prove it to you."

Frank blanched and inched out of the apartment.

"Frank?" the old man called.

Frank froze.

"I know why Lynn left that monster with Eva. I know that she wanted to go home with you that day. I don't blame you. You don't have to watch your back."

Frank nodded. He backed out of the apartment.

Tanya ran the comb through her hair quickly. In her rush, she lost more hair than she disentangled. Throwing on her best Harley shirt, she rushed out of the bedroom.

Henry sat in the kitchen, eating Oreo cookies and watching her.

"Make sure you clean up around here before you go to see Mr. Wright."

"Yes, ma'am." Henry bent to receive her kiss on his cheek. Straightening up, he groaned slightly and put a hand to the small of his back. His gesture made her realize that Henry was aging, something she had never thought about before. She never thought about it before because her child would stay four years old forever.

But something did get under his skin. Something had troubled him. He'd told her about how Mr. Wright had spoken angrily to Lynn. He knew, even in his simple little world, that something was not right, just like he'd known that Mr. Wright needed him. When Tanya left for work, Henry let himself into the Wright's unlocked apartment. This morning he'd told his mother that he was sure Mr. Wright was going to do something bad to Lynn.

Maybe Henry was developing and maturing. Before, Henry would never be troubled by bad vibes coming off people. She'd seen the kids at school gang around him and call him names and he'd emerge from their cruel little circle unruffled. She'd thought that he would remain blissfully unconcerned about Mr. Wright's troubles.

Nothing could be further from the truth. After Henry's first night with Mr. Wright, he'd come home, collected his comic books, his Nintendo, and a few packages of cheese n' crackers. He stuck the items into a bag and announced that he would be going to Mr. Wright's apartment from now on. She'd questioned him and gotten a very composed answer. "Because he's way too sad to be by himself."

Things were changing now. Henry was becoming troubled. But Tanya couldn't deal with that right now. She ran down the stairs, jumped in her car, shot out on Decatur towards downtown. Tanya was in a big hurry to speak to the President. She found a place to park, tried to avoid locking her keys in the car and streaked for the Horseshoe Casino. She closed her eyes to the gaudy fading carpet and the glaring lights from the machines.

Sal, her boss, caught up with her just as she was about to clock in. "He wants to see you."

They both knew who "he" was.

"I know," Tanya said. "I've been wanting to see him, too."

"Well, excuse me," Sal shot back.

Tanya punched in, then quickly tied her apron around her waist. She dashed toward the private dining room, running into Sal.

Her boss did his best to avoid her, but his unwieldy stomach got in the way of a quick getaway.

"That gut is getting unmanageable," Tanya snapped. "Time to lose some weight."

Sal sucked in his hefty midriff just as Tanya disappeared into the private room. He was still trying to think of something to snap back at her when the door opened again.

Tanya poked her head out. "Hey boss, can you get us an apple martini?" Her head disappeared back into the private room and the door slammed again.

Tanya returned to the center of the room where the President sat, two laptops standing at attention on the coffee table in front of him. She'd never been graceful, but she was trying to now. In as dainty a voice as possible, she asked him if she could sit down next to him.

He looked at her, boyish and handsome, his hand patting the sofa in front of her. "How are things going with your neighbor?"

Tanya flipped her hair. She couldn't have stopped herself. The habit had been ingrained in her muscle movements from the time she first discovered the beauty of boys. Even if this boy was the President of the United States. "You get right to the point, don't you?"

"I don't have time to beat around. Somewhere in the world, a terrorist is about to shoot a plane down. In another place, one of the earth's Teutonic plates is about to move, and somewhere else there is a young hero waiting for the President's acknowledgement. I've learned to live in the moment. I've been here three days and it's really been amazing. It's like time has stopped to allow me to connect with people."

His genuine, honest smile loosened something up in Tanya. She was about to tell him how her son has to stay with her neighbor every night because he is so messed up in grief and how angry she is at that stupid law that allowed this to happen. But, instead, she did something completely out of character. She burst into tears, then spent a flustered few seconds searching for a napkin.

The president handed her a napkin, letting his tanned smooth hand linger on her arm. The other hand, he raised in the air.

In her corner of the room, Ruth, the secret service agent, sat back down.

Tanya couldn't control herself. She kept thinking of the Wrights, two old people who never hurt anybody, both enjoying life, and now one was dead and one was shattered because of this stupid law.

The President waited for her sobs to subside. He couldn't take her in his arms. That would be unseemly, but he did tip his chin slightly towards hers, their two heads forming a tent.

Tanya could only manage a muffled apology. Eventually her sobs subsided. "It's so degrading to sit in front of the president with snot rolling off my face."

"Just think of me as a guy named Brad Pitt."

"You're not helping."

"Well, I'm kind of worthless as a comfort with Nervous Nellie over there in the corner, twitching her trigger finger every time I move."

Ruth did not change expression. She scanned the room alertly.

"You are so kind and I'm so undeserving."

"Feeling better?"

"I'm feeling crappy."

"Don't say that. Why would you say that?"

"Because I came here to really chew you out for supporting that reprehensible law that got my friend killed, but you've been so nice to me."

President Pitt shrugged.

"I feel crappy because a man who had knocked me down and roped me up like an animal came into the bar acting all chatty and apologetic. And I couldn't help wishing he'd roped you up."

Ruth's head shot up. She stared directly at them.

"And he was asking about you, too."

Ruth stood up.

Tanya got the feeling that she wasn't coming over to order a drink.

CHAPTER EIGHTEEN

Henry clomped down the stairs to his apartment, happy to be away from the old man and his noises. The first thing on his mind was popping his Tiger Woods game into his Wii and golf-swinging away. Frank could take care of Mr. Wright. At first, Henry enjoyed being with the elderly man, but now he said a lot of scary things that didn't make sense to Henry and they didn't sound right. Like how he was going to make Lynn feel the way he felt. And then he would get on the phone and yell at people. Lately he would yell things about getting 'the big lug' a job.

Henry was a big guy. He worried that they were talking about him. He didn't know how to work. He couldn't get a job. Mr. Wright would slam down the phone and then smile at Henry. He never told Henry he was going to make him get a job. So Henry would relax. Just a little.

Henry searched for the Tiger Woods containter. But then, just outside his door, he heard a large clopping noise. Someone big, bigger than Henry, was walking up the stairs. Henry waited and listened.

This giant pounded on Frank's door, just above Henry's apartment. "Lynn! Lynn!" he bellowed.

Without realizing the effect he could have on an angry man, Henry bolted to the door, threw it open, looked up and hollered, "Lynn's not here. She drove away."

"Mind your own business. Lynn!" The man went back to banging on Frank's door.

"Her boyfriend is in that apartment." Henry indicated the Wright's apartment, just across the landing from Frank's.

Henry watched the large man turn and look at the apartment door. Henry saw his face and decided that he was just a large man and not a giant. He slumped a little. Henry became emboldened. "She already has a boyfriend."

For some reason that Henry could not figure out, the man smiled. He looked ten times friendlier. "I'm her brother."

Henry scrunched up his nose and examined this man casting shadows down the stairwell. "But Lynn is a child. I'm bigger than Lynn."

"I can see that." His tone softened, almost friendly now. "I guess I could ask Frank where Lynn is."

"No!" Henry shouted. Some germ of an idea lit in his brain. Something that made him shout urgently at this perfect stranger.

"Come down here. Come down here now," he insisted. "Wait in my apartment. It's urgent." Henry had been watching crime dramas with Mr. Wright. He'd learned some important new words.

"If you think this is really necessary."

Henry nodded.

The man stomped down the stairs, clinging to the rail. His ankle bent a little sideways and he grimaced, but he still managed to smile at Henry. "Name's Big John."

Henry's eyes widened and he gasped. "I knew you were the big guy Mr. Wright talked about. You better get in here fast." He stepped back and waved insistently until Lynn's brother followed him inside.

Big John looked around the apartment. His eyes went to the lawn chair and then to the table with the plastic flowers. "You live here alone?"

"No, my mom lives here. She picked out those flowers. See? They match the flowers on the couch."

Lynn's brother nodded. "Well, I guess you didn't call me in here to talk about your decorations."

Henry shook his head slowly. "No, but my mom says I should always make small talk before I get into the large talk."

Big John nodded. "And what is the large talk?"

"It's about the old man across the way. His name is Mr. Wright."

"Yes? Do you mind if I sit down? My ankle is really starting to hurt."

Henry pointed to the couch. "Oh, yes. And do you want something to drink? I can get you anything but my mom's last beer."

"No, just the large talk."

Henry nodded. "Well that Mr. Wright across the hall is always talking about how he's going to make Lynn feel bad the same way he feels bad. His wife just got killed and he thinks Lynn could have stopped the killer."

Big John opened his mouth, but he had suddenly gone dry and he couldn't talk. He motioned for Henry to continue.

"Mr. Wright shouts into the phone a lot, something about getting the big lug a job so they could get close. I thought he meant me. But, I think he meant you. I think he is going to kill you."

Lynn drove down Decatur, her mind filled with all the things she had to do. Hiring an assistant never crossed her mind.

She made it halfway home before she hit the big traffic jam at Decatur and Charleston. Police cars, lights awhirl, lit up the whole intersection like some cosmic emergency disco. Traffic cops, pointed vigorously, trying to get the cars to use up every inch available to clear the road. But people wanted to get a good gander at the spectacle of a four car pile-up before they moved on. Mash a huge smoking truck with an expensive Jaguar and you had a winning crowd-pleaser that wasn't going to move away any time soon. Lynn toyed with the idea of jumping the curb and then cutting across Wal-Mart's parking lot; they let people camp in their parking lot, they should let people cut through it. Lynn scanned the parking lot and the sidewalk for pedestrians. She considered herself a careful driver. She glanced over at the mass of police officers dealing with the mess on the opposite side of the road. They weren't going to bother with a curb jumper on the east side of the street when it looked like Evil Knievel had just ridden a tornado down the west side of the street.

Before she swerved into the bus lane, something caught her eye. Walking away from the mess, was the unmistakable loping gait of her mechanic, Mike. Head down, greasy hair covering his face, he walked with a purpose.

Lynn had no use for this man. He worked on her car, that was it. He murdered an old lady and now he was heading toward the Wrights' and Frank's apartment. Lynn chewed on her lip. She had to get out of here. She had to head this monster off. Time to put her little Kia Soul to use. Time to stop thinking about jumping the curb and doing it. She yanked the wheel to the right sharply, applied some pressure and a prayer, then hung on tightly as the car jumped the curb. She knew it would never handle the same way again. At this point she just hoped it would run.

It did. She headed north, paralleling the road. But when she got to the last exit, she met with traffic three lanes thick, their bumpers married to the car in front. Drivers leaned forward, their mouths set in tight stressed lines. She'd get into the lane over their dead bodies.

Lynn picked her target. She watched cop shows. She knew how to profile. There was her target. A middle-aged man in an older Camry. The driver left her an inch. She punched the gas. Her Soul leapt forward and she got the corner of her bumper between the Camry and the car behind him.

The Camry inched forward, but Lynn wiggled her way in. When she got close enough to where the man could hear her through his open window, she said, "I could kill you. It would be legal." The man let her through.

The next two lanes before the center divider were a piece of cake after the first one. The other drivers noted her insanity, heard her heartfelt threat and let her through.

Now she was on the center divider, contemplating her next move. People had made a northbound lane out of the center divider and they were honking at her to get moving. People had just gotten past the massive traffic accident that had stolen thirty minutes of their life and they were bound to make it up.

To her left, Mike walked. She hoped he wouldn't look over and see her. How would she behave toward him? A murderer who wasn't a criminal. What kind of world was she living in?

He murdered Mrs. Wright. Everyone had loved her, thought she was so cute. Lynn didn't like her, couldn't bring herself to like the old lady, though she could be a catchy conversationalist.

Mike murdered Mrs. Wright to shut her up. Mrs. Wright had already called Lynn to tell her that Mike was the kind of guy who would let the woman work all day and then he would walk on her all night. "He's trying to take advantage of you," the old lady told Lynn. "He's playing you for a sucker."

What the old lady failed to see was that Lynn didn't give a fig about Mike the Mechanic. She couldn't get that through Mrs. Wright's thick hide.

Mike had enemies. Frank. Lynn loved Frank.

And now Mike the mechanic was taking his greasy black fingers and heading to Frank's apartment. Lynn could see him a half-block away. She could only ride this center divider until she got to Alta, a block away. Then she would have to turn left on Alta or merge with the mess on her right. Barring the chance that Mike the Mechanic gets a ride, he had a four mile walk ahead of him to get to Frank's apartment. She had time.

Or so she thought. A large RTC bus pulled up out of nowhere, stopped by the curb and scooped Mike up.

"Shit!" Lynn cursed, banging the dashboard.

For no apparent reason, a car stopped, letting her make a U-turn so that she could catch up to the bus. Lynn swore she saw a bright light beaming down from heaven. She zipped in, only to get caught at the Charleston light.

Her Good Samaritan pulled up alongside her at the light. The window rolled down, revealing a young guy with thinning curly hair and yellowing teeth. "I saw you on Shark Tank. I watch the show all the time. Your idea was the best."

So pleased with his compliment, she forgot to tell him to get out of the house more (and maybe see a dentist or two). "I'm actually trying to catch a bus," she yelled.

He laughed.

The light turned green and she lit out after the bus. The Soul squeaked, but Lynn kept after that bus. A good feeling crept up inside her.

She could have done a few things better that day. At this point, she could have pulled over, phoned Frank or even the police to warn them about Mike's arrival. But she wanted this. She wanted this feeling of the wind screaming through her windows and her hair, the tires protesting as she urged them on. Her heart beating as she raced up Decatur, the bus would soon be in her sights.

Wait, where was the bus? Lynn peered up the road and couldn't even see the tall RTC's taillights. That driver was making time. Lynn punched the Soul's gas pedal. When she hit sixty, she was between the Half-Price Lawyer's billboard and the flower shop selling bouquets for funerals. But she would not take her foot off the gas.

She would pass that bus and protect Frank.

She passed the bus.

Except that the next light was red. The smug bus pulled up alongside Lynn. Lynn glanced up, but the windows were darkened. The bus revved its engine.

"You got to be kidding," Lynn muttered.

The light turned green and the bus shot off. It was not kidding.

Lynn didn't stand a chance. The Soul was a big boxy wind catcher with two wonky tires on the front and a tiny engine. She was forced to get behind the bus. In two hundred feet, she could turn into her lover's apartment building. She was almost there.

Then the bus stopped. Tailgating behind it, she was stuck. She watched impatiently as a whole village of tired hardworking people got off the bus and lumbered toward the next transfer point. They walked slowly, but amongst their small compact bodies, an alien moved. Tall and white, his body lithe and bouncing with purpose, Mike stood out. Finally the bus moved off.

Lynn drove past him, praying he wouldn't see her. Her green Soul stood out. Loud green car with a scraping sound. How could he not see her?

"Lynn," he shouted.

Ahead of her the locked security gate beckoned.

"Lynn!" More insistent this time. The shout jumbled the security numbers in her brain.

She checked her rearview mirror. If he ran, he could catch her. She looked at the gates and her foot pressed on the gas.

CHAPTER NINETEEN

Frank's usual weekday night schedule consisted of going to his studio and painting. But his life wasn't normal now. His life left normal when he fell in love with his stalker, the crazy woman who became a multi-millionaire overnight. His rival for Lynn's love was an old-lady-killer and his arthritic old neighbor was a former Mafia Man who, despite the old man's assurances otherwise, would light a match if Frank were near gasoline. So, everyday life for Frank was over.

He stepped out on the balcony, craned his neck and checked out the lights from the Gold Coast and the Palms. Those would go on forever; that's how he knew life for everyone else was still normal. Traffic continued to buzz along Decatur. People called to each other across the dark parking lot, swing shifters glad to be home. All pretty normal. Except for something that caught his eye as he stood on the balcony surveying his domain.

Lynn's bright green Soul shot through the parking lot. He broke out in a grin. She could not stay away from him. For him, this was an extraordinary moment. Never had he had a woman leave his apartment and then come racing back a half hour later. Despite saying that she had a hundred things to do, she had raced back to him. He watched her car zip up to the curb. The window rolled down. She stuck her head out the window. The thin tendrils of her hair snaked around her face.

"Frank," she yelled. "Run! He's going to kill you."

Frank froze on the balcony, confused. While his mind processed her words, he saw Mike the Mechanic come walking up toward the apartment. Frank did not believe in abandoning a woman, but there was a man out there who was bound and determined to kill him. He darted back into his apartment, slamming and locking the door behind him. Normally, Frank wasn't this self-centered, but, normally, he didn't have a murderer hot on his trail. Fear seized him. He ran back toward his bedroom and locked himself in the adjacent bathroom. On the whole, he behaved like a goosed schoolgirl.

After two minutes of cowering, he started to feel a little stupid. Bullets were not blowing through the door, nor was there a maniac pounding on it. People don't kill other people in the middle of the day.

His cell phone rang. Lynn! Why didn't he think of the cell phone? Hands shaking, he managed to answer it.

"I'm fine." Sarcasm dripped from her voice. They had moved from phase one of adoration in their relationship to phase two: sarcasm. "I can take care of myself." Her accusatory and self-righteous tone managed to shrink his manhood.

Frank gulped. At this rate, phase three was right around the corner. Contempt. He had some major damage control to do here. He tried to clear his throat so that he could say something commanding and manly. A squeak pushed its way out.

"Thank you, I feel the same way, but I had to stay down here and deal with it." Her voice spoke volumes. "Mike would like to come up and have a word with you."

A wad of odd and confused words spewed from Frank's mouth. He couldn't force a sensible thought out.

"My thoughts exactly." With that remark, she ended the line of conversation.

He heard their feet clomping up the stairs. *You have ten seconds. How do you prevent yourself from being murdered?* He shot out of the bathroom into the kitchen. He stuffed the butcher block of knives into the fridge. He thought about putting one in his pocket but that would only hurt him more than it would hurt Mike.

The doorbell rang.

He tried not to hyperventilate, but if his life was going to continue like this, he'd have to buy some Depends. He wiped his hands on his pants so that he could grip the door handle, then he opened the door and jumped back.

Lynn and Mike stood shoulder to shoulder on the threshold.

"Mike really likes that painting you did of me." Her voice was flat.

Emotions churning, Frank did not comment.

"Can he have it?" Lynn raised her eyebrows and waited for his answer. "How come I never saw it?"

Frank swallowed. "Because I did it before I liked you."

Lynn simply stared. Behind her the lights of the far-off casinos blinked on and off, blips of light in the night sky.

A door opened beneath them, distracting them all from this awkward tense moment. Lynn looked at Mike, gauging his reaction to a newcomer. Mike kept staring at Frank.

The three of them stood in the chilly December air, letting the newcomer come up the stairs.

"Mr. Frank?" Henry's deep voice, oddly innocent called up the stairs.

Mike tensed.

Frank found his voice. "Henry, just go home."

Henry wasn't following orders that night. "Is that the man who killed Mrs. Wright?" he asked simply.

Mike stood there like a peacock. When he turned toward Henry, Frank's knuckles slammed into the mechanic's arrogant nose.

Blood splattered all over Lynn's chest, the red soaking into her dark t-shirt.

Mike's body staggered for a minute, too stunned to realize it'd had the stuffing knocked out of it. Then, finally the mechanic's knees buckled and he crumpled. He tried to get up, his legs scrambling out for purchase, but it was futile.

With the taste of blood and victory, Frank was not letting the mechanic get to his feet. Every time Mike tried to get up, Frank delivered a flying boot to his chest. This happened a few times until Mike realized that his efforts were pointless. Defeated and hollow, he remained prone.

During this fight, Lynn had not stood idly by. She'd made a valiant attempt to get Henry to go back down the stairs, but one hundred and eleven pounds of woman could not budge three hundred and fifty-three pounds of stubborn man. But now that Frank was done with his mission, she demanded that Frank make Henry go home.

"Lynn?" A man's voice from Henry's apartment called. "What are you doing?"

"Nothing," Lynn answered modestly.

"Who the hell is that?" Frank asked. He kept his foot near Mike's face. Frank felt like the hero and he didn't want anybody else stealing the limelight.

"My brother," Lynn said.

Big John clomped up the stairs. He towered over Henry. Frank was sure that he would tower over him too but the big guy stopped, surveying the scene. "Who is that?" Big John's eyes fell on Mike's prostrate figure. With some effort, Big John bent down on one knee to feel the mechanic's pulse. "He's alive. What the hell is going on here?"

"That's the bad man that killed Mrs. Wright," Henry piped up, his shrill voice rising.

Mr. Wright's door opened, startling the group on the landing. Henry's voice was loud enough to wake the dead. All eyes turned toward the old man. He didn't say anything, standing in the cove of light from his apartment. Behind him, Frank could see Mrs. Wright's quilt laid out on the couch, as if she had just gotten up to get a drink and would be coming back. Lines of concern were etched deeply into the widower's face. The fiery anger he'd had earlier had burned itself out. They were in trouble here; Frank could sense it.

"Mr. Wright, maybe you should go back inside." Frank tried to keep his voice gentle, unchallenging.

"Mr. Wright, go inside." Henry came up the stairs. Even in his simple capacity for understanding the situation, he knew that something was wrong.

Mr. Wright held his arm out and Henry walked to him, smiling as the old man draped his arm around the younger man. "This is my good friend," Mr. Wright announced to the group.

Frank did not relax, but all he could do was wait.

Deftly, Mr. Wright's arm tightened around Henry and he swung the young man around until he was facing the apartment door. The group saw Mr. Wright's head tilt toward Henry, saw his lips murmur something into the young man's ear and then Mr. Wright released him into the apartment, shut the door and turned back to face the group. "Better that he be lost to sight," the old man said. Then, from behind his back, Mr. Wright pulled out a small handgun.

Immediately, the crowd moved to disperse. All except for Big John, who remained on knee next to Mike the Mechanic's prone figure.

Mr. Wright's voice, loud and commanding, stopped them. The gun in his hand helped. His gnarled liver-spotted hand held the gun steadier than most men his age held a Bingo dauber.

Frank's heart leapt to his throat. If he lived through this night, he hoped the memory would not. Right now, he stood in the direct line of fire of a grieving, bitter widower with nothing to lose and a law to protect him. "Now, Mr. Wright, don't do anything crazy." Frank slowly withdrew, backing into his apartment.

"Don't leave, Frank." Mr. Wright's words were quiet and calm. His eyes surveyed the others. "Don't you all think that the only thing worse than dying is the few remaining moments you have right before you know your life will come to an end?"

Nobody answered, their eyes on the pistol.

From the ground, Big John's movements startled them all. Watching the big man with the bad ankle rise to his feet was like watching someone balance on a tight wire while having a seizure.

Mr. Wright appeared calm.

John's breathing sounded as if he had just walked a couple of miles with a fully loaded school bus on his back. "Sometimes, I think it would be great if I would just be no more," Big John declared. He took another deep breath. "Look at me, I'm obsolete. I'm a driver in an age when self-drive cars are the rage. I'm a big guy that can't do manual labor because my lungs are chronically obstructed." He took another deep breath. "And my ankle is permanently fused into a fucked-up angle by a cheap quack that my parents grabbed at the last minute, so I can't run after anybody."

"What are you doing?" Lynn hissed.

"What does it look like? The old man's got a loaded pistol and five people he wants to shoot. His dilemma is that he can only shoot one and he knows it."

"I can shoot more than one," Mr. Wright snarled. "I don't care about any stupid one-kill law. I'm an old man with nothing to live for. I could kill you all."

"Then kill yourself?" Big John questioned.

The old man nodded, his eyes locked into Big John's, his pistol arm locked and pointed on the big target.

"Here's what will play out in reality," Big John said. "Here's what will happen as soon as you pull that trigger. Before you get a chance to gloat in self-admiration, the rest of us will jump you and hold you down until the men in white coats come and get you. They'll lock you up in a padded room. They don't put mirrors in padded rooms so it will be a little hard for you to indulge in your narcissism."

The old man held onto the gun. "Narcissism? I got my pride, sure, but this animal killed the love of my life. I was supposed to be protecting her. The things we went through together… you young people have no idea. Our generation didn't expect things to be given to us. We worked hard for what we got. And then some pretty-boy president comes along and makes this rule that allows people to take away what you value most in your life. And you!" He turned toward Lynn. "You knew what was going to happen and you just left. You left that maniac with my sweetheart. I should shoot your brother just to let you know how loss feels."

Tears flowed down Lynn's face.

"She's showing off," Mr. Wright spat out.

Nobody spoke. They knew arguing with a crazed and desperate old man would be pointless.

Mr. Wright turned back to Big John. "I should shoot you and let her feel the hollowness I feel. I should teach Mrs. High and Mighty some humility. What's your brother worth?" Mr. Wright asked Lynn.

Sobbing, Lynn answered, "Everything. Just shoot me. I caused your wife's death. She got into the accident because of me. Just shoot me."

Mr. Wright raised his gun.

Frank saw the glint of metal. The barrel of the gun focused on Big John like an evil eye.

In that instant, Mr. Wright's apartment door opened and a dark blur hurtled out of the apartment. The blur rammed the old man, knocking him down. The gun went off. A deafening crack rent the air, then a muffled cry.

Three bodies went down. First Big John as his left leg flew out from under him, then Mr. Wright and finally the blur that had started it. A flood of blood pooled out from the three.

Stunned and disbelieving, Frank looked at the mess in front of him. In the background, apartment doors opened and slammed shut again, a baby cried. Lynn's screams finally moved Frank to action.

Unless he wanted to get blown to beyond the Strip, he'd better find that gun. He dropped on his knees, his hands clawing around the pile of bodies for the gun.

Big John's eyes were glazed and unblinking. Frank was sure he was gone, but he would have to cover up for Lynn. He yelled at her to call for an ambulance while he frantically clawed around the pile of bodies, looking for the gun.

"I've got it," Lynn said.

Frank whipped around.

Lynn pointed the gun at the pile of bodies.

"Are you crazy?" he screamed at her.

Henry, the blur, rolled off the pile of bodies and looked up at her. Mr. Wright didn't move. Then amazingly, from beneath the old man, Big John managed a hysterical laugh.

"I wouldn't let Mr. Wright hurt John. John's a nice man," Henry declared.

"Get your ass out of here," Frank screamed at the bulking boy-man. "Lynn, put the gun down. Henry call 9-1-1."

Henry obeyed. His lower lip jutted out, but he ran into Mr. Wright's apartment.

Lynn kept the gun pointed at the old man, though it was clear from his ragged breathing that he wasn't going anywhere anytime too soon. But now that Henry had moved, she had a clear aim at Mr. Wright. She looked up at Frank, a glazed look in her eyes. "I still have a murder coming to me."

"Lynn, stop! That's not what this law is all about. It was made so that good people could get rid of bad people. That was the idea. But the law's major flaw is that good people don't get rid of other people. They don't make judgments. They don't kill people. They work out their problems, just as a civilized society should do."

Lynn's face scrunched up as if she was being force fed bad dog food. "No, what people learn to do is to put a coat of varnish on evil. If this old fart had murdered my brother, society would say that he'd temporarily gone insane. That he's a war veteran, a man morning for his lost love when you and I both know that he's a murderer. It'll be up to me because I'm the closest into seeing what is really going on. I have a right to take this motherfucker out."

"Is somebody calling an ambulance?" Big John groaned from the bottom of the pile.

This unnerved Lynn. "Oh, God, John I hope so. Frank, go check."

"I'm not going anywhere. Put the gun down and check for yourself."

Lynn did not move. She held her stance, then suddenly she tossed the gun down and ran into Mr. Wright's apartment.

"Is the old man dead?" Big John huffed out.

Mr. Wright's chest rose and fell slowly. "No," Frank answered.

"Well, his face is covering mine and his breath smells like he's dead. It's like someone is making me wear a burqa made out of a corpse." A curtain of the old man's long grey hair hung in Big John's face. "Really, Dude? We're almost brothers-in-law. Can you knock this old fart blanket off me?"

"Sorry." Frank had always heard not to move someone in an accident. "I guess I'm a bit befuddled." As gently as he could, Frank rolled the old man off of Big John. Even in the darkness, he could see a death shroud around Mr. Wright's face. The old man groaned and looked pleadingly at Frank. Night did not conceal the dark hollows under Mr. Wright's eyes, the result of sleepless nights, nor the old man's hair, allowed to grow long and straggly. His clothes billowed around his thinning body, highlighting rather than camouflaging the fact that he hadn't eaten much lately.

Lynn stepped out of Mr. Wright's apartment. The glazed look was gone; now she appeared worried. A pool of light from the apartment flowed out from behind her, illuminating the old man's pale face. He looked up at them, his eyes half open, his breathing labored.

"Can't we cover him?" Lynn asked, curling her lip at the sight.

Frank sighed, suddenly feeling very weary. "Just go get the blanket off the couch." He looked up, suddenly remembering something.

Mike the Mechanic was gone.

CHAPTER TWENTY

Tanya got sent home early that night. She'd said that she hoped that a rodeo rider with a few loose screws lassos the President. The twitchy Secret Service took it as a threat. At forty-seven, she was too old to care about their feelings. She had gotten her point across and that's what counted.

Sal and Ruth sent her packing for the night. The last she saw of President Pitt was his rueful smile as the Secret Service ushered her out of the room. She really just wanted to go home and go to bed, so that was fine with her. Her bed swam enticingly in her head as she pulled into her apartment complex.

Two ambulances came flying out of the entrance, shattering her daydream or any thoughts of sleep. Instinctively, she knew something was wrong. This premonition was confirmed when she drove up and saw Frank and Lynn standing on the balcony outside their apartment. Lynn faced her dead on. Frank averted his eyes.

Tanya drew her leather coat around her shoulders. Back in the nineties she'd gotten it at a Grateful Dead tribute concert off her stoned boyfriend. The coat represented security. She grabbed for the car's door handle. "Where's Henry?" she yelled.

Frank wouldn't show her his face; instead, he went back inside his apartment. Lynn stayed, facing her. To Tanya, Lynn always had the appearance of someone who didn't give a shit about somebody else.

Tanya took the stairs two at a time. "I saw the ambulances. What is going on? It's ten o'clock at night. Where is my son?" She screamed this last question into Lynn's face.

Lynn's face remained a mask of calmness. "He was in the ambulance."

"What happened?" Tanya screamed.

More people came out onto their balconies, gleaning the leftover excitement now that the officials had come and taken the bad guys and the gun away.

Frank came out of his apartment. "Your son is fine. He demanded to ride in the ambulance with Mr. Wright."

Tanya opened her mouth to speak but Lynn cut her off.

"That crazy old fart had a gun. He was going to kill my brother."

"Geez!" Tanya took a step back, grabbed the railing and lowered herself to sit on the top step. "I can't believe Henry was in that mess. Didn't anybody try to stop him from getting into the ambulance?"

"He said nobody could see him in his camouflage shorts." Lynn managed a small smile at this.

Tanya dropped her head in her hands.

"Actually, when Henry is bound and determined to do something, nobody can stop him," Frank said.

Tanya nodded. "I suppose I should go and get him."

"I'll drive you," Lynn said.

Tanya's head shot up. "Seriously, bitch? The last time you were in the car with my friend she ended up in a horrific accident. You gotta be kidding me."

"I wasn't driving. She was driving. I wasn't even in the car."

"That's true," Frank popped in. "Mrs. Wright drove Lynn to the airport because I was avoiding her."

Lynn looked up at him with reverence. "You don't avoid me now, do you?"

"No, I don't."

"I'm going to throw up," Tanya said.

"Good, I hope you do. Because you used to try to destroy my love life," Frank said.

"For which I'm grateful for," Lynn cut in. "You kept the women away so I could walk in and take the prize." She looked up at Frank who smiled back.

Tanya dropped her head back into her hands.

"There's another thing that needs to be said," Frank called down. "Mr. Wright and Big John are at the hospital together. I hope both are closely watched. Mr. Wright threatened to kill Big John."

Lynn uttered a curse word and hauled Tanya to her feet.

Tanya wrenched her arm free. She was close to clocking the psychotic woman and knocking her on her ass. In fact, if her cell phone hadn't rung precisely as she was winding up for the punch, Lynn would be out cold. Tanya fished the phone out of her purse, looked at the caller ID. Her eyes grew wide.

Lynn stopped tugging on her arm. "What? Who is it?"

"It's Mrs. Wright."

Lynn shuffled to her other foot and stared at Tanya. "It can't be Mrs. Wright. Answer it."

Tanya answered the phone. She brought the phone slowly to her ear, as if she expected it to breathe fire on her.

Across the wireless, a voice raspy and rough coughed out one word. "Tanya," it said.

Stunned and confused, Tanya looked around, expecting television cameras and a laughing host jamming a mic in her face. But when she looked up, Lynn's inquiring face was all she saw.

Mr. Wright watched the wordy nurse bustle around the room, her mouth moving a mile a minute, her sleek long dark hair trailing alluringly across her shoulders. He never liked garrulous women, but this one had large boobs to focus on while she yammered on, so he could tolerate her. Taking the longest path possible, she explained his condition to him. When he could tolerate the deluge of words no longer, he spoke up. "That is the most tautological ton of crap that I've heard shoveled into my snout. Now stop this silly jabberwokking and tell me what is wrong with me."

Suddenly turning taciturn, she said, "Nothing."

Mr. Wright stared at her steadily until she relented.

"Alright. You got the wind knocked out of you. You're old. We don't want you so we are sending you home tonight."

"Thank you, my dear."

"You are quite welcome."

"Would you like to go out sometime?"

"Don't push it. Your clothes are at the foot of the examination table. We couldn't seem to find your underwear."

He winked at her.

She rolled her eyes and escaped.

Chuckling, he picked up his wife's cell phone out of his pocket. Seeing one of her possessions instantly sobered his mood. Her face surfaced in his memory. He chased it away and called Tanya. As soon as the phone rang, a coughing spell racked his body, making speaking difficult. "Tanya," he croaked out, then broke out again in the irritating coughs he couldn't shake.

"My god," Tanya whispered.

"I'm fine," he croaked into the phone.

There was a heavy silence. "Mr. Wright. Oh! Oh! I feel so stupid. I thought. . . Well, the caller ID said that you were Mrs. Wright."

"Oh, of course. You thought my wife was calling. I'm sorry." Mr. Wright cleared his throat. "I just grabbed her phone because my battery was dead."

"We were just coming to the hospital. Is Henry with you? Are you all right? What happened to Big John? What happened to you?" Tanya wanted a whole account of his injuries.

He just didn't have the energy to answer her questions. It was late and he wanted to go home. He'd have to figure out some way to get her to stop babbling. "I fell right on my penis. The nurse said if I want to date again I would have to find somebody really understanding because my-"

"That's enough. I'll just come and get you."

Mr. Wright smiled. "I'll be in the waiting room reading children's books and religious tracts, but take your time. They're all in Spanish and I'll have to get somebody to translate, but I'm sure this will keep me busy."

"I said I'll be there as fast as I can." She hung up.

Mr. Wright got dressed. He didn't like the way his red sweater hung on him, or how he had to tighten his belt just to keep his pants up, but right now he had other things on his mind. He still wanted to kill someone. He still felt slighted at the way his love had been taken from him. He still wanted somebody to pay for Eva's death. He opened the door to the room and nearly ran into a huge chest. "Henry," he said. "You scared the shit out of me."

"Not supposed to swear," Henry countered sternly. "Not supposed to shoot people."

"Not true anymore."

"It's wrong to shoot people. Church says so. Mom says so. Everybody in the whole world knows you are not supposed to shoot people."

"No, it's okay now. There is a new rule out. I shot John because I was angry."

"Mr. Big John didn't hurt you."

Revenge was complicated. He couldn't explain to Henry how he wanted Lynn to feel what he felt. How he felt she was responsible for letting Eva die. He would get the murderer himself. "How is Big John doing?"

"He says a bullet in the knee hurts more than a punch in the head."

Mr. Wright nodded. "What is Big John like?"

Henry's demeanor changed from a demanding disciplinarian challenging Mr. Wright's morals to a blushing schoolgirl. "He likes pretty ladies. Me too." Holding his large hand over his mouth, Henry giggled into it, then fanned his face.

Mr. Wright studied the younger man. "You really need a father, Henry."

"You're too old."

"I'm tired Henry. Leave me alone for a while."

Henry shuffled off. "I'm going to go see Mr. Big John."

And I'm going to pay your mother to kill him.

Just then, Tanya came whipping around the corner, dragging that psycho, Lynn. Mr. Wright hadn't accounted for another person, especially not Lynn.

The two women skidded to a stop in front of him.

"We thought you'd be dead," Lynn blurted out.

Mr. Wright couldn't tell if she was disappointed or relieved. "If second-hand smoke or diseased people coughing on me for all these years couldn't kill me, then I guess a knock from a person as big as a small pickup truck is not going to do it." He was making a jab at her nose plug business.

"My nose plugs save lives," she said defensively.

"Go see your brother," Mr. Wright said. "He's down the hall." He pointed the way. "Stay here, Tanya."

They watched Lynn walk away.

"Gad, she's a pain in the ass," Tanya said. "Non-stop talking all the way here."

"I want you to kill her brother."

"What did you just say?" Tanya stared at him. "Did that blow to your head do more than they thought?"

Mr. Wright looked directly at her. "She left my wife in the room with a homicidal maniac. I want her to feel what I'm feeling now."

"Okay. I know this is a dangerous question to ask a deranged man, but why can't you do it yourself?"

"Because I want to kill somebody else and I'm only allowed one murder," he snapped.

"No need to get hostile. Can't two mature adults have a civilized conversation about killing people?"

"Can't you just keep your voice down without becoming so loud?"

"Do all men get so mean after a certain age?"

"Do all women start off so bitchy before any certain age?"

"They get this way from dealing with men," Tanya said. "Why would you ask me to kill for you?"

"Because you are a barbarous piece of trailer trash. And you always look like you need a monstrous amount of money."

"I'm not some degenerate that would kill a nice guy for a little bit of money."

"Is it so degenerate to commit a legal act so that you could earn enough money for Henry to live on for the rest of his life?"

Tanya's mouth opened. She closed it. Her face whitened. She stepped back and then plopped down on one of the vinyl waiting room chairs. Her voice came out raspy and strained. She looked up at him with pure hatred in her eyes. "You are a bad and horrible man."

"I can offer you a lot of money for killing Big John. How long could Henry live with the money you've saved up for him? Two years? That's if he could take care of himself. We both know that he can't. He'll need caregivers almost round the clock. He'll end up in some state run facility. The first time he does something they think is wrong, like taking a walk outside, they'll tie him down or drug him up. He'll turn into a vegetable. You know this is true."

"Stop! You are a vile man."

"The truth is cruel," Mr. Wright said gently. "You have to decide. Do you want to be virtuous and leave Henry broke or do you want to be lawful and leave Henry well taken care of?"

"I hate you." Tears streamed down Tanya's face.

Mr. Wright nodded.

"I suppose this leaves you free to go after the man who killed your wife."

Mr. Wright shook his head. "It won't be me. It will be somebody else."

Tanya stared at him. "So you aren't going to kill anybody?"

"I will. I'm going to kill myself. How do you think I'm going to get the money? I'll name you and the person who kills Mike as the benefactors and then I'll kill myself. Suicide is now legal. The insurance policy will pay you off."

Tanya took a tissue out of her purse and wiped her nose. "I used to think good would always win."

"You're not young enough to be that naive. The strongest and the smartest win."

"Well, I guess you're number one." Tanya turned her face away from him.

"You wouldn't be such a loser if you'd noticed that the strong survive. I used to think you were so tough, watching you taunt poor Frank mercilessly every time he took a girl home. Now I see that you're just a little girl in a leathery body."

"I said I'd do what you asked. Why don't you just bug off?"

Mr. Wright was about to answer her, but just then Henry came down the hallway.

"Mom, mom!" he cried, his loud voice echoing through the halls. His nose ran snot. Several people turned to stare at the large blubbering man. He ran right into his mother's arms, his knees bending and his head curling downward so that he fit neatly into her arms. "The doctors said they have to take Big John's leg off," he sobbed into her chest.

Mr. Wright drew closer to hear the young man's muddled words. When the meaning of the words sank in, he felt an odd stuttering in his heart. He stepped back, clutching his chest.

Tanya lifted her head so that Mr. Wright could catch her full hateful look. "Not so victorious now, are you?"

Mr. Wright didn't know what to say. The man that he had just tried to murder would be suffering for the rest of his life. Suddenly, he wasn't sure if he was winning or losing.

Henry's sobs continued.

Tanya pulled away from her large son. Ignoring Mr. Wright's chest clutching, she focused on Henry. "Henry, I want you to go sit down over there, right now. I'm going to talk to Mr. Wright about what we can do about this."

Henry did not sit down. Instead, he stood up taller, towering over his tiny mother. He faced Mr. Wright like a champion boxer, posing for the start of a match and he didn't back down when Mr. Wright hunched over. Henry's face was purple with rage. "You did this! You did this!"

The pain in Mr. Wright's chest let up, allowing him to step back. In three years of living above Henry he'd never seen the boy-man look like this. Anger turned the child-like part of him into a man to be feared.

"Henry!" Tanya shouted. "You need to sit down. Now!" The scariest thing for Mr. Wright was the fear in Tanya's voice. She had lost control of her son. She jumped in between the two men, pushing Henry back with all her strength.

Two men in security uniforms strolled down the hall, one of them reaching for his club.

"Police!" Tanya hissed at Henry.

Henry stopped yelling. He hung his head and scurried off to one of the chairs.

Mr. Wright figured Tanya was the type of mother who taught her son to fear the law. Mr. Wright's own mother used to tell him that if he didn't keep the lawn mowed, the police would come and haul him away to prison. When he grew up, he moved to an apartment. He still lived in an apartment.

"We're fine." Tanya tried to head the officers off. "My son just got a little upset."

The thinner one gave her a foul look, but he started to walk away. The heavier remained, itching for a fight. "Keep your family fights at home," he said.

"Keep your repulsive stomach behind your belt," she retorted.

"No need to be distasteful." The skinnier one had halted his retreat. "Although that gut is disgusting." He gestured at his partner, a snide look at his face.

"Shove off," the fatter one said.

Like two old maids, the dreadful duo bickered their way back down from where they came.

Tanya still wasn't going to get her chance to light into Mr. Wright. A herd of medical students ambled by, some giving the group curious glances, especially at the large man quietly sobbing on the bench. Mr.

Wright could tell that something had changed in her.

"I just thought of something. You know what it is?"

Mr. Wright shook his head. He could tell by the wicked gleam in her eye that it was not going to bode well for him.

"According to our depraved Department of Justice, it is legal to kill someone, but it is not legal to assault someone. So, according to our perverted system of justice, you could go to jail for the damage you caused to Big John's leg." She smiled. "So what do you think of that?"

Mr. Wright did some quick thinking. And he could throw her reasoning right back in her smug little face. "I'll tell you what I think. If it weren't for that degenerate son of yours, Big John would still have both legs. He barged into me. I wasn't going to shoot, but he knocked into me, and that made the gun go off."

"You are despicable," she spat.

"As reprehensible as this may be, if you pursue this, I will tell the police about your son's part in it."

Henry watched them. He knew something was going on. "Mom?"

Tanya gave him a pleasant smile. "Mr. Wright was just telling me that he didn't mean to shoot Big John, that it was an accident. He was telling me what a hero you were."

Henry thought a moment. "I called the police," he said.

"Yes, you did," Mr. Wright agreed assiduously. "You did it very quickly."

Henry sat down, satisfied.

Mr. Wright sighed. "I wish my problems could be resolved that easily."

"You have a lot more problems to resolve than he does."

"I thought we were good here. I'm not going to ask you to kill Big John anymore," Mr. Wright said.

"Yeah, but you gave me a view into the future and a taste for money. And now I want the money. I'll tell Big John to press assault charges if you don't pay me off."

Mr. Wright had a violent urge to strike her. "I told you if it weren't for that awful shove your kid gave me, the gun would never have gone off." He saw fear in her eyes. "You want me to tell the cops how your brutal son caused the loss of John's leg? Because I will tell them."

"Henry's not homicidal. He's handicapped. He was also

temporarily insane, fearing for the life of his friends."

"The courts will see a brutal man, dangerous to society."

"These are turbulent times, old man. I hope you are strong and rich enough to convince the courts that Henry forced a loaded gun into your hand."

"He knocked my hand. He caused the gun to go off." He knew Tanya was no weak-kneed kid. She looked like she'd been around the block a few times. He could see hard times in the harsh lines of her face, and the leathery texture of her skin. Wiry muscles bulged in her thin arms and she had a spry graceful way of walking.

"If you don't pay me to shut up, I'll tell the courts that you tried to pay me to kill someone. That's illegal and you'll go to jail."

The courts had left that law in the books, leaving the one-kill law to be for people who found someone intolerable in their lives, not for rich people to get more than their share of kills.

Mr. Wright sat on the bench. He would have to give her his retirement money. Thankfully, his four daughters were all married to well-off husbands who would provide for them so he didn't have to worry about them. Now he would have to live in some nursing home and room in a small dark space with another elderly man, the two of them growing even older together.

The odd thing was how bad he felt about Big John's leg. He'd meant to kill Big John so that his sister would suffer, not confine him to a life of misery. That was too much.

CHAPTER TWENTY-ONE

Don strutted down Fremont Street looking and feeling virile and indestructible in his black leather vest and his tight Wrangler jeans. It was the National Finals Rodeo in Vegas and packs of cowboys roamed the streets, checking each other out. A few women in tight clingy dresses looked over at him and giggled. Don knew that they were not used to seeing a man who was all male. He'd looked at the other men. Some of them wore pastel colors and had soft bellies hanging over their jeans.

He approached the Grand Canyon Gentleman's Club, his eyes caught by the life-sized videos of enticing young women scantily clad in string bikini bottoms and two stars in strategic places. Out front stood a woman in a low-cut dress, smiling at all the men who walked by.

Next to her stood a man in a Justin Bieber haircut and acid-washed jeans. He smiled at the men too. He kept his head down, but batted his eyes up at Don. "Well, there's a strapping young man." He sashayed his hips at Don. That was the last thing he did.

Don charged the young man. His left hand grabbed a fistful of the man's t-shirt and his right fist drove into the man's gut. He pinned the guy up against the video dancing ladies.

"Ooh, how macho," he squealed, then coughed in Don's face.

Don jumped back, releasing his hold.

The young man straightened his hair and his shirt with quick and flighty effeminate flips of his hands.

Don felt like he'd hit a woman. He almost apologized. Instead, he decided to get out of there. Above his head, the ceiling of a million bulbs blazed to life. Everyone stopped what they were doing, craned their necks upward and stared. Queen came on singing about how they were the champions and light-animated cards and queens danced across the sky. Only the vendors with the carts kept their eyes downward, watching the crowd and watching their merchandise. People would steal Mardi Gras beads or glass paperweights with whole families engraved inside them.

Don headed down Fremont Street until he saw the Horseshoe. He entered the dead quiet of the lobby and looked toward the bar.

Sal spotted him immediately. Tough old Italian guy, wearing a wife beater tank top. "Hey, my man, you're back!"

"Hey," Don returned. He wished Sal weren't so chummy. It's not like he wanted to be remembered.

"What'll you have?" Sal got down to business.

"Ummm, what do you have on tap?" Don didn't want anything. He wanted a clear head when he went to kill the president.

Sal listed their beers on tap and grabbed a glass and looked questioningly at Don.

"Surprise me," Don said. He was about to ask him about the president when he was nearly deafened by an explosion. Dirt and chunks of ceiling pelted him. People screamed into his ears. A gigantic encompassing dust cloud closed in on him. An invisible wall of forced air knocked him off his feet. A pile of blasted plaster sliced his hand as he went down. His eyes went up to see helicopter blades and bits of sky. Speech was impractical. He couldn't reign his thoughts in enough to speak; a loud groaning sound came out of his mouth. In another blink, another loud explosion detonated. His eyes squeezed shut, but he did not lose consciousness. When he could open his eyes, he saw and felt a wall of flame. He choked on the dirty air, forgot where he was and figured he must be dreaming.

Then, from out of the dust and the screaming chaos, a figure stepped out. The man, despite being covered in filth, carried himself with dignity and strength. He yelled something that Don couldn't hear. When he got closer, Don could make out his face. He looked oddly familiar but Don couldn't get his brain to process who this man was. The dusty hero yelled something and all Don could do was stare at him. The man came closer and, wrapping wiry thin fingers around Don's arm, pulled him to his feet. Don screamed in pain.

Then he stared at the man, his face backlit by a line of fire. What he saw was stranger than a hallucination.

"It would be wise to get out now," the dusty president commanded, then fell into a paroxysm of coughing. With an unusual amount of strength, the fifty-eight year-old president half carried, half pulled Don toward an exit.

They picked their way through carnage. A huge blade of a helicopter lay where the Horseshoe's kitchen used to be. Now Don knew he was hallucinating, just as sure as he had hallucinated that the president was escorting him out of the building, or what was left of the building.

Hours later, Don woke up in a completely different environment. Stark white walls and the mild smell of antiseptic filled the air. He tried to clear his mind, but all he could see was the vision of Brad Pitt walking out of a dust cloud to save him. It was quite some time before he realized that there was somebody in a white coat standing in the corner.

"Where is President Pitt?" he demanded. "Brad Pitt carried me out of the building."

"Delusions, confusion, slow processing brain." The Indian doctor spoke into a tiny recorder, his sing-songy accent giving Don the feeling that he was being mocked rather than noted. The doctor whipped out a tiny light and flashed it into Don's eyes. "Pupils responding," he told the tape recorder.

"Do you think I saw a ghost?" Don asked.

Finally the doctor stopped talking to his little friend and made direct eye contact with his patient. "You don't think Brad Pitt pulling you out of the fire is a little unrealistic?"

Don blinked. "What happened?"

"One of those little tourist helicopters made a wrong turn. It was supposed to be going to the Grand Canyon. Instead, it lost power and fell through the roof of the Horseshoe."

"That sounds completely feasible."

The Indian doctor did not miss Don's sarcasm. "It does sound a little unreal, but then, imagined things don't break your leg. Now young man, I have to go. Seventy-eight people were brought into this hospital tonight. I will never be out of a job in this Utopia." And with that he opened the door and whisked out, leaving a nurse in his wake.

She stared at Don, her eyes behind the thick lens magnified.

They roved his face and then rested on his hands.

"Look, this is all very romantic, but aren't you supposed to be helping me?"

"I know you. This is not a romantic encounter. You were the one who tried to strangle Mrs. Wright."

"I did not strangle her," he shouted. He tried to get up but a sharp searing pain stabbed through his shoulder. "I was trying to hug her. I thought she was my grandmother."

Plump hands were placed on plump hips. "Then why did you run?"

"Because everybody was screaming." Don rubbed his throbbing arm. "What is wrong with my arm?"

"We think it's broken." She continued to stare at him.

"You *think* it's broken?"

"You heard the doctor. We have seventy-eight victims, some with way more than just a broken arm. A helicopter crashed through the roof of the Horseshoe. One moment it's full of life, the next moment, it's full of death. I've already seen the videos on TV. There were people coming out covered in blood and yet, still helping others. Now, we have twenty people in line for the x-ray machine, plus you, a criminal. So, as soon as we get around to x-raying that arm, we'll do what we got to do, be it surgery, amputation or just nailing some pins in it. And then you can be on your merry way to jail." She practically danced out of the room.

Don looked down at his body. He still had his tight Wranglers and Western shirt on, although they were now in tatters. He scrutinized the sides of his body and his jeans and did not see any holes or huge masses of blood. A dull pain came from his left shoulder. But that was it. He'd been bucked off a horse and felt worse than this. Clenching his teeth, he got up from the table, slowly. He had to hug his left arm, but the pain was tolerable. Better this pain than going to jail. Ironically, if he had killed the old lady, he wouldn't be going to jail.

He pushed the door open and peered out in the hall. Pandemonium reigned. People yelled and moaned. The hallway was lined with the injured, the worst ones were the ones that stared hollowly up at Don as he walked by. Medical personnel walked around barking orders. Nobody had time for him. He walked down the hall, avoiding looking into the eyes of the ones far more wounded than he was. They slumped against each other, still covered in blood. The smart ones had learned that if they were able to demand attention, they were well enough not to need it.

Don made his way out the emergency room door to the ambulance dock. Out here, the yells and demands were drowned out by the sound of ambulances roaring up, sirens deafeningly loud. After he saw what they unloaded from the first ambulance, he avoided looking at the rest. The noise, the pain and overall fatigue fused together. He stood there, in a fog.

"Bus that way, medical help that way." A man pointed while yelling in Don's face. "Either way, you can't stand here."

Don jumped. The sight of human suffering compounded with his own pain nearly overwhelmed him. He headed in the direction of the bus stop, having no idea if he still had a rental car. He'd parked eight blocks from the Horseshoe.

He found the Charleston bus stop and got directions from a homeless man. Heading east, he rode the bus back toward downtown. The area segued from the land of strip malls to large warehouses, some with restaurants in front and signs advertising art galleries and an artistic Ironworks shop. The bus then passed a building that looked like it had withstood a nuclear bomb. What the hell was happening to this city? "My God," he said.

"Believe it or not that was designed by a professional architect, Frank Gehry," a voice behind him said. "That piece of work is typical of the guy's career."

"It looks like something Godzilla vomited. They give people that do stuff like that jobs in this town?"

"Works for me," the man said. "I could take LSD and come to work and they'd promote me." He sighed and looked at Don. "May I ask what happened to you?"

"A helicopter dropped through the roof of the Horseshoe Casino."

"No shit. How'd you survive that?"

"President Pitt pulled me out."

"Yeah, my sister used to have that fantasy a lot."

Don sighed. He had no idea whether the president made it out or not.

"If you want to get back there, here's your stop. Maybe Vice President Clooney will help you find your car."

CHAPTER TWENTY-TWO

Lynn found Tanya sitting on a bench in the hospital waiting room. Henry stood over his mom, keeping a careful watch on her.

Lynn approached the two, clearing her throat to get their attention.

"Tanya, I want to go to Frank's." Her voice, normally so demanding and thoughtless, came out weak and tired. Seeing the pain her brother was in had gotten through to her: that other people had problems. That his problems might be monumental and that her needs would have to take a back seat. She had never stopped and considered these things before.

Tanya looked up, shoved her bra strap under her tank top and then did a double take. Her harsh grey eyes rested on Lynn's face. Then she did an odd thing. She stood up and put her arms around Lynn.

Lynn was not sure what to do. She stood there for a minute, smelling the smoky essence of Tanya's hair, looking over the smaller woman's shoulder at her large son and feeling a tightness in her chest. Lynn endured the hug for a while. "Can we just go," she asked, trying to keep the impatience out of her voice.

Without a comment, Tanya released Lynn, grabbed her purse and motioned for Henry to follow them.

Nobody said a thing until the three of them were buckled into Tanya's car.

"Where did the old fart go?" Lynn asked. Her new-found humanitarianism did not extend to the old man who had shot her brother.

"Mr. Wright said he was tired and wanted to go home. Mr. Wright said he was hurting from falling on the ground," Henry piped up from the backseat.

"What are you? The official Mr. Wright spokesman?" Lynn snapped. She did not care if the old man was tired or not. She wanted him to pay for what he'd done.

"Spokes*person*," Henry grunted, shifting his large frame in the small back seat. "Mom says you should always say 'person' at the end of a word instead of 'man'."

Tanya almost smiled, instead she concentrated on the road. Even at ten at night, the roads were not deserted. Enough industry people had gotten off work and were frequenting the bars along Charleston. Tanya concentrated on merging into traffic safely, then staying the speed limit as the cops knew this was about time for Vegas' second rush hour.

Suddenly, her cell phone rang. "What else could go wrong?" She dug in her pocket for the offending device.

"You could get a $350 fine for talking while driving," Lynn informed her.

Tanya gave her a defiant look and brought the phone to her ear. No sooner had she swiped the answer button, than a flood of words squawked out of the little phone. Tanya pulled the phone away from her face, but listened contentedly. "Oh, my God, what? When?" She looked over at Lynn. Tanya's face had gone very pale.

"Momma, what is it?" Henry asked from the back seat.

Tanya turned away from her phone. "Shhh!" she said, then pressed the phone back to her ear. "No, I'm fine. I got sent home early. Have they heard from Sal? Have they heard from the president or any of his people?"

"What's happening?" Lynn asked.

Tanya put the phone down. "My friend is watching the news. She says a helicopter dropped down on the Horseshoe." Tanya pulled the phone up to her ear and listened some more. "They aren't divulging much more. They don't have any number of survivors or deaths. They don't know if Sal got out, or if anybody else came out of the building."

"Wasn't the president supposed to be there?" Lynn asked.

Tanya nodded. She suddenly felt middle-aged and bone-weary.

But she also wanted to call her mom.

"He didn't leave, did he?"

Tanya shook her head. "He said he needed to be someplace where he could go and relax."

"He told you this?" Lynn asked, a little incredulously.

"He told me a lot of things."

Lynn snapped out of her gloom. "You got to meet the President? Did you even vote at the last election?"

Tanya shot her a dirty look. "We are going to get Frank."

"What do we need him for?"

"Because we are going to go downtown and see if we can find the president."

Lynn looked at her as if she had truly gone mad.

Tanya was undeterred. "We'll need all the muscles we can get."

"And we're getting Frank for that?"

"Flabio's busy this week."

"Let me get this straight," Lynn said. "You want to go downtown amidst the fire, dust and chaos to look for the president. "You didn't even exercise your right to vote, and yet you are going to put a posse together to save the president. The Women's Suffrage Movement was all in vain because of women like you. You won't go to the polls because they're in an area with a lot of homeless people, yet you want to go where a terrorist barbequed his plane over a casino? Well, I elect not to go."

Tanya wasn't listening. She had the toe of her boot leaning on the gas pedal and they were flying up the road. "You got any of those nose plugs on you?"

Lynn nodded. She kept her face straight ahead. Strip malls and empty parking blew by her peripheral vision. "Maybe you should slow down."

"Maybe you should pull out some of those nose plugs. Downtown is going to be rife with dirt, grit and smoke. Later, when we're interviewed about how we managed to survive all that, we'll say Lynn's nose plugs saved the day."

"Okay," Lynn agreed.

"I want to go find the president too," Henry piped up from the back street. "I'm big and strong and can find the president."

"We'll see," Tanya said. She pulled into the driveway of their apartment complex. At this time of night, the place was quiet. Still, ever since she'd been hog-tied, she scanned the area before she pulled in.

Lynn was wired now. Before Tanya could even pull into her parking place, Lynn was on the phone, calling Frank.

"Tell him if he doesn't come down and get in this car I will spend the whole night telling you what a lousy catch he is."

Lynn shot her a dirty look and stuffed her phone back into the enormous bag she carried. "He's coming down. And he is not a lousy catch. AND he is good in bed. I can vouch for that."

"Stop." Tanya held up her hand. "If my son starts repeating this smut, you'll answer for it."

Frank came jogging down the stairs, taking them two at a time. "I just saw the news. They've confirmed that the President was in the building, but still no sign of him." He climbed in the back seat, next to Henry.

"I know he was there at ten o'clock, when I left." Tanya backed the car out of the parking place.

"We'll find him," Frank said. "But why are we risking our lives to find this guy when every Secret Service agent and their mother are out looking for him?"

"Because I think that it's important that we show him that human life is sacred, that humans are worth saving," Tanya said.

Frank had been fumbling for his seat belt, but he froze and looked at her. "Have you been smoking opium?"

Tanya turned around in her seat. "Why would you say something like that?"

"Because I've never known you to be human," Frank spat out. He leaned back in his seat. "This guy really got to you, didn't he?"

"Put your seatbelt on." Tanya pulled out on Decatur, leaving rubber on the road. She drove north for almost five miles, until Decatur ended into the North Las Vegas Airport. Then she turned right and headed east on Rancho, paralleling the airport. Normally, the airport handled tourist flights and privately owned small aircraft, but tonight military helicopters circled the airspace.

"That's a mess of aircraft up there," Lynn noted. "It looks like we're under attack."

"Well, this is big," Frank said. "I wouldn't be surprised if they've got the whole downtown roped off."

"Tuck and roll," Henry sang out. "I'm going to tuck and roll under the ropes."

"He plays too many video games," Tanya explained.

"Then he's probably the most experienced one here," Frank said. "We're going to have to really think this out."

"I know a great place, it's near downtown, and it's dark and completely abandoned." Tanya headed east on Bonanza. They passed the Las Vegas Review Journal Building, all lit up with cars pulling into the parking lot.

"I bet they're excited about this," Tanya said, watching the frenetic movement of cars pulling into the parking lot.

"They're all probably out to find the president. And if one of those media sharks gets ahold of them, it'll take a Kardashian getting married to distract them."

"We're not giving up," Tanya declared. "We're going to find President Pitt."

Frank looked at his watch. "I gave up reruns of *Project Runway* for this."

Lynn was not put off by Frank's interest in the models. "Shelf your lust, darling. It's not every day that you get taken on the adventure of your life. Up until the time you met me, your whole life was on the backburner. And then I happened." She smiled back at him.

Her assumption that his life was nothing until she came along offended him. And then he thought about his life and realized that she was right. He didn't want to think about it anymore. "So, Tanya, what did the president say to you to make you so gung-ho on saving him?"

"He knew what it was like raising a child like Henry. He knew about the troubles we'd gone through, like he'd gone through them himself."

"Well, he did have five or six kids, didn't he? And his wife had cancer," Lynn said.

"At least they have money," Frank said.

"Money doesn't cover everything," Tanya said. She fell silent.

"Love does," Lynn said. "I was more thrilled when Frank finally came around than when I got the money for my business." Turning to Frank she said, "Love is the best thing in the world; right, Darling?"

"It's great," Frank agreed.

Tanya suddenly stomped on the gas, watching her passengers' heads lean back with the force.

"Wow, you are really serious about this," Frank said, when he had recovered.

"No, I just had to shut the two of you up before I vomited."

"Where are we going, Mom?" Henry called from the backseat.

"So glad you asked." Tanya finally slowed the van down and turned left into a dark parking lot. Gravel crunched under the wheels as they drove up to a long, low building, its sides crumbling from neglect.

"Is this place what I think it is?" Lynn looked out at the building, her eyes trying to decipher the huge sign laying on its side.

"I'd forgotten about this," Frank whispered almost reverently. He scooted to the middle of the back seat and craned his neck up so that he could see the roof of the building. His eyes fell on the old windmill, lying on its side. "How could they have let the walls just disintegrate?"

"Mom, what is this?" Henry asked.

"This is the Moulin Rouge," Tanya answered. "This is where black people stayed back in the days when they weren't allowed to sleep on the Strip. We may think times are rough, but at least we're more accepting of each other."

"Yeah, we accept them, or we shoot them," Lynn said.

Tanya slid out of her SUV and took a moment to drink in the atmosphere of the old place. "I can't believe this is the only place in Las Vegas that Sammy Davis Jr. could get a room. We've come a long way."

"Tell that to the black kid who got shot on his way to buy a candy bar," Lynn said. She looked up at the old windmill lying behind the building and then back at Tanya. "Tell me, why exactly are we trying to find the president?"

"I got the chance to meet him. He's a really good guy. I feel like we connected."

"I want to bring him home," Henry said.

Tanya smiled at her son. "Yeah, I want to bring him home too."

"You know, he might not even have survived," Lynn said gently.

"Let's just get going," Frank said. "We're leaving the car here."

Tanya nodded. "From here, we can walk up the street and climb up to the railroad tracks. From there we can walk along the tracks and get to downtown without the traffic and the checkpoints." She pointed to the railroad bridge, about a half a mile away. "We'll need to move the car around the back. Everybody in."

When they got in she put the car in gear and drove around the back.

The back of the Moulin Rouge looked as non-descript and decrepit as the front. Signs of a homeless settlement with scattered sleeping bags and litter lined the rear-door entry. The parking lot backed up to a field and across the field stood a simple log ranch house.

"That's the old Binion Ranch House," Lynn said.

Tanya nodded. "This area is packed with Old Vegas' ghosts."

"It's dark," Henry said. He looked apprehensive, his eyes seeking his mother's face.

"We'll be okay," she told him and motioned for the rest of the group to follow her.

Without words, the group tailed her across the parking lot, the crunch of their tennis shoes on gravel the only sound. Then, in a clear voice, Henry began reciting the twenty-third Psalm. For a while, the group said nothing, but when he got to the part about "thy rod and thy staff comfort me", the women joined in.

Frank found their soft voices, led by Henry's baritone, oddly comforting as they trudged through the night. The group finished the verse right at the base of the hill, where the sidewalk went down under the underpass and a dirt path led up to the tracks. A mile away, the bright lights of Fremont awaited them, but here, they were in a different world of dark, worn-out warehouses. A mile away, tourists in brand-new wrinkled clothes stared excitedly at everything happening around them. Here, homeless people, wearing seedy clothes, stared vacantly at the nothingness around them.

Tanya thanked Henry for the verse.

The group stood for a second, assessing the dirt path leading up to the tracks. Their eyes went to the road. If a   police car happened by, they would be stopped and questioned for trespassing.

While the group hesitated, a twig snapped behind them.

Four heads spun around.

A man with long scruffy hair faced them, his dirt-encrusted hands clutched at his sides. Under his filthy coat, he wore an oxford shirt that had seen better days. His pants weren't too raveled, but they were held up by a raggedy belt and one hand. "Spare a quarter?" he asked. His voice was sober, solid, but there was no denying the pitiful, pleading tone.

Tanya reached in her pocket and gave him a ten dollar bill.

The man thanked her profusely and shuffled off. They watched him turn the corner and disappear into the back of an old Dodge Rambler. He ducked his head down and slammed the door.

"Ahh, the nomad's life," Tanya said.

"He was a smelly vagrant," Lynn countered. "I can't believe you gave that derelict money."

"Medication wearing off?" Tanya asked her.

"He needs money. His clothes are ugly," Henry said.

The group shushed him.

"Just because he's homeless, doesn't mean he's a bum," Tanya defended him.

"Ladies, ladies. Can we just get on with our humanitarian mission?" Frank asked. He was a little surprised at Tanya's generosity, but he decided to keep his comments to himself and get the ladies moving. "There's going to be a lot of security from here on. After all, a plane crashed through a building where the president was staying and now he's missing. We're going to have to be quiet and inconspicuous. We can't parade in like Nancy Drew or the Hardy Boys."

Henry laughed.

"He's right," Tanya said. "Henry, you got that? Voices down."

Henry saluted her.

"All we have to do is walk along this railroad track. It parallels Main. When we get to Fremont we can take the little service road that leads from an employee parking lot out to Main." He started up the dirt path to the tracks, relieved when he heard the others following behind him.

"Let me walk behind Frank," he heard Lynn say.

"You don't have to be so jealous," Tanya snapped. She barreled ahead of them, dragging Henry behind her.

"My mom knows martial arts," Henry blurted out loudly. "It's better we're ahead."

Frank rolled his eyes. He let mother and son take the lead, then followed them. Lynn followed him. "Can we just have a few peaceful feet? After we find the president and become big heroes we can all go back to our separate lives. That okay, ladies?"

Silence answered him. The group trudged on. Frank could hear the rhythm of the ladies' feet. Henry brought up the rear, his big feet clomping out an uneven beat.

The silence was okay for now, but Frank worried about Lynn. When she made the money on Shark Tank, she handled it with calmness. Now with the stress of her brother's injury, her new business and her new boyfriend, namely him, he could see a little of her unravel. He'd tried to talk to her about it, but she'd shut him down, saying she was fine.

Lynn was not fine. In the last few days, her personality had changed subtly from minute to minute. Her appearance started to lag. One day she hadn't brushed her hair, the other day she'd arrived with a scary-looking stain on her skirt. He'd gotten her to take a shower, only by going in with her, so that she thought he was just behaving as a normal male. And really, the sponge had worked magic with them, so he let worried thoughts fly away.

A low rumbling sound vibrated his feet, bringing him sharply back to the present. The roar of an engine from far off followed. His brain took a while to register, almost too long, but when he realized what he heard, he shouted at the top of his lungs. "Train! Make a break for it."

They were in the middle of the bridge, with no room to get to the side, but the train was still three hundred feet off and they only had to make thirty feet.

Lynn panicked and grabbed his arm. He wanted her to get moving, but she reached for him. Ahead of them both, Tanya and Henry were already running for the far side of the bridge. They made it across the bridge and were scrambling down the hill on the other side.

Frank and Lynn could still beat the train if they hurried. They had time if they turned and ran. . . now! Lynn kept holding on to his arm. He seized her with both his hands, spun her in front of him and half pushed, half-carried her toward the direction Henry and his mother had run. Lynn took four long stumbling steps before her brain hooked in and she started to run, Frank hot on her tail. They made it to the other side of the hill, just as the engine came up behind them, breathing smoke and fire.

Lynn's face pale face appeared even pastier in the moonlight. She sank down to her knees in the gravel hillside, her lungs spent and burning.

Tanya ran back up the hill, her face flushed and crunched with anger. "What were you doing, stopping to take a picture?" she screamed above the roar of the passing freight.

Frank ignored her, his attention on Lynn. He had to wait until the train passed before he could talk to her. In the time it took for the twenty cars to pass, her breathing had slowed and her eyes had lost some of the wild look. When the quiet had finally returned to the night, he asked, "You holding up okay?"

"She's fine," Tanya snarled. "We're sticking to the plan. If she can't walk, she can go back. Or you can carry her if you want."

"Nobody's going to carry me," Lynn said.

Though her words sounded strong and determined, Frank could still see the spirit and the courage eroding from her face. Normal stresses on a bipolar person were hard enough, but the pressure of creeping along a train track at night in search of the president could denude someone with Lynn's illness. And though they had never discussed Lynn's psycho-tropic drug use, Frank knew that the drugs could weaken a person.

"Losing your nerve?" Tanya goaded.

"Don't," Frank warned, his eyes narrowing on Tanya.

"Just take her home and run a nice bubble bath for her. We'll take care of everything here." Tanya was twice Lynn's age and twice as tough and Frank resented her for taking advantage of Lynn's illness.

"Nobody is going home," Frank hissed, more determined for Lynn to make this trek than was wise. "We're all going to keep on marching with our ears open and our mouths shut. We are going to find our president."

"Amen," Tanya said. With a final glance down at Lynn, she turned and scrambled back up the hill.

Henry trotted up after her like a well-trained puppy.

Frank offered his hand to Lynn. "You ready?"

"Come on," Tanya called from the ridge. "We don't have any time to waste."

Lynn glanced up at her and then turned her large eyes on Frank.

"We don't have to do this if you don't feel up to it." He left his hand extended for her to take if she chose to.

"No, we're not going to go home and fritter our lives away. We are going to have a good life together." She put her hand in his. "We're going to spend our money recklessly. When this hunt is finished, we'll join other hunts and other causes. We're going to live."

He squeezed her hand. "I don't want you to go through hell and then drown in the high water."

Lynn laughed. "You crazy man. Look, we both know I have a pretty severe mental illness. I'm going to do my best to take care of myself, but I'm not going to hide in a corner and wither away. I'm not going to let your concern for me enfeeble me."

He pulled her up into a hug. "Alright, woman, if you are bound and determined to sap the strength out of me. . . well, then let's do this." This was the closest they had come to talking about Lynn's illness. It took a train nearly crashing through them to make a breakthrough in their relationship.

"You punks need some help getting up the hill?" Tanya stood at the top of the ridge, near the railroad tracks, her slight silhouette straight against the midnight sky. She looked down on them, the queen of the railroad tracks.

"Shrivel up and die," Frank yelled. He helped Lynn up the hill. When he got close enough to Tanya, he shot her a look that would shrink a man's appendage.

Tanya was no man. She was the kind of woman that wreaked havoc on weaker men.

Frank held Lynn's hand, tugging her along like she was a sack of treasured loot.

Tanya stared at the two of them. "Frank, you should just save yourself." She laughed when the couple simultaneously flipped her off.

The obscene gesture strengthened Lynn's resolve. Gently, she took her hand away from Frank's. "Come on, what are we doing squandering all this time?"

"'Bout time," Tanya agreed. "Let's go." For a few seconds, she gave them a look of admiration.

The four, newly resolved, continued down the tracks toward Main and Fremont Streets. The only sound they made for a few minutes was the crumple of rubbish being stomped under their feet. Garbage lined the railroad tracks as if drawn there by a magnet.

"What a nice romantic moonlit night among the dregs of society," Lynn said. A smile widened her lips.

Tanya took up the mood. Chest out, chin lifted, she marched on. "We're on a life-changing, very important hike through the wastelands of Las Vegas."

"We're out to save the free world, using a diabolical plan concocted out of the emptiness of our combined heads," Frank said. And with that, he threw back his head and laughed. The group laughed with him. *We've become punch-drunk.* The crazy night, the lunatic mission, the breakthrough he and Lynn had; all reinforced his feelings.

Lynn looked up at him, her light brown eyes glowing in the moonlight. Her thin hair flew around her face, giving her a wild, carefree look. He realized that as crazy as it sounded, he was in love with her. At first, he'd avoided her, then he thought he'd fallen for her because of her money, but now he realized he'd fallen for her.

Even Tanya succumbed to the magic of the night. She stopped nagging. She'd glanced around to check on her troops, but instead caught Frank smiling at Lynn. Tanya watched for a few steps, then turned around and continued the trek, for once leaving Frank alone with his happiness.

They approached where Main Street came closer to paralleling the tracks. It was time to leave the tracks and hit the little side road that led up to the street. All they had to do now was walk the short block, cross Main Street and then they would be at Fremont Street, the heart of the downtown area and the eye of the storm.

"Why is it so quiet now?" Lynn turned and peered at him in the dark.

The group's campy spirit dimmed. Something wasn't right.

Frank contemplated the sky over Fremont Street. When they got to the street leading up to Main Street, he surveyed the area.

"I'll keep an eye on the road," Henry said.

"Shh!" Tanya admonished. "Just be quiet and follow us. I need you to mind me now."

"I can look after myself," Henry said. "I'm big. I can guard you now, Mom."

Tanya sighed. "You guys help me keep an eye on him."

Henry disregarded the last comment and walked alongside his mother.

"Looks like the police have neglected this area." Lynn's voice sounded as if it might crack, reminding Frank of a small child who got passed over when the teacher was distributing candy.

Henry looked at his wristwatch. "It's midnight, Mom. I can guard you." Henry drew himself up to his full six-foot-eight inches, displaying his aptitude to do an alert vigil.

"Fine." Tanya relented.

Standing tall, Henry surveyed Main Street, then the little road they had just walked up. On their side of Main Street, a half-full parking lot sat quietly in the moonlit night.

Across from them rose the back of The California Hotel, its lights still determinedly lighting up the night sky. Beyond that stood the opening to Fremont Street, its neon ceiling conspicuously dark. No street people, no tourists. Not a soul walked the streets.

"What do you think happened here?" Tanya asked.

Frank's throat went dry. He desperately wanted water and then maybe, something stronger. He looked into the faces of the other two women and saw the realization dawning on them.

"They've blocked off the streets, but have called off the search," Lynn said.

"Let's go looting," Tanya said. "All I want is some bottled water."

"I hear something," Henry shouted.

"Shh!" Tanya said. "It's just a car starting up. Oh, cry me a river!" Sweat dampened the top of her lip.

Frank's armpits were wet with tension and the effort he'd used to get to this point. "Wait, where is it, Henry? There's not a soul in town and then you hear a car. That's where we should go!"

Lynn's eyes lit up with excitement. Frank squeezed her hand.

The air had a sinister feel, as if something tremulous and dangerous lurked around the corner.

Henry pointed to the small parking lot across the street, dark now and quiet. "There," he said.

Frank looked in that direction. Suddenly the interior light of a car flashed on, then off almost as quickly. "Come on," he said to Henry, and then without another moment's hesitation, he was off at a run, toward that car.

Henry followed him.

The two men cut diagonally across the street, making a beeline toward where the light had gone on. Henry's heavy boots, clomping behind him gave him courage.

Behind them, the two women followed.

CHAPTER TWENTY-THREE

Don figured he had a watertight alibi. He'd been taken to the emergency room. His name and vitals had been recorded and, like most emergency room visits, he'd been placed in a room and forgotten. The patients who made a bloody mess of the space around them got seen first. Others, like himself, sat in the little cold rooms, time eating up the prime of their lives. So his alibi for at least four hours was flawless. Nobody knew he had bolted and nobody had expected him too.

Don wasn't quite sure of his motives in coming back to the scene of the crime. He wanted to find his car. That was indisputable; but even more, he wanted to find the president. What he planned to do with him when he found him was another thing altogether.

There would be security to deal with. Even now, three miles from the scene, a helicopter roamed the air, its searchlight scanning the area.

Don wanted to call his father; but he was afraid that his old man would berate him with names if he tried to explain what had happened to him last night. What had happened was that he'd seen the human side of President Brad Pitt. Whatever policy the man had made or allowed while in office, however it had affected Don's family, didn't matter after what had happened tonight. Brad Pitt had saved his life. The president had pulled Don out of the dirt and turmoil and had lead him out of harm's way.

Then he'd run away.

His father would tell Don to grow some cojones and take the bastard out. He reminded him how the president's policy on green-only housing by 2020 had ruined the last of the family fortune. Green housing was expensive and it'd cost the last of the family's nest egg to come up to code.

Thoughts of how his father would pressure him to do the family honor by doing away with the president made Don's knees get weak. That and the blood he had lost in the explosion left him feeling shaky. He needed to rest.

This dark area of downtown wasn't exactly filled with inviting cafés or warm family restaurants. Tony Hirsch's revitalization of downtown had gone on for a limited number of blocks. The bottom-feeders of society still pressed on the borders of the gentry. A block outside of the boutique stores and trendy lunch counters lurked the people who couldn't afford to live there. They were the people who earned their keep by scrubbing the dirt and serving the people who kept the sophisticated shops open.

Don found a porch with an iron-railing leading up to a banged up door. He and his family would probably live in a place like this if they had not inherited land and a house from the generations that went before them. He was no better than those people, only luckier. But his father wasn't happy with that. He had some misguided idea that their family should be aristocratic ranch owners, that they were somehow entitled. Fatigued, Don sat quietly down on the lowest step, intending to rest for only a minute.

Behind him, the door opened.

Don jumped up and turned around. A solemn little boy with straight shiny black hair and almond-shaped eyes faced him.

A woman appeared behind the little boy. She threw a slim olive-colored arm across the boy's chest and to Don, she threw a string of invective, half-English and half-Chinese.

Don was too tired to argue, too tired to listen but suddenly, a phrase and a name came up among the string of words. He distinctly heard her mention the president's name and then "no" afterward. "Wait, what? What did you say about the president?"

Her answer was a quick shove off the porch and the slam of the door.

Powerless with fatigue, he moved on. Normally he wasn't so soft that he would let a woman bully him, but he'd changed. Tonight, he'd seen what one group of people could do to another group. He couldn't get his mind off those poor people dripping blood at the hospital. All of them had just been wanting to go out and have fun and now they probably all just wanted to go home and have peace.

Presently, he came to a cement block wall with a small u-shaped area built into it, built for a huge dumpster to park in. Instead, Don parked himself in the inlet. He had two miles to go before he made it to the Horseshoe and he needed to rest. The way he felt now, it would be implausible to get there. In the distance, he heard the faint hum of a helicopter. Lifting his wan face up to the sky, he could see the big metallic bird sweeping the 'hood with a wide beam of light. When it swept over him, he ducked, squeezing his eyes as tightly shut as he could.

The light swept away, taking his fatigue with him. Overjoyed to be passed over, energy surged within him. The two miles didn't seem so far now. The sidewalk was lined with convenience stores. A few people ventured away from their stoops to squint up at the activity in the sky. Ahead, the stratosphere lit the way, like a beacon to guide him. He continued north, his route taking him to just east of where the disaster occurred.

A plume of smoke drifted up to the night sky. Aside from the helicopter moving farther away, the night was relatively quiet. He hit Bonneville and headed west toward Main Street, then walked in front of the plaza hotel. A pack of news vans had gathered there.

He continued south to the dark parking lot where he'd left his car.

"Hey, buddy, where are you going?" A voice barked at him from behind some cars.

Don thought he would have a heart attack. He squinted along the dark row of cars until he saw a man skulking by the Honda, Don had rented from a really cheap place called "Shambles-rent-a-pile-of-shit". In the year 2019 "shit" was made legal. People would have complained but in that same year, killing was made legal. Complaining about a four-letter word would have been like being sent to hell and then complaining about the poor ski conditions. "I'm trying to find my ride," he snapped at the nosey intruder.

"Well, I'm trying to find somebody *with* a ride."

It felt like this man and Don were the only two people in the world.

The man stepped out of the shadows, his hand casually in his pocket. He turned a boyishly good-looking grin on Don, despite the dirt and grime in the creases of his forehead.

"You . . . you . . ." Don looked up and down the empty street, trying to find somebody to witness this. "You pulled me out of the rubble when the bomb exploded. You saved my life. You are the president."

Brad Pitt, 50th President of the United States, moved closer. Despite the ordeal he had just gone through, his hair almost shone and he carried his frame like a king. Don could tell this was no ordinary man. The president grinned his perfect-toothed smile that had earned him fame in the movies. "Yes, I know who I am." His bemused expression held no malice. He looked up at the sky, taking in the distant helicopters. "Just another monotonous moonlit night in Las Vegas, eh?" His laugh, warm and comforting, broke through the night air.

"Is this your usual routine when a disaster hits, wandering around the streets?"

"No, I thought I'd try something new and refreshing for a change. Usually, when a disaster hits, I'm bundled up and told what to say and do and then released on a short leash to stand up in front of a selected bunch of reporters. I've found this getting out and doing what I want quite enjoyable." He rewarded Don with one of his star-power smiles. "I imagine that it won't be long until the Secret Service finds me."

Don could only stare back, still in shock, still not quite believing that the President of the United States was standing in front of his beat up foreign car, asking for a ride. "Mr. President, are you all right?"

"I've never been better, I'm running away from home."

Don wiped the sweat from his brow. Why was he sweating on a chilly December night? "So that's why you are looking for someone with wheels?"

"You got it. Would you mind giving me a lift?"

Don swallowed. "No, not at all."

"Good, because I think there are people out there trying to kill me."

A coughing spell fell over Don.

The president patted him on the back.

Don knew he should probably warn the president that the police were after Don, but when he caught his breath, lifted his head and stared into the kind eyes of his nation's leader, what he said was, "My car is right here."

The president got away because of snot.

The end of Henry's nose filled with snot. He hated running in cold weather, but he knew they were out to find the president and he had to hurry. The cold temperature made his nose run and he had to stop and get rid of all that nasty stuff.

He stopped, wiped his nose and then had to rest because he was really out of breath.

And that is the reason that the president got away.

His mother and Lynn caught up with him. He was leaning against a small Nissan pick-up, trying to catch his breath.

"My poor baby. I shouldn't expose you to such conditions." His mother took out a handkerchief and wiped his nose. "What kind of mother am I?"

"What kind of a mother lets a twenty-four year old man wear clothes like these?" Lynn pointed to his green-stripped knickers and his Kiss T-shirt.

"Shhh," Frank called. His hiss came down to them from two rows up.

Henry's mother wasn't finished wiping his face. "You want to live?" she yelled back at Frank.

Frank stood up, his head way above the level of the cars. He looked angry, like he wanted to march over there and hit Henry's mom. And then he did come over. When he got within reach, he grabbed Tanya's arm.

Henry didn't know why she didn't turn around and deck him. But then Frank bent low to Tanya's ear and said something which made her stop and listen.

Tanya put her handkerchief away. In a very calm voice she told Henry to kneel down because his head was sticking up.

Frank kneeled down. Lynn did too. So did his mom. Henry followed.

"The president is in that car," Frank whispered, pointing to an old Honda, four rows up. "He's in the passenger seat and there's some guy in the driver's seat with spiky hair. That's all I can see, except the guy doesn't look very tall."

It was like a football huddle with all of them in a circle. Henry put one arm around Frank and the other around his mom.

"When I got here, the president was outside the car. I could have gotten him if you'd been here to help me," Frank scolded.

Henry put his arms down. He'd didn't deserve to be part of this group. Now he would have to tell the American people that he'd let the president get kidnapped because he'd had to stop first and wipe snot from his face. Tears welled up in his eyes.

His mom's tiny little hand patted his shoulder.

The tears stopped.

"Henry, we may still be able to get the president out of the car. I need your strength," Frank said. "You are the strongest person here." In the way of macho men everywhere, Frank raised his fist and the two men fist bumped.

Henry looked at his mother.

Tanya bit her lip, twisted a strand of hair around her finger and then gave him the nod.

Henry grinned. He needed a chance to make up for his mistake and this was it. With a final look at his mother, he turned and followed Frank through the rows of cars. They zigged and zagged through four rows and then at the last row, Frank motioned him to squat down. Finally, they came up to a rusted-old car with two men sitting inside.

Frank put his finger to his lips.

Henry's smile dropped. He already knew he should be quiet, but he made a criss cross sign across his heart, and put his finger to his lip, silently signaling to Frank that he would be quiet.

Frank looked at him very seriously. He bounced his fist in the air, then bounced it again. This time the index finger stuck out. He bounced it again. This time two fingers stuck out.

Henry got that he was counting. He knew that something should happen on "three". But what? Henry tightened his muscles, ready to spring.

Frank bounced his fist in the air and three fingers came out and he motioned frantically to the car, already running toward it himself.

Henry followed suit. The two men reached the front doors of the beater simultaneously. Frank pulled open the driver's door and Henry pulled open the passenger door and, before the two men inside had a chance to react, they were dragged out of the car.

President Pitt's thin arm slipped out of Henry's paw and the president fell, sprawling out in the dirt.

What was going to happen to Henry now? What did they do to people who threw the president on the ground? *I must fix this.* In one motion he reached down, hooked one arm under the president's legs and one arm around his shoulders and hefted him up as quickly as his strength would allow. Henry had difficulty balancing with the extra weight. He released the president into a standing position gently, still keeping one arm around Pitt's shoulders.

In return for his efforts, the chief executive officer dealt Henry a quick blow to his head that sent him staggering back. Unfortunately, Henry pulled the president down with him.

"Get him, Henry!" Frank yelled. He had the driver neatly pinned against the side of the car.

The president was on all fours, trying to get to his feet.

Henry wrapped his arm around the president's waist and lifted him off the ground.

"Henry! Put him down." His mother and Lynn came running up behind him.

"Tanya?" President Pitt asked. The words were choked out.

Henry loosened his hold around the President's waist.

"I'm so sorry. This is my son. We came to save you."

CHAPTER TWENTY-FOUR

Brad Pitt felt a heaviness in his heart. He looked up at Henry, Tanya's overlarge and ambitious son. President Pitt knew Henry was developmentally delayed. She'd talked about him all week, not once mentioning the word "burden". Some women would consider a twenty-four year old with the mind of a four year old, a millstone, but not Tanya.

Henry dropped his arm from around the president. His innocent face scrunched up. He apologized. "I'm sorry I dropped you in the dirt."

"Don't worry. I'm sorry I cracked you in the mouth. Did you lose any teeth?"

Henry felt around in his mouth and shook his head.

"This was actually the most fun I've had in a long time," President Pitt said.

Don coughed, drawing attention away from his famous passenger. Frank was still leaning into him with his forearm pressed against Don's chest.

"That's the man who hog-tied me." Tanya made a motion to attack, but Frank fended her off with a quick raise of his elbow.

"I look like a lot of other guys," Don said. He held his hands up.

"Liar," Tanya shouted. "You think you can just attack somebody and there won't be any consequences? And now we catch you trying to take off with the president in your car?"

"Wait, Tanya, this man did not force me into his car," President Pitt said quietly, laying a hand on her shoulder.

Tanya whirled toward him, her eyes big with worry. "Did he try to influence you in any way?"

President Pitt laughed. He was probably the first president in U.S. history who had run away from his job. It was a terrible onus to have on his presidential reputation. "Tanya, dear," he confessed. "I asked him for a ride."

Tanya looked at the president as if he were crazy.

President Pitt maintained eye contact. "I did. I asked for a ride."

"Why? Why would you do that? I'm sure one of the Secret Service agents could have arranged a helicopter for you."

The President shook his head. "We don't even know if any of them survived the bomb. Tanya, thank God you weren't there! It was horrendous."

"I was there," Don said. He jerked his head toward the president. "He pulled me out of the wreckage. The man saved my life."

"If you all don't mind, I'd like to go with Don." President Pitt felt the weariness in his bones. *I am not prepared to argue with these people.*

"Well-known grown-ups, especially presidents, can't just run away," Henry said.

"I got to say, I've never heard of a president just running away and if one ever did, it's not widely known. I'll be famous for the one who drove the president away," Don said.

"I think running away will make you the most notable President in history," Tanya said. She looked at him so intimately that he had to look away. Her next question ruined the spell she had cast on him. "Don't presidents have a cast of shrinks standing around to examine their heads when something like this happens?"

"I have the best shrink ever." He placed both his hands on either side of her head. "You. You are the best unsung psychologist around. Do your friends know how good you are?"

"My mom is the best?" Henry piped up.

"Yes, she is," the president said. "She helped me by talking about you."

Henry frowned, not comprehending.

"She helped me each day by talking about what she had to do to be a really good mom to you."

"Then why are you running away?" Henry asked simply. "If my mom helped you by talking about being my mother, why are you running away? My mom never ran away."

President Pitt couldn't answer the question. He looked at Tanya. Her eyes shown with pride and love, but she didn't say anything. "I just need to go where nobody knows my whereabouts. I need to go to a place where I can just sit and think . . . alone. I need to think about this law that I let get passed. My week at the Horseshoe with Tanya and you, Frank, and other people really helped me to understand what people in America really need. We don't have a huge throne or castle in this country for our leader. What we have is far, far worse. We have a staff of people that control me. They teach and press me into speaking to a selected representative of the American people. But what I learned this week from talking to real people was that Americans are far different from a composite that the government put together. On cold unfeeling paper, the one-kill law sounds like a law that should work. It sounds like a way to make people self-govern. But what really happened was that your friend got murdered."

The moon shown on the little group that night, lighting each of their faces. For a while, President Pitt stood there as if on the edge of a cliff, deciding whether to jump or not.

Then, from the back of the crowd, from Tanya's large son, came a sniffle, pathetic and desperate. Tears poured down Henry's face. "My mom doesn't want you to leave. She really likes you."

Already the strings of freedom were pulling at the president. He had to go, but he feared that Henry's sniffles would turn into a scene-making wail.

"I'm not going to cry," Henry said, as if reading the President's mind. "But it's mean to leave your friends."

"Oh, just let him go." A woman stepped out from the shadows. She had wispy blonde hair and an angry face. She looked slightly familiar, but as hard as he tried, the president couldn't place her.

"*Shark Tank*," Tanya supplied, reading the president's mind.

President Pitt smiled and nodded. "I'm a big fan of the show."

"She's famous," Tanya continued when the woman didn't say anything. Tanya turned to deal with Henry. "Let him go, sweetheart. It's okay. Everything will be okay."

"Yeah, everything will be okay. Mama said so." Henry nodded to the president, then stepped back to the group. "I'm not going to cry," he said.

Don's cell phone suddenly chirped. He pulled out the phone and held it close to his ear. In the glow from the screen, his face appeared pasty white. He looked up. His pale countenance focused on the president. "Sir, let's go. I have to go."

The President turned toward the others. Henry sat in the dirt, his big head in his hands, crying.

"Please, let's go, Mr. President." Don held his arm out, gesturing toward the car.

President Pitt took a good look at the young man he had picked out to be his driver. His spiky yellow hair looked like the Bart Simpson cartoon character, but his sallow yellow face made him look old and worn. With a quick nod to the group, the president made his decision. He was going to bolt, just jump in the car with this strange distraught young man and go.

Don started the car.

Sunlight streamed in through the plantation shutters. So odd to see their bright homeliness in a hospital room, but that's how Desert Rose Hospital rolled. Lynn loved this rehab facility with its beautiful garden and free soda machine. The therapists were pragmatic and didn't take any excuses. She loved them for that. They were hardasses with her brother, so she didn't have to be. They brought him drugs if he complained of pain and then they followed up with their little sliding boards and dragged his ass out of bed.

Lynn was alone in the room, her brother had been carted down to the rehab department earlier. She lingered in the bedside chair, watching the news. It seemed like the whole country was in an uproar. The president was still missing and presumed dead. The reporter announced that since it had been seventy-two hours since the president had been seen, they were making arrangements for Vice-President Clooney to run the country.

A nurse popped into the room with a tray of meds, her attention caught by the announcement.

"Things are going to change now," Lynn said.

"Oh, totally." The TV screen held the nurse's undivided attention.

"No, I meant with my brother. He must feel like he's not intact."

Something in Lynn's voice made the nurse turn away from the TV. "Oh, honey, he's intact and in one piece. He was uninjured in every other part of his body." Then she left the room, leaving a bad taste in Lynn's mouth.

Lynn was there the day the doctors had told him he would lose the leg. He'd cried the whole night. It was Lynn, not their mother, who sat by his bedside. It was Lynn, not their mother, and certainly not Big John's doctors, who had fought for the best rehab facility. Lynn became the adult. In an hour, though, Lynn would have to go to work. She still did most of the work required for her business. She was the accountant, the shipping clerk and she contacted the labs for fresh product ideas. They were now in the process of inventing an industrial strength nose plug system that was fire-retardant.

With a sigh, she got up and headed down to the rehab department's therapy gym.

The hospital walls narrowed in toward her as she made her way to the gym. Pictures of beautiful canyons were posted along the whole span of the hall, making a patient's walk, or their roll in a wheelchair down to therapy-hell feel like a hike into far desert canyonlands. She kept her eye on the range of beautiful pictures so that she would not have to see what she knew she was about to see. And that would be the extensiveness of the damage that the loss of a limb was wreaking on her brother.

She made it to the doorway, poked her head through and was immediately surprised by the immenseness of the therapy area. It looked like a football field-sized space. In the far corner, a glassed-in-pool serenely waited to drown some cripple. Lynn shook her head. Where did this morbid negative thinking come from? In the other corner of the gym stood rows of exercise mats, their surfaces cold and flat. A group of staff in matching blue polo shirts and a ragtag group of patients in wheelchairs gathered around the mat in the far corner. Curious, Lynn was drawn to the group. So focused on what was going on, she almost ran into the Cadillac in the middle of the room.

"Defies comprehension, doesn't it?" A small compact woman had emerged through an office door. She spoke as if she needed a large word to make up for her small size. "It's a training car. Patients use it to practice getting in and out of. Can I help you find somebody?"

"I thought they had taken my brother here for therapy, John Buttoni?"

A grin broke out on the woman's small face as if someone had told her a joke. "Oh yeah, he's over there." She shot off toward the corner where the crowd had gathered as if she'd been fired from a canon.

Lynn hustled after her.

Suddenly Lynn had a wild urge to get out of there, away from these party people. She really just wanted to get to her brother. This was his first day of therapy and the apprehension and tension she felt for him was killing her. This woman wasn't leading Lynn to her brother but toward some unbroken person who was laughing and entertaining the group. She reached out a hand and stopped the little woman. Lynn's voice came out a little harsher than she intended. "I just want to see my brother," she hissed.

The woman's face darkened. "I am taking you to your brother."

The backs of the staff stood like a blue picket fence of polo shirts, blocking her view of the show. She couldn't correlate this light heartedness to a rehab hospital where things were supposed to be white-coated and solemn. Laughter in these walls felt barbaric. "I want to see John," Lynn demanded.

The blue backs parted. Sitting on the mat, was her brother, John.

Nobody in the room said a word. They just stared at her until she felt like an uncultivated beast that had just swung through the jungle to destroy their party.

The sight of her brother, his left leg missing, completely unsettled her. He had just lost his leg. He was supposed to be looking desolate and needy. She expected to see him isolated, not surrounded by a crowd of adoring fans.

"What's going on here?" she asked, tempestuously.

"Hi, sis," John called out brightly. "They're trying to see if I can slide from the highest point here . . ." He patted the mat table he sat on. It was raised up as high as it would go, about four feet. "To there." He pointed down to his wheelchair. A board bridged the gap between the two, angled downhill to his chair. "Oh, and I have to do it without touching my leg to the ground."

The whole group howled with laughter, startling Lynn.

"Come on, do it before I give you a shove," one of the blue-poloed employees yelled.

"No rough play," Big John said, shaking a finger in her direction. He pushed down on the mat, stood on his remaining leg and lifted his bottom up and over onto the top of the board.

Her brother, missing a leg, actually planned on sliding down the board unrestrained. She looked around, searching the faces in the room for one reasonable person among them, but they all looked eager to watch her injured brother complete this crazy feat. She was sure he would fly down and bash his head on the cold, hard tile. Surely, a supervisor would show up and put an end to this madness. She wanted this rowdy bunch of miscreants to be sent back to their holes where they couldn't hurt her brother. Turbulent clouds of gas fought inside her stomach.

Finally, a supervisor showed up.

Big John seemed even more excited by the sight of the slender man. "I'm not only going to do this without touching, I'm going to have an unbroken record for speed," he said passionately.

Nobody, not even this supervisor, was going to stop the hijinks. She would have to do it herself. "I don't think you should do that," she said to Big John.

They all turned and looked at her as if she were the one who was mad. She was mad, but they were crazy. Her face turned red under the pressure of their stares. Her brother had probably already told them she was mentally ill. "It's a bit deranged, this sliding thing, don't you think?" Her voice sounded weak and sheepish.

All the heads nodded maniacally, agreeing with her.

"My brother has always been crazy but this . . . this." She pointed to the slide contraption John was now sitting on.

Big John's smile dropped. "Oh, sis, you were always such a party pooper," he said, exasperated.

All eyes fell on her. Lynn seethed, every cell in her burning with anger. "This is foolish. These people are supposed to teach you how to live and how to get around. Instead, I come here to find you embarking on some ill-advised stunt. I didn't pay for you to have madcap adventures, I paid for you to learn how to cope with . . ." Momentarily flustered, she pointed to where his leg should be. "I paid for you to learn how to cope with a missing leg."

Big John's face softened. He held out his hand to her. He looked so eager, like a young pup reaching for his mother that she came forward. He took her hand and looked deep into her eyes. "This . . ." he gestured to the board underneath him . . . "may look crazy to you, but it is helping me learn to cope."

He clutched her hand tighter. "Hit or miss, here I go." Suddenly he pulled his hand away and launched himself down the sliding board.

Lynn screamed, but the blue-polos surged forward, hands outstretched toward him, but without touching him. By the time she opened her eyes again, her brother was sitting in the wheelchair, lopsided and flushed with laughter. The wall of hands reached for him, to keep him from toppling over. They grabbed at his clothes, at his arms and in a massive group effort, they propped her laughing brother upright in the chair. When they were finished, they backed off, leaving her brother looking like a happy victim of a mass mugging with his clothes askew. A cheer erupted from the group and hands that had been outstretched to catch him now slapped him on the back.

"Wooo!" he hollered. "When my heart calms down, I'm going to do that again."

"You should be restrained," Lynn snapped.

Big John lifted his hand for a high five.

At that moment, seeing him so gleefully triumphant, something loosened in her. Before she knew it, she was high-fiving him back. The crowd cheered. Hands patted her on the back. The crowd dispersed, leaving her, Big John and one of the blue-poloed therapists standing there. He was a heavy-set man with red hair and a belligerent expression.

"Well, should we get started?" he asked Big John, seemingly unimpressed with the stunt.

"I'm ready," Big John answered, still breathless with excitement. "I want to do that again, please?"

The red-headed young man looked at him sternly but the smallest smile tugged at the corners of his mouth. "We have to do some exercises first."

"My brother has a tendency to play around a lot."

"I noticed." The therapist pressed his foot down on a button and the mat lowered. When it was level with the wheelchair he patted the mat.

Big John slid over obediently.

"Face down," the therapist ordered.

Big John rolled his eyes, but immediately flattened himself on his stomach. He groaned.

"Keep flat on your stomach. Don't you lift up, not even a little."

With two meaty hands, Linebacker pushed on Big John's bottom until he was flat.

Big John groaned again.

"And don't roll your eyes at me, I can see through your head. You will stay flat for ten minutes." He slapped a ten pound weight on Big John's backside and walked away.

"Sis, take the weight off me."

"No, he ordered you to stay there."

"Please, Sis, don't leave me with that monster." Big John wailed loud enough for everyone to hear.

"I could pass you on to Liz," his therapist yelled back. "She's so mean, her husband asked for a transfer to Siberia."

Big John burst out in laughter.

"I don't know why you think this is such a joke," Lynn snapped.

Her brother lifted his head. "What choice do I have, Sis?"

"Keep flat or I'll call Liz. It's your prerogative," Linebacker yelled across the room.

"Your wish is my command." Big John turned his face back down.

"I wouldn't mind if your visitor just sat on you," Linebacker hollered.

"I wish you'd both shut up," Lynn snapped.

"I have to stay on my stomach, Sis, so I can stretch the front part of my short leg. I have to do it so I can wear a prosthesis, okay? It hurts to do this. Now I can stay ten whole minutes out of sheer willpower or I can make the ten minutes go by with joking and horsing around. Just talk to me, okay? That's all I need."

So Lynn talked. She talked about her business, she talked about Frank. She admitted, rather shyly, that she was back on her medication.

Her brother smiled at her. "That's great, sis."

"Ten minutes are up," Linebacker called from across the room. He was pulling another lady's stump so far back behind her that it looked like it took all of her resolve not to chew the rest of her leg off to get away.

"Thank God." Big John rolled over on his side, knocking the weights off. He threw his one remaining leg over the end of the bench and pushed himself up to a sitting position with a doggedness that made Lynn look away.

Big John took her hands. He looked into her eyes. "This is a commitment I'm determined to make. I'm going to walk again."

Lynn finally found herself smiling. She couldn't help but admire his guts.

He still held tightly to her hands. "When they first brought me into the hospital, they asked me to write my Last Will and Testament. I told them there was no need. I wasn't going to die."

A shadow fell over her brother. She looked up to see Linebacker staring down at Big John. The therapist's arms were crossed across his chest. "Feeling lucky punk? And don't give me any attitude or the reps will be doubled."

Big John rolled his eyes and flopped back down on the mat. "I'll be okay, Sis. You better go now. Mom's coming to see me this afternoon. It'd be nice if you went over to see her in the evening. You know she's kind of a mess."

Lynn nodded. Tears rimmed her eyes. She gathered her purse. Her brother seemed so accepting. Why couldn't she? All she wanted to do was punish the old man who had done this to her brother.

She turned to go, determined to do just that.

CHAPTER TWENTY-FIVE

"I can't win," President Pitt said while watching the retreating backs of his rescue party. "At first, I felt like a little boy being let out of school and now I feel like a heel for deserting the very people who tracked me down all night."

"Yeah." Don's face was pasty white. He stared at the cell phone screen.

"Did you get bad news?"

Don swallowed. "Yes, really bad news."

President Pitt flung his hands in the air. "Well, come away with me. We'll live like Thelma and Louise until somebody throws a net over my head. Until then, we can be victorious."

"What would we do?" Don asked, tightly.

"I don't know. What have you come first in?"

"Bull riding," Don answered.

"Really?" President Pitt gave him an admiring smile. "I guess that's what we'll do. I'll overcome my fear of bulls and we can travel the rodeo circuit together. Do we have to finish first to win any money?"

Don shook his head.

"Well, then that's what we'll do. As long as we come out ahead a few times and make a few bucks, life will be good. Cheer up boy, we're going to succeed as bull riders." In the dark, the President's perfect teeth shone. He gave Don a disarming smile. "Now what was your bad news?"

Don looked over at him. He kept his face tight. The President's charm failed to get an answer out of him.

President Pitt didn't dwell on it. He acted like a kid let out of school early. He flashed Don the "V" sign for Victory. "Whatever it was, boy, we will triumph over it."

Somehow that remark triggered something in Don. "My father wants me to kill you." Don punctuated his words with a quick stomp on the gas, sending the car racing forward. At this point, they left the last line of houses, and were now in the darkest part of the road, where civilization ended and the desert began.

The night the cops came and hauled the old man away, Tanya sat in her apartment. She felt relieved that Mrs. Wright wasn't around to see this. Then again, if Mrs. Wright had been around, they wouldn't be hauling her husband away. At least the police handled the arrest in a quiet gentlemanly way, aside from the handcuffs. The morning had started out with a chill, and one of the police officers very kindly assisted the old man into a sweater.

She stood on her porch, sending him off with a frosty stare.

He returned her glacial glare with one of his own. The old dog wasn't beaten down yet and for that she admired him.

The policeman gave her an unfriendly look. He took Mr. Wright's arm and helped him down the stairs.

She watched them until they were in the police car.

Henry came up behind her, startling her. "They taking Mr. Wright away for shooting off Big John's leg?"

"Yeah, baby. They're just going to question him. He'll get out in a few hours." She did not tell him that he would be under house arrest, that he would have to endure a trial.

Henry looked sad. "But I pushed the gun."

"No, honey. That's not true. You had nothing to do with hurting Big John."

Tears ran down her son's face. "Yes, I did. I'm just a big dumb retard."

"No, Henry, don't say that." But the germ of an idea had already taken root.

Brad Pitt looked at the wiry young man who drove him out into the dark night of the desert. He looked physically strong with sinewy arms and broad shoulders. "So that was the phone call that made your face go white? Your father commanding you to kill me?"

The young man maintained a thorny silence. His foot grew heavier on the pedal. His shoulders went rigid, as if he would just drive on all night without stopping or talking. Only his eyes gave him away. They appeared strained around the edges, belying a frailness that the young man was trying hard to conceal.

"So your name is Don?" President Pitt asked. "But that's all I know about you." He didn't expect an answer and he didn't get one.

The car continued into the night. They drove past the turn off to the Mt. Charleston Ski Area. President Pitt's mind drifted off to happier times when his family went skiing. "I miss my wife."

This triggered something in Don. He looked over, taking his eyes off the road for a split second. "Do you think it was such a wise decision, letting the one-kill bill pass?"

President Pitt shrugged. "I thought it would be clever to make a law that would force people to govern themselves."

"You're educated. Didn't you realize what would happen?" Don asked, turning a tired eye toward him.

"Truth be known, I dropped out of college in Missouri with two credits to go. Hollywood beckoned." The president shrugged. "Still, I like to think of myself as an enlightened person, but nobody can fully predict everything."

Don gave him a discerning look, as if he were trying to figure out if the President was for real or not.

"You really are going to kill me, aren't you?"

"You are very perceptive."

President Pitt felt his nerve endings flare up. "Do you think that's sensible?"

He was answered with a shrewd smile and a carefree shrug of the shoulders. "It's not illegal," Don answered smartly.

"I thought you were sane. I wouldn't have gotten in the car with you if I thought you would do something stupid."

Don looked over at him, surprised at how whiny the distinguished President of the United States sounded. "I'm doing something stupid? You allowed this idiotic bill to pass. You didn't put any immunity clauses in it. You have the best security system in the world, and you ran away from it. You don't, for once, think that one of your constituents would see this as a free chance to off you. And I'm stupid?"

President Pitt stared morosely out the window for a few seconds. "Maybe I should just open the door and roll out. That would kill me. Or would you try to stop me?"

Don smiled. "Of course I would try to stop you, but how could I possibly be fast and strong enough to stop you? The fall would kill you. And guess what? That would leave me free to kill again legally. So feel free."

President Pitt sighed and leaned his head against the window. "Why did I have to run away? I'd be retiring in eight years at the most. Who runs away when they only have eight years to go?"

Don was not forthcoming with his answer.

"Great. Now you are going back to being quiet?"

"I'm introverted. Plus, I'm thinking private thoughts."

"There's no reason to be timid. Tell me all your thoughts. How many times in your life are you going to get the chance to discuss the weight of your world with the president? Don't hold anything back. I'll be dead in a few hours anyway," President Pitt said diffidently.

A small smile cracked Don's lips. "What gave me away?"

"If you really were going to kill me, you wouldn't be so sociable."

Both men laughed.

"So what are we going to do?" President Pitt asked.

"Drive," Don offered. "And then we're going to need to get jobs."

"I might have some connections," the President said. "Say, is Death Valley around here?"

"About an hour up the road."

"Can we go?" The President's eyes shown in the dark car. Once again he looked like an excited little boy.

"The road is our oyster, but it will cost money to get into the National Park."

"I think I have a pass. And I have a good idea for getting us some food."

Linebacker shot Big John a look that would wither Hercules. "Here's your leg." He slammed a prosthetic limb on the table. The replacement leg looked nothing like a real leg. Basically, it looked like a large bar with a cup at the top and Big John's size fifteen shoe on the bottom.

"It's so beautiful, I think I'm going limp." John waved his hands in front of his face like a fluttery beauty queen.

Linebacker didn't crack a smile. He looked at the metal contraption. "If you wore this with a pair of shorts, this bare barred limb would definitely kill off any interest that a strong-stomached lady might dare to show. On the other hand, it will get you from here to there."

"You've just blasted away my dream of becoming the sexiest man alive."

Linebacker looked at him, his square angular face set stonily. For a second, Big John thought he saw the hardness ebb away. He swore he thought he saw the tough physical therapist's face crack, just a bit. But when Linebacker opened his mouth, he said, "You sexy? Perish the thought. Now, let's stop talking and put this on." He squatted on one knee in front of Big John, took a large cup out of the top of the leg and placed it on Big John's stump.

It felt snug, but there was no pain. Big John relaxed a little. He was sitting in his wheelchair, his huge physical therapist down on one knee in front of him. John's face scrunched in concentration as he studied how the cup fit over the stump. From the corner of the room, Big John saw a group of people enter. He could not resist. He placed his hands over his chest and posted a big goofy smile across his face. "Oh yes, yes, I will marry you," he gushed as loudly as he could.

Linebacker reddened. He looked over at the group of people, apparently a family checking out the facilities. He scrambled to his feet.

"Oh, don't look so sad, so worried. Did you think I would say no?" Big John tried to grab for Linebacker's hands but the flustered physical therapist dodged him. "I would never do or say anything to make you unhappy, my love. Do not look so dejected, my darling."

"I am not dejected," Linebacker said with a quick glance to the group of people. "We are not getting married."

Big John conjured up a tearful voice. "Oh, how you loved me," he wailed.

The group quickly shuffled out of the gym.

Big John burst into laughter. "Oh, that's some funny shit. I know I'm going to pay for that, but it will be worth it."

Linebacker waited out the laughter. "If you are done with your pranks, I would like to get started."

Big John wiped his eyes. "You know the really bad thing is I don't even know your name."

Linebacker pointed to a name badge that looked absolutely tiny anchored to his left pecs. "It's Lindsay," he said pointing to his name.

"Lindsay? Your name is Lindsay?"

"Don't even go there." Linebacker's stare was fierce.

Big John threw up his hands. "I didn't say a word."

"Now, we are going to get on with trying this prosthesis on you."

It was a statement, not a question. Without another utterance, Big John let Linebacker explain how to put it on, what to do if it became loose. He finished up by impressing on Big John how important it was to report any skin breaks from the prosthesis.

"I give you my word of honor," Big John promised.

"If you have something rubbing and you think you can just macho your way through it, I guarantee you, those wounds will become enough of a problem that we would have to remove more of your leg."

This sobered Big John up. "I vow to take care of my leg."

"Good, because I don't want to waste any more of my time on this kind of talk. We're going to try this leg on. If it doesn't fit or work well, we'll have a consultation with the prosthetist." With that, he knelt down again, grabbed the prosthesis and pushed it up on Big John's stump. He placed two hands on Big John's knee and pushed the shortened leg toward the floor until he heard three distinct clicks. He almost smiled.

Big John did not. It was a little painful before and now it felt too tight.

Linebacker grabbed the back of Big John's wheelchair and pushed him up and between the two parallel bars.

Automatically, as he had been drilled to do, Big John locked his wheelchair. "I guess I just pull up on these?" He placed his hands on the two bars in front of him.

Linebacker pulled a belt from out of his pocket. Deftly, he cinched it around Big John's waist.

"You don't want me to get away, do you?"

"Enough chit chat. You will lean forward first and then you will pull yourself up to a standing position. You may notice some discomfort around your knee joint.

"I already noticed some discomfort."

"Stand first, report later." Without further dispatch, Linebacker squatted down in front of Big John and put both of his meaty paws on the belt around Big John's waist. Then he pulled.

Big John felt his whole body going forward. Every muscle in his body screamed. His knee felt like someone was stabbing at it and his good right leg, the real one, felt like it would buckle. On the bars, his knuckles were white. He could see the strain in Linebacker's face, the tension in his huge arms. Despite all the feedback that Big John's muscles were giving him, Linebacker was holding him up. Big John couldn't breathe. "Down," he managed.

Linebacker lowered him gently, watching Big John's face he gasp for breath. "Breathe in through your nose. Breathe out through pursed lips. Again, and repeat."

"What?" Big John asked.

"Do it."

Big John obeyed, breathing in through his nose a short quick snort and then a quick exhalation out.

"Slowly. Purse those lips on the exhale."

Big John thought about taking a swing, but instead he listened and obeyed. To his surprise, his breathing slowed down and he was able to get a few more words out. "Somebody rescue me."

"We are going to do it again."

"Again? I need to rest."

Linebacker smiled a sweet, slow smile. He patted Big John's knee. "Sure. I'll let you go back to the common area and you can watch *Password* and *The Price is Right* with all the other old people. I just thought you wanted to walk."

Anger and humiliation crowded into Big John's brain. He hated the bully standing in front of him. Hated him. Big John was so overwhelmed that he couldn't find the words to express himself. He wasn't sure he had the breath to do it anyway. He managed a half-strength cuss word, scooted forward in his chair and grabbed the bars. "Okay, let's do this."

Big John stood four more times after this. Each time, he swore that that stand had taken the last of his strength and each time,

Linebacker commanded him to do it again. Like a dejected robot, helpless to disobey, he would stand again. Twenty minutes of this and Linebacker announced that they were done.

Big John breathed a sigh of relief. "What made you decide to finally quit? Did you hear my muscles screaming? Did the pungent sweat of my efforts finally get to you? Did you see the defeat in my eyes or notice the shakiness of my movements?"

Linebacker let him go on with his long-winded pity party and then he spoke. "No. I was tired. Now wheel yourself back."

.

CHAPTER TWENTY-SIX

Lynn wanted to see Frank. She had just left the Rehab Department where she'd watched her brother put on a brave show. She felt volatile and shaky. Frank could diffuse her nerves.

She pulled into the rambling apartment complex and found a space by his building. She sat in her car, looking up at his arched bedroom windows. So many memories. Right next door to Franks', the Wright's apartment stood. The old man lived there alone now. The old man who was responsible for the loss of her brother's leg. She would press charges. Right now she didn't want to think about that, she just wanted to be in her boyfriend's arms, hearing him deliver a tautological argument about how everything would be all right.

She opened her car door. As if on cue, like a little monkey hearing the treat bin open, Tanya appeared on her balcony.

Lynn never really liked the little dried up bean that was Tanya, despite the fact that she owed that little bean something for chasing away Frank's female suitors. Lynn pressed a smile on her lips and squinted up at Tanya who was watching her intently. The sun had just risen to the apartment roof and now glared into Lynn's eyes.

"I need to talk to you," Tanya declared.

"Coming." Lynn grabbed her purse, got out of the car and shut the door. She glanced over at the Wright's place. The curtains were drawn tightly against the winter sun.

"Hurry up. I got to go to work soon." Tanya disappeared and opened her front door before Lynn had made it halfway up the stairs.

Sweat glistened along Lynn's forehead, despite the cool winter day. She thought about all the work she had to do today on her nose plug business; some of it would need her brains but most of it would demand her elbow grease.

"You're lucky you don't have to have a job," Tanya said. Like most people Lynn met, Tanya had no idea what a huge undertaking it was to run a business.

Lynn finally made it to Tanya's door. "Yeah, I'm lucky I don't have a job. Wait, how is it that you have a job? I thought they blew your place up."

"Lucky for me, I have the type of profession that is marketable. My boss got on the phone and started calling people. I've got a full-time job tending bar at The Four Queens."

"That's quite an accomplishment."

"You're darn right it's an accomplishment. If they like my performance, I'll get a raise." Tanya waved Lynn inside her apartment.

To Lynn, the place looked like something right out of the seventies, right down to the dogs painted on black velvet shooting pool and the crocheted owls on a stick. "Creative," Lynn commented, pointing to the owls.

Tanya shut the door behind her. "That piece took me the better part of a day."

Lynn sniffed the apartment, detecting a dank moldy smell. She had since cleaned her own apartment up and now wasn't tolerant of other people's housekeeping negligence. "I take it you didn't bring me in here to talk about the art of crocheted owls."

"My Henry ran and knocked the gun out of the old man's hand. That is how your brother lost his leg."

Lynn didn't know how to react. The sentence was delivered with all the aplomb of a sledge hammer meeting an ice sculpture.

Tanya spoke as if directing a play. There was no apology in her voice. "That's what I'm going to tell the police."

"Why would you do that? They'll take Henry away."

Tanya shook her head. "No, they won't. He's not in his right mind. He was trying to defend Big John, not hurt him."

"Why would you risk this?"

"Because if I tell the police that, the old man will give me enough money so that I can breeze through my retirement."

Lynn let her purse crash to the floor with an angry thud. "No! That's not the way this is going down. I want that dangerous old fart in jail. He brought the gun out with the intention of killing my brother. Don't you understand that?"

"I need money," Tanya said. "I barely make enough to support us now. What is going to happen to Henry after I'm gone? You think he'll be able to hold down a job? You think he'll be able to earn his own living? You are lucky. You won five million dollars to ply your trade. You don't have to exert yourself. The rest of us have to toil away to eke out a living. You want to make yourself feel better? Go ahead and press charges on the old man. Just remember me, grinding away to support my boy."

Lynn controlled herself during the speech. "You and Henry will manage."

Tanya's face turned red. "So you are going to go ahead and press charges? After all that I told you. . . "

Lynn nodded.

Tanya crossed her arms on her chest. "I hope things go well for you. Maybe you'll get the old man in prison for the rest of his life. You can celebrate by going out and buying a new car."

"You taking digs at my Soul?"

Tanya didn't answer.

Lynn picked up her purse. "Now, you listen to me. I think Henry can hold down a job. I want you to bring him by my warehouse tomorrow morning. I think Henry can perform the duties of a floor stocker quite well."

It took a few seconds for Lynn's words to sink into Tanya. Lynn could see the minute the words hit home. She watched a reluctant grin spread across Tanya's thin lips. "Really?" Tanya wiped a tear from the corner of her eye. "You won't regret this. Henry is a good cause."

"I'm arranging a job for him, not a charitable donation," Lynn said coldly. "He'll be a floor stocker. He'll be expected to carry out his duties. If he can pull it off, he'll get a 1% raise every three months."

"You know he's . . ." Tanya looked toward the ceiling. ". . . different."

"I was with Henry a couple of nights ago. I saw how he took to tracking the president. Don't worry. I have a foreman who can mold a chunk of clay into an ideal employee. Henry will be a piece of cake."

"Wow," Tanya muttered. "You are like a model employer."

Lynn looked at the older women directly. There was an edge in her voice. "If he screws up we'll give him the elbow. I and my people don't play."

"I guess not."

"I'm going to go now." Lynn started to walk out but guilt nagged at her for playing so rough. "I used to be different too. I still am. I've learned in these last few weeks that you can't blame your problems on someone else. I have to take my medication to function. I've come to realize that. Henry may have to be taught how to do things several times. We all have to do what we have to do to survive. But we can't make excuses."

Tanya nodded. "I understand."

Lynn spun on the heel of her shoe, escaping before things got too mushy. She wanted to see Frank.

He must have heard her coming. Before she could knock on his door, it had swung open. She picked up her step and the next thing she knew she was running into his arms.

He pulled her into his apartment. She felt the warmth of his arms and his breath in her ear as he murmured sweet whispers in her ear.

She told him what she had done and he praised her and hugged her closer.

"Maybe Henry will move over into management and take over your job someday." Frank sat her down on the sofa. "So now that you've given Henry a job, his mother doesn't have to throw him under the bus for Mr. Wright's retirement money. You are a good person, Lynn." He wrapped his arms around her, felt her stiffen.

"I've got so much to do today," she said by way of apology. "I can't relax."

"You listen to me, Lynn. Everything is going to be okay. Your brother is going to get better. He'll get through this. Mr. Wright can keep his retirement money. He'll be able to live to a ripe old comfortable age."

Lynn started to tell him what her plans were for the old man, but suddenly, someone was banging on Frank's front door.

"Hey, I'm working here," Frank yelled.

The knocking escalated until it sounded like they were going to barge through the door.

Lynn jumped up, alarmed.

"I'll get it." He stood up and was about to answer the door when it swung open.

Lynn's brain stopped functioning when she saw the face of the man standing in the doorway. She reached up, grabbed Frank's arm and pulled him down on the couch. "What are you doing?" she hissed in his ear.

Mike the Mechanic answered the question. "Acting like a brave boyfriend, I'd say. Putting on the performance of his life." Mike was dressed in what looked like an execution jacket, a long heavy dark hooded thing.

Lynn gasped.

"Surprised to see me?" A sinister grin spread across his face, the smile not reaching his eyes. "I love your reaction, Babe."

"What are you doing here?" Lynn asked.

"I have a score to settle with this guy." He jutted his grizzled chin at Frank.

Frank stood up slowly, hoping that the little guy would see Frank growing before his eyes. He kept his hands in his pocket. "Why don't you just turn around and leave, no harm done."

Mike's face reddened. "This girl is meant for me."

Lynn sat up, watching the two men.

Frank didn't look down at her. He never took his eyes off the mechanic. "Don't worry, Baby."

Lynn could barely breathe. Mike was severely disturbed. He'd already killed a helpless old lady.

Mike turned his face toward her, his eyes pleading. "Lynn, just come with me. I won't bother your friend here." He held out his hand, surprisingly clean. He looked at her quietly, but his foot tapped vigorously, betraying his agitation.

Her stomach felt unsettled, like she would vomit anytime, but she knew what she had to do. She stood up slowly. "I'll go with him," she told Frank. She kept her voice calm.

Frank's handsome face darkened.

"It's okay." Lynn held her flat hand out to him, gesturing for Frank to stay seated. She prayed that he wouldn't do anything stupid.

"No, it's not, Lynn. Stay with me. He doesn't care about you the way I do."

Lynn felt tension emanating from Mike. She shot Frank a warning look.

Mike stepped forward, stretched out a slender forearm and clasped her hand in his.

Lynn wanted to scream when she felt his claw clinging to her hand but she forced herself to stay calm. She knew that if she showed her fear, it would anger him more. Trying to smile she said, "I'm going to go with Mike, so we can talk." Her eyes quietly pleaded with Frank not to try anything heroic.

"Come on." Mike's hand moved up her arm, grabbing her above the elbow. He took possession of her, yanking her toward the front door.

Despite her best efforts to remain cool, the sudden jerk on her arm unnerved her. She cried out and stumbled forward.

That's when her big hero made his move. He shoved *her*. She went crashing forward, right into Mike's chest, the two of them sprawling forward, Lynn on top, skinny Mike padding her fall. Frank's fist blurred past her head, crashed into Mike's jaw and knocked his head back into the carpet. The mechanic lay still.

"Owww," Frank said, nursing his hand. "That hurt like a son of a bitch. You're going to have to get up by yourself, Babe."

"Oh, my hero," Lynn sneered.

Wincing, Frank looked down at Mike. The mechanic's chest rose and fell, but he did not move. Satisfied that he was the big hero, Frank went to the freezer and got himself some ice while she scrambled off the prostrate mechanic

"Geez, Lynn, I think you stepped on his hand getting up. I think you hurt him." Frank stared down at Mike, frowning.

"Really? I suppose the crack in the jaw you gave him just got his attention. I think you were the one who took the hit on the head."

"What are you getting mad at me for?"

Lynn sighed. "Let's just call the police."

By the time the police arrived, Frank was still nursing his hand with a pack of ice, the mechanic was still lying on the floor groaning and Lynn had paced back and forth thirty-two hundred times.

"She's the mean one," Frank told them, indicating Lynn.

"I am in a bad mood," Lynn admitted. "When you have to call the police to take the trash out of your living room, you are not in the best of moods."

"This is my house," Frank said. "My fingers are in ruins."

"We'll get your statements. We better call an ambulance for this one." The officer looked down at Mike, who had finally started to stir.

Mike turned his face away, averting his eyes. Already, a light discoloration had formed around his right eye.

"How much of a beating did you get?" The cop squatted next to Mike, peering at the space above the mechanic's eye.

Suddenly, something filled the doorway, blocking out the light.

Everyone in the room looked up, including Mike.

Mr. Wright stood there, utter devastation on his face. He let out an animal cry and before anybody could react, he charged into the room, his foot smashing into Mike's head.

Lynn understood how seeing the man who had killed your wife could be your undoing.

Before the cops could wrangle the old man into one of the bar stools across the room, he had managed to ruin the younger man's chance of modeling. Blood poured out of every orifice on Mike's face. "You have destroyed my life," Mr. Wright screamed. Fury and turmoil wracked his visage.

Mike scooted away, his head marred and bleeding, but at least he was able to sit up. He looked like a shipwreck victim, stunned and bloated.

One of the cops reached down and hauled Mike to his feet. "Come on, Romeo, it looks like you've been knocked off your horse."

The moment Mike stood up, a deafening gunshot rent the air.

Lynn screamed, "Save me!"

The mechanic fell to the ground, this time with an outpouring of blood from a hole in his chest.

When her head cleared enough for Lynn to realize what had happened, she saw Mr. Wright standing by the bar stool with a smoking gun.

Chaos broke out. Lynn ran toward Frank. The two policemen dived for the old man. Lynn never made it to Frank. The two policemen knocked her down in their rush for the old man. She landed a few inches from where Mike lay, gurgling noises coming from his mouth. Behind her, a string of expletives lit up the air. The cops, swearing and grappling, got the gun from Mr. Wright. They handcuffed him and hauled him toward the door. The last thing she heard was the old man's laughter as they dragged him away.

CHAPTER TWENTY-SEVEN

Lynn sat in her brother's hospital room. She had just related the whole story to Big John. "The poor creature," Lynn finished, still seeing Mike's dull eyes. "I think he's going to live."

"Poor creature?" her brother asked. "That guy killed an innocent old lady. He tried to take you away."

Lynn never told her brother that at one time, Mr. Wright had wanted to kill him.

"I smell a skunk," Big John said, suddenly. He sat up straighter and sniffed the air.

"What are you talking about? I don't smell any such thing." Lynn did hear heavy footsteps coming down the hall.

"You smell it now?"

Before she could shush her brother, Linebacker had barreled into the room, scowling. "You put your leg on," he barked.

"My sister's here."

Linebacker barely turned. He grunted towards her general direction.

"I'm fine, thank you. How are you?" Lynn asked.

The big guy had already pushed past Lynn. He grabbed the prosthesis from the nightstand and thrust it in Big John's face. "Did I not tell you to have this on before your therapy time?" he hissed.

Big John shrugged. "So I'm a lawbreaker. What do they do with first offenders?"

"We cut off the other leg. I expect that to be on by the time I return." He strode out.

Lynn watched until the thick-shouldered man was completely out of sight. "What crawled up his butt today?" When she turned back around to face her brother, she caught him furiously stuffing his stump into the cup of the prosthesis. "Hey, what's going on?"

"I don't think he was kidding." Big John didn't relax until he heard three distinct clicks. "Okay, it's locked on. Sis, come down to the gym and watch me walk."

She smiled. "Relax, big brother, you are going to do great."

"I know, Sis, I got to go. If he has to come up here one more time, he's going to start removing limbs." He yanked his pants leg down over the prosthesis and scooted from the bed onto the wheelchair.

"You afraid of that jerk?" Lynn asked.

"That jerk is the one who is going to get me up and walking." He rolled for the door, rounding the corners of the bed expertly, like a prize barrel racer. Lynn had to jog to catch up to him. Just before he rolled into the hall, he stopped abruptly, and turned his chair around, nearly landing her in his lap. "The answer to your question is, yes, I'm afraid of him. Now come watch him work miracles."

Lynn hurried after him. She wanted to see her brother take his first steps.

CHAPTER TWENTY-EIGHT

Tanya sat in the ugly, cold grey waiting room of Metro's holding tank, yawning. Normally, she napped at two in the afternoon. Today, instead, she found herself in a musty old police station, staring at the cavernous hall.

Finally, the deputy brought Mr. Wright to her. Tanya stared at the old man as he slowly walked toward Tanya.

Mr. Wright signed all of the release papers, went through the manila envelope of personal items they returned to him, and stuffed his belongings into his pockets. The watch went on his wrist. When he finally finished, he had nothing better to do but shuffle towards her.

"So I heard you bailed me out." Mr. Wright simply looked at her. "Funny world this is. You pull a gun on somebody, but you don't have to stay in jail that long because it's legal now."

Tanya nodded.

"So I guess I'm yours. What are you going to do with me? Slap a collar around my neck and walk me around the yard?"

In spite of herself, a small smile broke out on Tanya's face. The humor of the remark so reminded her of her lost friend, Mrs. Wright. "No, not until enslavement becomes legal."

"Enslavement is legal, they call it marriage." The old man suddenly realized what he said. He clutched his chest and sat down on the edge of a hard wooden chair. "Ohh! I miss her so much."

Tears formed in Tanya's eyes. "I do too." She placed her hand lightly on the old man's shoulder, their grief the only bond between them.

"We got hitched sixty years ago today," he said, his voice cracking.

Tanya stood up. "You can't honor her memory by going around shooting people. I don't care whether it's legal or not." She patted him on the shoulder and pasted a smile on her face. "Now come on, you old fart. I've come to take you home."

"Why did you bail me out?"

Tanya told him in the car. "Lynn offered Henry a job. That simple act of kindness pushed me to stop blackmailing you. It pushed me to be a little kinder. President Pitt and his congress got it wrong. We don't need to kill each other to make the world a better place. I think Lynn got it right. We need to practice more kindness."

"I guess she's forgiven me," Mr. Wright said. "I'm guessing that she's dropped the assault charges."

"She has, otherwise I would never be able to bail you out." Tanya drove past rows of shabby houses filled with people who couldn't afford to fight the placement of a detention center in their backyard.

Mr. Wright scratched his chin; the whiskers made a bristly sound. "Why did she forgive me? I fired the gun that shot her brother's leg off."

"She never came by to tell you?"

The old man didn't answer. Instead he fixed her with a long hard stare. "I'm too old to wait all day for the answer. If she'd have come to the jail to forgive me, do you think I'd still be here?"

Tanya smiled. Mr. Wright's answer was a fair one. "She said she forgave you because the leg that her brother lost was the one that had all the pain in it."

"So now that the leg is gone, he doesn't have the ankle pain and, for that's she's grateful?"

Tanya nodded.

"Well, that's pretty fucked up."

Tanya burst out laughing. She snuck a peak at the old man.

He had allowed himself a small smile. "Well, that is the high point of my life."

Tanya looked over, but all she could see was the top of Mr. Wright's head. She was afraid that he was crying or breaking down. She called his name gently.

He lifted his head. Dry-eyed, he said, "I would like to go see Eva's grave. She's buried at Palm Mortuary, there on the eastside."

Tanya's face fell. Palm Mortuary was located in a depressed side of town. "There? You buried her there?"

"It's too late to be spending money on prime real estate for the old gal, don't you think? I was going to buy her an oceanfront estate somewhere along the equator. Problem is, I spent all our money on the mansion I'm living in now."

Tanya nodded. "I think you made a mistake."

"That's because you live on the bottom and we lived at the top." Mr. Wright stuck his nose in the air. "I wouldn't expect you to understand. Just take me to the cemetery."

"To the cemetery, it is, sir." Tanya turned down Eastern. Over their shoulders, in the distance, the Stratosphere rose up. "It's not so bad on the bottom where I live. Someday you'll get old and won't be able to climb the stairs."

"I ain't there yet." He turned to look out the window. The older houses spun by, eclipsed by a strip mall.

Tanya figured he was mentally preparing himself to see his wife's grave. "So what are you going to say to the old girl?"

Mr. Wright turned to face her. "I'm going to tell her that I think everything's going to be all right. I'm going to tell her that I think that her friend . . . you . . . is not so bad."

"Really? I'd love to be a fly on the wall when you say that."

Mr. Wright laughed, but his eyes moistened.

Tanya pretended not to notice. Instead, she concentrated on making the left turn into the cemetery. She pulled as close as she could to the gravesite, but he still had to walk a few feet. "I'll let you go by yourself," she said as she shut the car off.

The moment of truth had come. The moment to see if a miracle would happen. Somehow Lynn thought miracles happened with a little more glamour than this. She stood on the side of two metal bars. Her brother, in his wheelchair, sat between the two bars. Linebacker stood in front of him.

A few scattered people worked out in the gym, their muffled grunts and groans ruining the magical aura that a miracle should have. Mostly bored old patients, working under the tutelage of their uptight young therapists.

"Okay, John get up. I'll follow you with the wheelchair," she said.

Linebacker gave her a look that would reduce a heroin addict to sucking on sugar. "We don't cut to walking right away," he said, stonily.

Lynn felt dense.

"We will first stand on the leg to see if it will hold you. Then, we will shift our weight from side to side. Then, and only then, if that works out well, will we take a step or two." Linebacker's clipped tones brooked no arguments. "To summarize, nobody gets up and just starts walking."

Lynn's face flushed. She took a deep breath and told herself to shut up. Then she told herself to be patient. If she needed to, she would stand in the corner until the shadows lengthened and wait for her brother to walk.

Linebacker strapped a belt around her brother's waist. He cinched it up, then motioned for Big John to scoot forward.

Big John did so.

Lynn watched her brother's face, tense with concentration. She watched Linebacker's face, also tense with concentration. He gave strict instructions to her brother, detailing exactly the steps it would take for Big John to stand.

Her brother grabbed the bars, squeezed and pulled. Linebacker pulled on his belt and together, Big John stood.

Lynn enjoyed the look of surprise on Linebacker's face as her brother slowly elongated his seven-foot frame until his head rose way above the physical therapist's. It suddenly occurred to her that, although the two of them had been working together for days, this red-headed punk had no idea how tall her brother was.

But now Big John towered over Linebacker, his face registering sheer joy at finally being able to stand on two legs. "I'm the king of the world," he quipped, looking down on his subjects.

Linebacker was the only one who wasn't smiling. "Shift your weight to your prosthesis. You are only standing on your good leg. You need to put some weight on the prosthesis."

Big John frowned and looked down. The prosthetic leg remained flexed, stubbornly refusing to straighten and accept its fair load.

"Well, King of the World, you are going to abdicate your throne if you can only stand on one leg."

Big John looked down at his physical therapist. "Renounce my crown? Never!" He tried to straighten his knee on the prosthesis. His face reddened.

Big John's knee couldn't straighten on the prosthesis.

Big John's face darkened with effort.

"Maybe you should give up for today," Lynn called.

"I refuse to leave this gym until I've taken a step." His face had gone ruddy with the effort. "I'm not going to surrender to a little piece of metal and plastic." With that he tightened the knee and shifted his weight onto it.

He buckled like a queasy schoolgirl at a One Direction concert.

Lynn inhaled sharply.

Linebacker jabbed his knee into Big John's buckled knee, pushing it back until it locked. At the same time, he gave Big John a bear hug, holding him up.

Big John pushed with his arms, getting himself straighter until he could lock his arms out straight. He threw his weight onto his good side. "I got it, I'm all right," he said several times until Linebacker backed off.

Lynn turned her fury on Linebacker. "I told you, you should have quit for the day. You could have dropped him."

"Knock it off, Lynn. I'm standing, see?"

Linebacker said nothing, just gave her a level look.

"I wash my hands of the two of you," she said. She snapped up her bag and stalked out of the room. She couldn't take this. She couldn't take watching her brother's daily struggle. She stomped straight back to Big John's room and flopped in the bedside chair.

Which is where Frank found her.

Catching sight of his broad shoulders, she lifted her head. She loved his easy, no-hurry walk. When he strode into the room, tension dissipated.

"Hi," he said, in that husky way she loved. "You cry here often?"

She laughed, then stood up and ran to him, throwing herself into his arms. "Let's run away together."

"Okay," he said. "After Big John is walking. After your nose plugs become a household name. After I make the big bucks selling a unequivocally awesome painting. Then I will spirit you away from this hellhole."

She laughed harder, but she saw his point. Now was not the time to give up, now was the time to seize the moment. "You are right. I was just sitting in here trying to snatch some pity time."

He responded by putting his arms around her and holding her

tightly.

"I love you more than when I was stalking you," she said and pulled away. "You have a bad look on your face. What is going on?"

"I was just worried about you."

She sighed. "You are going to have to tell me eventually."

"Your mechanic lover has not died yet. He's still hanging on in ICU."

"I can't believe he's still alive."

"I'm going to kill him, Lynn."

Lynn gasped. "No, he's going to die anyway."

Frank wrapped his arms around her, pulling her back into his chest. "Mr. Wright failed because he was emotionally distraught. I will not fail."

"No!" Lynn struggled but he held her tight. "I'm not going to let some worthless law turn you into a cold-blooded killer."

"I'm not going to be a fruitless boyfriend that just stands around while this deranged asshole comes and carries you off or kills you. This is precisely what the one-kill law was made for."

"You are a successful, talented painter, a loving man. I won't have you turning into some kind of a savage. Please!" She looked up into his eyes. "You are a fruitful boyfriend. Good things come out of you."

He sighed. "I hate it when you twist me around your finger."

"Promise me you won't do anything stupid."

"I promise. I'm just worried about you." Frank brushed a hair away from her eye.

"If you want to help me, go down to the gym and see how my brother is doing. I can't bear to watch that physical therapist torture him."

"Sure."

As soon as the clomping of Frank's boots could no longer be heard, she picked up the phone and called Mr. Wright.

CHAPTER TWENTY-NINE

Henry was learning a lot on his new job. He was finally a man now, bringing home bunches of money. The most important thing he learned was that he needed to suck up to his new boss.

From his first day on the job, Henry had to take in buckets of information. His boss told him the one thing that he better not forget was where the mop was. Henry's co-workers told him what he really better not forget was to snag the last donut before the boss caught him. So he had two things that he better not forget.

By his second day, he had learned more for this job than he did trying to get to level three on the new Avenger World War III game in 3-D. When he got home, he would tell his mom what he learned. Then she would go through some appropriate behavior lessons with him. For example, it wasn't appropriate to tell a lady he thought she was pretty. It wasn't appropriate to tell her she was ugly either. It wasn't appropriate to occupy the toilet too long and if somebody happened to ask him what he was doing in there, it wasn't appropriate to tell them.

His job was to take the big boxes of nose plugs off the truck and place them on shelves, according to what the work orders told him to do. He found his job captivating.

What surprised everybody was that Henry could read. He'd always loved to read. He couldn't do a lot of things well, but he could read. And that really helped with this job.

Henry found he could keep up with the work easily. He could empty the trucks in just a few hours, get inside the break room, get the last donut and eat it before the boss walked in. Then he'd go into the bathroom that nobody seemed to know about and complete his business. By then, it was lunch time and he could schmooze with the other workers.

Henry found them friendly. They taught him how to make it look like he still had a lot of work to do. One showed him how to walk slowly with an abstract look on his face. "You want to look like an intellectual," the man had said.

"What's an intellectual?" Henry asked.

"That's someone who no one would ask what they're doing because they'll get a long philosophical answer back."

"What is philosophical?" Henry asked.

"Anything that is unrealistic and boring."

The answer was complex, but Henry got the message that he should just try to look smart. The look came easy. Henry was a deep thinker. Sometimes he'd put his head down and think about what would be worse, banging your head against concrete or eating dead birds. He never told his co-workers what he was thinking about, but they told him that he had the look down so well that he should put it in his resume.

Henry had to ask what a resume was. He was told that it was the *Reader's Digest* version of your working life. He didn't understand that, but he decided not to ask.

Today, he'd been on the job ten days. He'd gone the past three without getting yelled at. He'd perfected his plan.

His plan was not really to have a long-term job here. His plan was to be able to sneak away so that he could get to the hospital and kill the creep who had killed his friend, Mrs. Wright.

He knew exactly how he was going to do it.

The truck with a full load backed in to the delivery dock. Like he normally did, Henry ran up to the truck as if eager to do his work. The other employees glanced at him, some with envy and some with a rolled eye or two at his enthusiasm. Then they got busy with their own work.

After five minutes of working, Henry announced that he had a large log that he had to get rid of. "That means a huge amount of poop," he stated, in case they hadn't caught on.

"Go profusely, my friend," one dude called out.

"Gross," declared a sour-faced woman.

"That toilet better not be overflowing," yelled his boss.

"It won't," Henry hollered. He ran to the bathroom and slammed the door. Watching through a crack, he waited until nobody was around to see him slip out of the bathroom door, then he sprinted as fast as he could. He had to run three times the length of his living room to make it around the corner and out of their sight. Luckily, winter was here. If this were summer and he had to run like this, he'd look like some of those dried up road kills he'd seen on the side of the road. He had to jam because he wouldn't have much time to make it to the hospital, do his duty and get back to work before he was missed. He really didn't care if he lost his job. If worse came to worse, losing the job wasn't that important. He wanted that creep dead.

Henry continued to run after he hit the road. The box cutter bounced against his leg, solemnly reminding him of his mission.

Gator Guthrie drank himself silly most nights of the week. His job, his life, his work. Everything! Everything drove him to drink. Tonight he had to work a twelve hour shift. It was just after nine p.m. on a Sunday night. Gator knew that nobody bought gas at this time of night. In fact, around here, nobody did anything at this time of night.

Gator ran the gas station convenience store about one hour south of Death Valley. Nights out here could hit freezing temps in the winter. A man had to sip a little sauce now and then to get by. Liquor kept the bones warm and the boredom at bay. Sometimes he overdid it and hallucinated. Tonight . . . well, he just kept chugging.

The room had started to weave when a car drove up. Gator leapt to his feet, trying to snap out of his stupor. He studied the car. He recognized the model, a Honda Accord with Nevada plates. He watched it pull up under the lights and stop by the pumps.

Gator stumbled to the doorway at the same time that the driver got out of the car. The grizzled drunk studied the young man, thinking he'd seen him somewhere. The blonde spiky hair looked familiar. "Hey, Bart Simpson," Gator called, chuckling.

The young man shook his head. "No, I'm not. Bart Simpson is not real. I'm here on special business for the U.S. Government. This is a top secret mission. I need you to give us some gas."

"I'm not allowed to give you gas."

The Bart Simpson look-alike frowned. "Is there somebody here that could authorize it?"

Gator grinned. "It's a thing that would authorize it. Money. You give me money, I suddenly become authorized to give you gas." The world around Gator spun and he suddenly wished that this hallucination would get on his skateboard and ride away. But the young man didn't.

The passenger door opened.

Gator squinted into the lights under the old awning. "Uh-oh," he muttered under his breath. "Here's where I get the shit kicked out of me."

The passenger had a perfectly groomed head of hair. He was a trim older man, but younger than Gator. He moved with authority and when he turned so that the light fully illuminated his face, Gator nearly fell on his butt. "President Pitt," he gasped. "You can't be here."

"I am here and I need a tank of gas. Your country needs you to give me a tank of gas."

Gator slapped himself, leaned against the door frame.

The president was still there.

Gator got him the gas, all the time slapping himself to see if the hallucination would go away. It did not.

In fact, the hallucination thanked him kindly, saying, "I will tell the American people that I was well-received here and treated kindly."

Gator coughed slightly, sending his vision into jitters. "Is this . . . normal . . . for you to do?"

"This is a pretty standard mission protocol trip," the president answered. "Usually I'm in disguise so I'm not recognized. We drive to places that are well-established as bastions of good citizenship and we impose on them in a variety of ways to test their loyalty."

"Uh-huh." Gator's head swam. He couldn't fully comprehend everything that came out of the president's mouth, and by the time he ran the sentence through his head again, the car was gone.

The president of the United States shrieked and cheered like a schoolgirl.

Don joined in.

"A pretty standard special mission protocol trip?" Don asked, laughter kicking its way up his throat. "Where the hell did you pick that one up?"

"I am an acclaimed actor," Brad Pitt said. "And, oh yeah, I am the president. Let's celebrate by going up to the next bar we see and having a drink."

"Hail to the Chief," Don said. "But we cannot go to the nearest bar and have a drink. You'd be recognized. While a bar load of drunks will be declaring you the sneakiest president around, the bartender will be making a call to turn you in."

"I've got a way this will work. We'll both pretend to be pissed out drunk. You go in and announce the president, and I'll come in, as messed up as I can make myself look. They'll laugh into their drinks without giving us a second look."

Don nodded his approval. "I pay you homage for the boldness of your suggestion. But don't push this." He fell silent. The road on either side was black, the moon nearly full as it rose over distant peaks. It was quiet out here in the desert. He cracked his window, letting the wind wake him up a bit.

Beside him, the president sank lower in his seat, the smile slowly slackening his face. "Alright, if I try to catch a little shut-eye?"

"Fine, we won't be anywhere near any lights for another forty-five minutes."

They passed the sign for the turnoff to the famous Rhyolite house made out of bottles. The unmanned fee station for the National Park came up on the left and Don drove brazenly past it, entering Death Valley illegally. He had the president in his front seat. What more could entering a national park without paying possibly do to his rap sheet?

The president stirred in his sleep. "You're a good ally," he muttered.

"Tell that to your henchmen, when they come after me."

"We're partners. They come after me, they come after you," Pitt muttered.

"Thanks, friend." Don drove on.

CHAPTER THIRTY

Mike opened his eyes. A slight beeping sound had awakened him. He looked around the room, trying to figure out where he was. His eyes needed time to grow accustomed to the light and his brain needed time to target his whereabouts.

A woman pushed the door open and bustled in.

He flinched at the sudden noise and piercing light.

She stopped suddenly. "Oh, you're awake."

He nodded. "What are you doing?"

"My routine rounds, but now that you're awake I'll have more work to do." She fixed him with an unblinking stare and reached down to take his wrist.

He yanked his arm away from her. "I asked you what you are doing."

"Generally, when a patient comes out of a coma, we take his pulse."

"I was in a coma?"

"The doctors induced it with medicine."

"Why? What happened?"

"You were shot by a jealous husband. We got the bullet out but it collapsed your lung. The doctors had to put a chest tube in to drain it."

"What's in my nose?"

"Oxygen. Don't take it out, you'll need that to breathe."

"I don't remember anything."

"Nobody ever does."

"What's that supposed to mean? When can I get my clothes?"

"You won't receive your clothes for quite some time. First, you have to get better and then we turn you over to Metro for processing. Apparently, you were shot in a fight over a woman. You tried to kidnap her. You'd be in jail but because of the coma, the hospital agreed that you were secure here without a guard."

"I'm going to call my friend. He'll come pick me up."

"You're not understanding me. You are not going anywhere. You are under-"

Mike flew up in bed, enraged. Excruciating pain filled his chest, knocking him back down again. "Listen, you bitch. I'll kill you if you don't get my clothes."

The nurse jumped back, fairly quickly for such a large round woman. She slapped a button on the wall.

"What did you do, you bitch?"

The door burst open. Mike saw a burly man barge into the room. "I'll help you, nurse."

"He threatened me." She ran out of the room, screaming about calling the doctor.

Mike looked up at the large man staring down at him.

"Shut up," the man said. He ripped off the pulse ox taped to Mike's finger and placed it on his own. In the brief time that the clip was off Mike's finger, the alarm sounded and then quieted instantly when Henry put it on his own. Henry looked at the meter. "You are okay now."

"Why did you do that?"

Henry answered with a pillow over Mike's face. Mike's world darkened. He struggled to catch a breath but the huge guy in the orderly uniform held the pillow firm.

Mike lay quiet now. The terrible man who had killed a sweet little old lady was dead, Henry was sure of it. In the pit of his stomach, Henry felt that he had done a great wrong by killing someone, but killing evil was more favorable than letting it grow. Now, he had to get out of the hospital quickly. He knew that killing one person was okay, but he didn't want to get caught. He didn't want anybody to know he had committed this horrible act.

Suddenly the door opened.

Henry whipped around, his body blocking the man on the bed, his heart beat wildly as a mean-faced nurse looked at him.

"I need you in room three to help us with that woman." She

started to leave but noticed that Henry hadn't jumped to her demands. "Come on, we need your superior strength NOW."

"I have to stay with this guy."

"He looks like he's not going anywhere soon. Let his nurse deal with him."

Henry's heart thumped in his chest.

"We need you in three now. X-ray's called twice! They need that patient," the nurse said.

Relieved that she wasn't going to look at the man in the bed, Henry agreed to come down to room three.

Satisfied, the woman backed out of the room.

Henry waited until he could no longer hear her heavy footsteps going down the hall. He opened the door. Miraculously, the hall was clear. He made a run for the stairwell, got his hand on the door handle when the same nurse hollered at him.

"It's faster if you take the elevator."

Henry grunted something and darted into the stairwell. He took the stairs two at a time. When he hit the bottom floor, he prayed that the nurse would not be standing there waiting for him. He tore off the smock that he had found in the break room, pulled open the door and dashed out into the lobby.

Don had been driving so many hours that his tired brain no longer worked correctly. The road climbed slightly and curved, demanding more energy and concentration than he had to give. The landscape changed from fields to gently sloping dark hills. A sign pointed to Zabriskie Point. He pulled in, needing to rest his brain.

Their car was the only one in the parking lot. The moon lit up the hills, its glow erasing the shadows from the steep trail in front of them. Beyond the trail, the bright stars pinpointed the night, bedazzling Zabriskie Point with their brilliance.

Feeling the car slow, the president stirred in his sleep. Don watched him open his eyes, saw his boyishly handsome face light up at the panoramic moonscape before him. He sat up, stretched and leaned forward. "Wow, that's effective. Let's go hike up there."

The view had done something to jazz up Don's metabolism. He found himself agreeing to a hike up to the top of the hill.

The two men got out of the car, stiff-legged and weary.

"Geez," the president said the minute the cold night air shocked his system.

"Let's just get moving," Don said. "The cold will get us going."

"Long as we keep mobile, we won't freeze. I can't believe how energetic I feel after that little nap." The president stepped along in a lively gait, motioning for Don to follow. "Feels good to finally be on the go."

"We have been on the go."

"Driving, not moving our muscles. A good steep hike will wake up that dormant tiger in you."

"So will inert gases and a match." Don craned his head up to the top of Zabriskie Point. Even from here, he could see wooden platforms built to contain the tourists and support the coin-operated telescopes.

"Come on, man. I've seen old ladies in high heels make this hike."

Don smiled and followed the president. He looked up at the moon and watched the president walk toward it. Keeping up with Brad Pitt proved to be pretty difficult, the president was in good shape. Don lit a cigarette and let Pitt chatter on about delighting in the joys of life and making the most of who you were. Don wasn't paying attention.

The beautiful atmosphere made the president high on poetic pomp. Don let him talk. He thought about his family farm back in Texas. Even in the dead of night, the old homestead wasn't as quiet as Zabriskie's Point. A farm was constantly in motion. The cattle shuffled or snorted in their sleep. There was always at least one pig banging on the trough, scrounging for a late night snack. "Hey, Mister President. I think I need some directions here." Don heard the president stop and turn but darkness prevented him from seeing Pitt's face.

The president walked back toward him, his face floating in the moonlit night. "I am in no position to give directions. My future's a little bleak."

"Should we talk about it?"

"Are you going to give me a sermon about what a bad president I am? Come on, be direct."

"I think I should send you home."

The president's face tightened and Don could almost see icicles forming in his eyes. "You want to make a speech to me about what I should be doing and what I did wrong? Go ahead, lecture away. But before you preach to me, you better make sure things are perfect with your own life."

"There's nothing wrong with my life."

"Well, I salute you. But weren't you the one who got a call from your father telling you to kill me?"

Don swallowed and turned away.

"You can't even face me."

Don shook his head. "Come on, let's just go."

"You want to go back to your father so he can put a ring in your nose and lead you around. You're not even a man. You just do what-
"

Don punched Brad Pitt, knocking his presidential words down his chief executive throat.

The president staggered and spat out a wad of blood. "Fists will solve everything, won't they?"

"I don't need your judgment."

"I have a right to judge you. I saved your life. I pulled you from the burning building. You owe it to me to listen to what I have to say."

"What do you want from me?"

The president crossed his arms over his chest like a prissy schoolgirl. "What do *you* want?"

"I want out of this stupid little escapade we're on."

"I thought we were having fun. Did your mommy put you on suspension and then die before she could take you off? Is that why you're so afraid to be so far away from home?"

Don charged, ramming the president. "You had seven years to go until your retirement and you're pulling this stupid little stunt."

The president stumbled back, closer to the edge of the cliff. Don stopped him by grabbing a fistful of the president's shirt. Instinctively, President Pitt swung, clipping Don on his injured shoulder. The two men hit the dirt, the president's head hanging over the cliff. "Your parents made a little mama's boy out of you," Pitt taunted, the muscles in his neck stretched taut with the effort of supporting his head.

All Dan had to do was leap up, shove the president and he'd go down the cliff. And then it dawned on him that that was exactly what Pitt was trying to get him to do.

"Oh, wait a minute." Don jumped to his feet. "I know what

you're doing." He reached down, grabbed a handful of the president's oxford shirt and hauled him up.

The president wasn't helping. In fact, he fought Don off. He threw a left punch, clipping Don in the eye. Don lost his grip.

The president flew backward over the cliff.

Don looked down the ravine and saw the president's mangled twisted body laying at the bottom. "Crap," he screamed into the night air. Pacing back and forth madly, he screamed manically. He stopped every few steps and looked over the cliff, but there was the president's form, folded and still at the base of the mountain.

Don looked up at the moonlight over Zabriskie Point. The deck and parking lot were empty, not a soul around except his and the president's. The president had gotten Don to push him over the cliff on the pretense of an argument. Don knew that he had to get out of here now. He could make it back to Vegas in darkness. He had a full tank of gas, the cover of the inky night and only two small towns between here and McCarran Airport. He walked to the car, got in and turned the key. He felt like singing when the engine roared to life. Don threw the car into gear and ripped out of the parking lot, hitting the curves as quickly as he could. Once the road straightened out, he had time to think. What if the president wasn't dead? Don hadn't climbed down the cliff to check the president for a pulse or any signs of life. Don was sure that the president had wanted to die. He drove on, but still, guilt ate at him.

CHAPTER THIRTY-ONE

For the third time that day, Big John found his face smashed into Linebacker's chest, grunting with the effort to stand up tall. But he couldn't. Each time he tried, he ended up plopping back in his wheelchair.

"We're going to do it again," Linebacker said, gently.

The softening in the tough physical therapist's voice and his pity fueled Big John. With a last effort, he gripped the bars, hauled himself up, and pushed his knees back into a locked position. He couldn't do that before.

"Wow!" Linebacker said. He stood back, letting Big John stand on his own.

"A wealth of emotion from you, my friend," Big John huffed out. Talking and holding himself in the locked position was difficult. Despite his concentration on keeping his elbows straight, movement from the side of the room caught his eye.

Frank, the love of his sister's life, stood watching him with a goofy smile on his face. Big John couldn't decide whether he resented or admired the guy. This guy had ignored his sister for years, but then again, she could be pretty bad when she didn't have her meds balanced.

"Please, enjoy our opulence," Big John said of the beige room. He sat down heavily, receiving a dirty look from Linebacker.

Frank looked around the gym. Beige carpet, beige mat tops. Even the open bag of Fritos sprawled across one of the mats did nothing to add color to the room. His grin widened. "An opulence of resources to get you back on your"-

Frank choked on the last word and suddenly became interested in everything around the room. He looked back at Big John. ". . . everything to get you better."

"You impressed, man?" Big John asked.

"Very much so," Frank answered.

"I'd be more impressed if we could get back to work," Linebacker said.

"Sorry, I gotta go. I'm this guy's bitch for another forty minutes," Big John said.

Frank coughed and looked at Linebacker.

Linebacker stared at him, a level gaze that didn't say anything.

"Okay, well, I'll go back to your room. I'll let your sister know how you're doing."

"Ahh, she's probably on the phone with some sales agent. Besides, I need a go-between in case this guy gets rough."

Frank glanced at Linebacker. He had arms the size of Frank's waist, except they were made up of muscle, not flab. "I'll just spy on you from my corner back here. I don't want to be the cause of you not walking so I'll just be quiet and watch. He glanced at Linebacker, whose frown had deepened. "I think your physical therapist means business."

"Yeah, I'm afraid of him, too. He's only allowed to use brute force on me, so you're pretty safe."

"I'll stay over here."

"Suit yourself. If I take any steps my sister's going to be sorry she missed it."

"You're not going to take any steps, if you don't get off your butt." Linebacker scowled down at him.

"Yes, ma'am." Big John's hands shot out quickly. He gripped the bars and hefted himself to his feet. "I did it again!" he cheered. Behind him, he heard Frank clapping and then the sound of his retreating feet. The door closed quietly.

"I guess it's just you and me, kid." Linebacker grinned down at him.

Mr. Wright arrived at the county hospital an hour later. He signed in, but when he put down the patient's name, whispered turmoil broke out among the volunteers.

"Don't send him up there," one hissed.

"He's got to know."

"I know but"- The speaker looked up at him. Her cheeks glowed red.

"I'm an old man," Mr. Wright informed them. "I'm going to go sit over there until the three of you can agree on something."

The three flustered young ladies took a few more minutes of arguing before deciding on a course of action. One of them picked up the phone. Covering her mouth, she whispered into the phone, all the while casting furtive glances up at him.

"You don't have to worry about me hearing you. At my age, you could scream in my ear and I wouldn't know you were there."

A few minutes later, a middle-aged man dressed in a sharply creased suit walked up to him.

"Not good," Mr. Wright muttered under his breath.

The man, speaking in soft, hesitant words, introduced himself as the hospital administrator. "Please, come with me," he said.

"Can't you just tell me what you have to tell me out here?"

The hospital administrator looked at him, worry and discomfort etching his young face into one of middle age.

"Oh, all right." Mr. Wright nodded his assent. He followed the man down a hall to an office where he could receive the bad news. Mr. Wright allowed himself to be ushered into a room decorated in a harmony of soft browns and soothing colors. He was waived toward a compact soft little chair that would suck all his masculine dignity the minute he tried to get out of it.

The man sat behind a large desk opposite Mr. Wright. He folded his hands and peered deeply at the old man, assessing him.

"Are we going to make some kind of a blood pact or what?" Mr. Wright asked. He remained standing.

The man laughed nervously.

"You gonna tell me something now?"

The man twisted in his chair. "So here's the deal. Your friend is not in his room."

Mr. Wright's heart beat faster. He leaned forward. "Mike is my son."

The administrator practically sputtered.

Mr. Wright tried not to smile. This was going to be fun. "Did they send my son someplace where everyone has matching toe tags?"

"No, no, nothing like that. He was . . . attacked this morning."

Mr. Wright said nothing. It took all he had to not jump up and down for joy.

The administrator read it as shock. "I'm very sorry. Nobody knew he had a father living in the area. We would have called you."

"Where's my son?"

"In accordance with our policy, we have to ship him out to another hospital. He's in ICU at Valley Hospital. We could call a cab for you if you are too upset to drive."

Mr. Wright nodded.

As soon as Frank left, Lynn darted out of her brother's room and headed toward the stairwell on the opposite side of the building. Taking the stairs two at a time, she made it to the lobby. Trying not to draw attention to herself, she forced her body to slow down and walk calmly through the lobby.

She pushed open the outside door and the gusty December wind pushed back, sending her hair flying in all directions. Dust flew in her eyes. The hospital had been built in an open patch of desert and nothing blocked the wind. She pulled one of her famous nose plugs out of her purse, but the flimsy material flew out of her hands. A nurse walking toward her gave her a sympathetic smile and continued on her way.

Lynn rushed on. She had a place to go and a job to do. She hopped into her eight-year-old Soul and revved the engine, singing praises to Korean carmakers. Within minutes she had hit the freeway and was heading toward the Strip. She made it to the county hospital in eighteen minutes. When she pulled up to UMC Hospital, she saw Mr. Wright standing in a taxi lane. She honked and pulled up to the curb.

His face brightened when he saw her car. With confidence and a zip to his step, he hustled over to her. Leaning down, he stuck his craggy face into her ear. "Come on, let's go kill the motherfucker." He hopped into her car.

"Where to?" she asked with alacrity. Her eagerness widened his smile.

"Make haste to Valley Hospital. That's where they moved him after someone tried to strangle him this morning."

"I know who tried to do that. I got the call from my foreman that Henry was missing this morning. I'm going to give the big galoot a raise."

Mr. Wright grinned, then looked out at the traffic racing by. "I'm going to enjoy this."

In a turmoil over what to do, Frank decided to do nothing. He just went home. He couldn't stand being in that hospital gym any more, despite Big John's optimism. He couldn't control Lynn.

Frank drove through the city streets, the western mountain range in his rearview mirror, and the outline of the city in his windshield. He loved this city. He loved his life now. Who would have thought that he could have fallen in love with his stalker?

Frank drove up to his apartment, ready for a beer and one of his hidden secret movies, the kind that he would never admit to Lynn that he watched. He planned to put his headphones on and close off the world for as long as he could.

But what he saw when he reached his apartment complex sounded an alarm bell in his head. Danger. Tanya, all five-foot-nothing of her, stood on her balcony, watching. Apprehension scraped his very core like sharp fingernails on a chalkboard. He locked the car, sighed and turned around slowly, hoping she would be gone.

She hadn't budged.

His unease increased as he climbed the first three steps and she still had not said anything. This was serious. Heavy with dread, he continued trudging up the stairs until he reached her apartment level.

"What?" he asked. Even her silence perturbed him. But then he saw her face.

Instead of her usual snide expression, tears poured out of red-rimmed eyes. She looked so terrible that she should have come with a warning before anybody bared their eyes on her.

"What's wrong with you?" His words came out slowly and full of dread. He really wanted that beer and movies he'd been thinking about.

"I think that Henry went to kill the man who murdered Mrs. Wright."

Frank glanced up at Mr. Wright's apartment and then quickly looked around. Nobody was out and it was cold enough that people wouldn't have their windows open. He knew murder was legal. His nervousness was instinctive. He was, after all, raised in a time when murder was morally wrong and illegal. "I'm coming in." He opened the door of her apartment and slipped in, closing the door behind him. Knitted owls stared at him from all four walls. He shook off the chill they gave him and made his way over to her balcony door. "Get in here," he urged.

She obeyed immediately, making a beeline for the battered couch. With shaking hands, she lit a cigarette. He watched the bright spot reach her mouth, flare up and recede as she exhaled smoke into the room.

"Why would Henry try to kill that man?"

She looked at him for a long moment, then spoke. "Henry's not the most brilliant guy in the world, but he is the most devoted. When I got the phone call from his employer that he was missing, I knew what he was up to."

The sudden ring of her phone made them both jump. She stared at Frank, then picked up.

Frank watched the worry lines etched on her face relax into a smile.

"Okay," she said. "Yes, I'll talk to him when he gets home." She hung up, wiped her eyes and stubbed out her cigarette. A plume of smoke escaped, drifting its way up into the ceiling. "They found him in the bathroom. He's back to work."

Frank nodded but something hung in the air between them.

"I feel kind of stupid. I guess I just panicked."

Frank didn't know what to say, but he sensed that she was waiting for some form of comfort. He said the first thing that came to mind. "You know, killing is legal now."

She looked up sharply. Frank froze. He didn't know what her beliefs were.

"Would you like a strong drink?" she asked.

And suddenly, the idea of boozing it up with her felt right.

She gave him a mischievous grin. "I got some rotgut that will carve a hole in your esophagus, blow out your asshole and leave you wanting more."

"Works for me."

CHAPTER THIRTY-TWO

Four hours later Henry arrived home. He put his key in the lock, pressed open the door and it banged Frank on the head. Frank's large body lay on the floor like a corpse, his mother's smaller body curled behind it. From deep in his chest, a cry of anguish sprang out.

His mother stirred. She sat up, rubbed her eyes and stared at her son for a good long time.

Alcoholic fumes permeated the air. Henry wrinkled his nose and looked at his mother for an explanation.

"We got into the strong stuff."

Frank remained where he was. Henry stared at him for a few seconds. The rise and fall of Frank's chest reassured Henry. "Is Mr. Frank an alcohol addict?"

"No, but he's so drunk right now that if you hummed a few bars, he could fake it." She burst out into peals of inebriated laughter.

From the floor, Frank groaned and begged her to shut up.

"Mr. Frank looks like the wino who lives in the park."

A day's grizzle grew on Frank's chin. Half his shirt had come untucked and one of his shoes was missing. Tanya couldn't remember how that had happened. For this, she was grateful. She poked him with her manicured toe. "You have to go home."

A loud, low, pitiful moan sounded from Frank.

"Will he die?"

"I wouldn't be that lucky," Frank mumbled. With his throbbing head clenched in his hands, he pulled himself up to his feet. "Your mother got me completely snockered. We talked about all of our problems, divvied up the blame and then drank some more." He sat at the kitchen table. "Mind if I sit here and try not to vomit?"

Tanya ignored him. "Henry," she said so softly that Henry had to squat down to her level to hear. "I know what you did today."

Henry pulled back, fear and worry etched in his face. "I'm sorry. Mama, I had to do it."

"Shh. Don't say any more." She put her arms around him protectively. She looked over at Frank, who had managed to sit without holding his head.

"Everything's fine," he said. "Except that my head feels like something that was used to play Fetch with."

Tanya turned her attention back to her son. "They called here to tell me you spent almost the whole afternoon in the bathroom."

Henry looked at her, amazement on his face. "They said I was in the bathroom?"

Tanya nodded. "You are going to go back to work, and you are not ever going to spend that much time in the bathroom again. Do you understand me?" She drew her man-child into her arms, holding him tightly until he fidgeted.

Valley Hospital was a large medical center four miles from the Strip. The lighted sign and lobby welcomed visitors, even in the wee hours of the morning. Beyond its circle of light stretched the once-nice middle-class neighborhood. Back in the day, the houses displayed their pride of ownership with fresh coats of color and armies of yard decorations. Now they looked like they were allergic to paint and lawn tools.

The gnarly old man and the thin young lady walked into the hospital together, past people in the waiting room who were dripping and coughing bodily fluids. The couple made it to the desk and waited while the receptionist ran out of things to fiddle with. When she finally looked up, they demanded to see Mike.

The woman gave them an antagonistic smile. "No visitors. He's in protective custody."

Mr. Wright's face crumpled. He suddenly looked like an old man, destroyed.

Alarm replaced hostility on the receptionist's face. "Sir? Are you all right? Shall I call a doctor?"

Lynn put an arm around him, expecting him to collapse. He held tightly to the counter.

"My son, my son," he wailed. "I'm never going to see my son again."

"Help him to a chair." The receptionist picked up a phone.

Lynn tightened her arms around Mr. Wright, leading him to a chair. He held his own weight, not leaning on her a bit.

"She on the phone?" he whispered.

"We're ten feet away. You can see for yourself, unless you've suddenly been struck blind with grief."

He winked at her. "Pretty good performance, huh?"

"Great one," Lynn agreed. "I'd give my whole allowance to see another of your performances. I almost forgot that he wasn't really your son."

The receptionist waved Lynn over. "You've been granted a visit." She gave them the room number and directions.

Before she'd even finished, Mr. Wright, forgetting he had been near to fainting from grief, shot out of his chair and smoked a path toward the elevators. He left Lynn standing there.

"Does he know how bad his son is? He's in a coma." The receptionist spoke in the soft whispered tones used when referring to the dead.

Lynn could never figure out that soft speech around dead people. This was the same woman who had just shouted at two live people. Lynn knew she should appear sad and worried. She really tried. "That's too bad. At least the nurses get to share his tray."

The receptionist snapped. "They don't do that."

Lynn nodded, wondering why the woman was angry. Maybe Lynn's voice wasn't as soft as she had intended. "You're probably right. It's pretty shitty food and pretty small portions. Well, nice talking to you but I better go catch up with my friend." She zipped away, reaching Mr. Wright at the elevators.

The doors opened and they stepped on. Mr. Wright avoided looking at her.

"Are we really going to do this?" she asked.

"*I'm* going to do this," he corrected, sternly.

"Right."

Mr. Wright sighed. "I have to admit, I'm a little nervous."

"Of course you are. We've been taught all our lives that killing is wrong. God hates murderers. And murder is pretty gruesome."

"You are not helping."

Suddenly they were at the sixth floor. The elevator doors opened to display long glistening white halls and a bustling nurses' station. He stepped out and froze.

Lynn joined him.

The elevator took off.

"We haven't committed a crime yet." Mr. Wright looked over at her.

"Not true. I parked in the red zone. That is still illegal."

"You should have mentioned that. I would have hurried the night's festivities along somehow."

Lynn nudged him gently. "I suggest we get on with this, that is, if we are still going to do . . . this."

Mr. Wright kept staring at the nurses. "Maybe we shouldn't."

A weight lifted off Lynn's shoulders. She whipped around and stabbed at the elevator button. "Okay, let's go."

Mr. Wright looked relieved. "I just want to get out of here. What was I thinking?"

The doors slid open with a loud, resounding DING.

They stepped back toward the elevators together, bumping shoulders in their haste.

"Hold it," a stern voice called out.

Turning slowly, the two found themselves face to face with two policemen. Behind them, the door to the elevator they had almost escaped in, shut.

"We'll need you to come with us," the middle-aged police officer said. He needed a haircut and a good night's sleep. He also looked like he wasn't in the mood to argue.

They followed him away from the elevators and around the corner and down another hall. The other uniform followed at a discreet distance. The leading policeman stopped in front of a hospital room and pushed the door open without knocking.

There, in front of them, lay Mike the Mechanic. Bruises decorated his collar, but the biggest shock was the tube sticking out of the middle of his neck. Lynn understood immediately that the noisy machine was breathing for him. Behind her, the old man gasped and stumbled.

"Monster," Mr. Wright spat. He looked at the officer. "What are you doing here?"

"We were just about to ask you that."

"We're practically neighbors." She nodded toward Mr. Wright. "I drove him here to check on his son."

"We forgot to bring flowers," Mr. Wright added.

The police officer gave him a withering glare. "Sir, I am approaching the tail end of my sense of humor. I'm verging on a nervous breakdown. I have wasted the last half of my career carting this man in and out of jails."

"He's a real piece of work," the younger officer snarled.

"Neal, please." He glared at his partner. "And now my captain has put me on duty to protect this guy. Somebody tried to kill him."

"Murder is legal," Lynn informed him.

The officer's bloodshot eyes fell on her. "One murder is legal. As policemen, it is still our duty to protect people. And this piece of garbage has not gone to trial yet."

"He killed my wife," Mr. Wright growled.

"So I guess you're not really his father?"

"What do you want from us?" Lynn shot Mr. Wright a warning look.

The policeman sighed. "We are supposed to question anybody who comes up to see him. We are supposed to stay here and guard him." He ran a hand through his hair. "He's supposed to be top priority with us. On the other hand, say we heard someone yelling bloody murder from outside the hall." He turned his head toward the doorway. When he turned back toward them, he made eye contact. His next words were slow and deliberate. "We would be justified to run out of the room to save that person, wouldn't we?"

The air hung heavy among the four.

"Maybe one of you would like to go and one of you would like to stay and talk with the patient," the policeman further prompted.

Sweat glistened on Mr. Wright's forehead. He looked at Lynn meaningfully, then nodded. "Lynn, go bring the car closer. I will stay and talk to my son."

Lynn hesitated.

"Go on," Mr. Wright urged. "Do it."

"Be careful out there," the other officer said. His right eye twitched.

Lynn could have sworn that the officer had winked at her. She stood up and took a last look at the monster in the bed. He had loved her. Sick and twisted as he was, he had seen something in her that he had loved. Although he had done something terrible, she, of all people, understood mental illness. Even though murder was legal, she wasn't sure she had the stomach for this. These thoughts ran through her head while she walked down the hall. Murder was wrong, notwithstanding the fact that it was legal. But she thought about the anguish Mr. Wright had gone through. She thought about Mrs. Wright's cheerful face. She thought about the harried-looking police officer trying to put Mike the criminal away to keep him from committing crimes and now having to protect him.

Thou shalt not kill. This saying ran through her head.

Her hand twitched on the cold hard door knob of the stairwell. She pulled it open and stepped in, but left her heel in the doorway so that the door didn't close completely.

She wasn't killing anybody.

Lynn took a deep breath, filling her lungs with air. And then she let it out in a primal deafening scream.

CHAPTER THIRTY-THREE

The next day dawned bright and beautiful. The sun shone into Mr. Wright's window. He woke feeling rested and peaceful, as if God had combined the serenity of the islands with the excitement of Las Vegas. His heart held a blend of passion and a new zest for life. Wanting to mingle with the natives, he knocked on Tanya's door.

She answered in a faded brown t-shirt, bloodshot eyes and an expression that would separate eggs.

"It's done," he said, gleefully. "It's done."

"It's seven a.m.," she snapped, attempting to slam the door.

He stuck his foot inside her apartment, stopping her from shutting him out. "I'm ready to attack life again," he said, his gusto pouring out over her.

"How can I incorporate that with something I care about?" she asked, drily. She tried to slam the door again.

He pushed his way into the apartment. "I murdered the mechanic."

"What?" Tanya backed up quickly.

"I murdered the mechanic who murdered Eva," he said, enunciating his words. "I feel so good."

Tanya glanced back toward the hallway. She lowered her voice. "Henry thinks he killed Mike."

"He attempted, but I succeeded."

Tanya sat down on the barstool. She put her head in her hands.

This was not the reaction Mr. Wright expected. "You are not happy?"

"I'm torn, Mr. Wright. I'm really torn up. You come in here like a delighted disciple of death and I just don't feel okay in my heart about cheering for this."

"I'm going to give you some counsel culled from the wisdom of my years. You know that Mike the Mechanic represented everything wrong. He murdered an old woman because she got in his way. She died a brutal, bloody death because she advised Lynn to be wary of him. Eva was your friend, you loved her. We all lost her. And now this man, wanted by the police his whole life, walks free. Do you think he's going to stop at one murder? So, yes, I'm the deputy of death and, no, I'm not going to apologize for it."

At the end of his speech, they were both crying.

Tanya looked up at him. "I understand," she managed.

The two embraced.

Tanya walked him out. When she opened the door, dazzling sunlight lit up her face and her surroundings.

"We're going to be okay," Mr. Wright told her.

Turning toward the sun, she smiled.

Mr. Wright continued up the stairs. He knocked on Frank's door. He had to knock several times before he heard Frank's heavy feet clomping toward the door. Cursing surrounded the sounds of fumbling fingers twisting open the locks.

Mr. Wright would not be deterred. As soon as the door opened he spoke. "I've come here to tell you to grab that girl with all your strength. Marry and hold onto her. Take everything that life gives you and work your fingers down to icicle points for the things that life doesn't give you easily. That's what I want you to learn from me, my boy."

Frank looked at his watch. "It's not even eight a.m. Man, you're ambitious."

"Life is too short not to appreciate everything you have while you have it," Mr. Wright said forcefully.

Frank squinted at him. "Why're you so pushy with all this sunshine shit?" Frank muttered and rubbed his forehead.

"Because if you lie down like a doormat, life will be the dirty shoes that wipe the shit from their soles onto you."

"I'm sorry. It's too difficult to concentrate on inspirational stuff while the dregs of alcohol are weighing down my brain. I think I'm going to have to be bold and slam the door in your face. Otherwise, my head is going to fall off."

Mr. Wright threw back his head and laughed lustily. "When that hangover loosens its hold on you and stops making you so apathetic, you'll remember my words and be grateful for them."

The door slammed. Hard.

Mr. Wright's easy smile remained on his face. He wasn't going to go home. He was going to go have breakfast with the guys, something he hadn't done in a long time.

With a bounce in his stride, he headed down the stairs.

In the end, it was Henry who saw Big John take his first steps. Earlier, he'd been in his room and heard the conversation between his mom and Mr. Wright. He'd known Mike the bad man was dead. But in his heart, things hadn't all been cleared up. His new friend, Big John, was still in a hospital, trying to walk.

So Henry, with his newfound knowledge of the world, learned the bus schedule. He slipped out of the house while his mother slept off her hangover.

He arrived in the hospital's gym to find Big John sitting in a wheelchair between two bars. He was staring at a huge red-headed guy with a name badge and a snarly look. The two men did not even notice Henry.

"I can stand by myself," Big John said, sounding like a pouty two-year-old.

"That doesn't amount to anything if you can't walk," the redheaded angry-looking man said. Henry made a big shadow himself, but this guy was even bigger. He barely fit between the parallel bars. His angry eyes focused on Big John and he said, "Come to me."

Henry watched, transfixed, as Big John pulled himself up to his full height, braced his arms on the bar, and shifted his weight to his real leg. With effort, he kicked the fake leg ahead.

The big redhead smiled, but he didn't come any closer. "Lock that knee, shift your weight onto it."

Big John did so, looking like a gigantic toddler on Quaaludes. But he did it again and again and finally he reached the redheaded worker. The two men stood facing each other.

"Was that not the greatest thing any of your patients has ever done?" Big John grinned down on the slightly shorter man.

The redhead nodded. "Equal to, anyway." He waved at someone and they pushed the wheelchair behind Big John, who was still grinning widely.

"That was like running a triple triathlon," Big John said, breathlessly.

"It was approximately equal to a stubborn donkey doing what he was told for once."

"Ouch!" Big John said, still with a huge grin on his face. "You got me to walk. Someday you're going to grow into a really decent therapist."

Around the room, people laughed.

"And someday you're going to mature into a fine version of an adult," the redhead said. "Now get your mass out of my gym."

"That's the extent of your praise for my first step ever taken?"

"The grand total of my praise will come in the bill. You'll see the cost of having to put up with you. We charge for the whole she-bang."

"What? You're charging me for the hole she banged? When did that happen?"

"You have a visitor."

"Why didn't you tell me?" Big John whipped around and smiled when he saw Henry. "Henry, my man! Did you see that?"

Henry nodded.

"Well, as one of the humans to witness my progress, what did you think?"

"It was kind of slow."

This made the redhead laugh.

Big John scowled at the redhead and turned to Henry. "Henry, this is Linebacker, my physical therapist. This man is a true miracle. He can walk, talk and completely function without a heart."

Linebacker nodded politely to Henry then turned back to his victim. "Tomorrow, the exercises increase. We need to intensify your program."

"Why?" Big John whined. "Why do we have to expand on something that takes forever as it is?"

"Henry said it. You walk kind of slow. We need you to develop some speed. We'd take your wheelchair away from you but at the speed you walk now, the food would be gone by the time you get to the cafeteria."

Big John's lip pouted out. Henry thought he was going to ask another "why?" question, but he simply looked down at his shoes.

Linebacker didn't seem phased by Big John's downtrodden look. "I'll go over next week's lineup later, when there aren't any witnesses around." He snickered at his own joke, then turned and walked out of the room.

"What's wrong with him?" Henry asked.

"The condensed version is that he is an asshole. But enough about him. So Henry, you got to see me walk."

Henry grinned down at him. "Yeah, I'm sorry I told him you were slow."

Big John waved a big paw in the air. "Forget about it. How are you doing? And what brings you to this neck of the woods?"

"I had to see if you were okay."

"I'm great. I'm walking. How's your mom?"

Henry shrugged. "I don't know." Henry told him about the conversation between Mr. Wright and his mom.

Big John thought about what Henry had told him. He seemed to choose his words carefully, like Henry's grandparents did when Henry asked them questions about what his mother was like in high school. "It sounds like the old man got his revenge," Big John allowed.

Henry nodded. Thoughts weighed heavily on his mind. "Big John, do you hate Mr. Wright?"

Big John's smile dropped. "Henry, can you get me out of these parallel bars?" He released his brakes and motioned for Henry to pull him backward.

Henry pulled him out from between the parallel bars. He repeated his question. "Do you like Mr. Wright?"

Big John, cornered, answered. "I'd like him better if I was sitting here with matching legs. You ask hard questions. It's like asking Mrs. Lincoln how she liked the play."

Henry thought about that, and decided that he didn't really understand what Big John meant. Henry knew he was a grown-up now, but he was still learning to talk like one.

"Come on. Let's go hang out in my room." Big John pushed on his wheels, sending the wheelchair spinning out of the gym.

Henry walked briskly to keep up with Big John. Keeping his eyes focused on Big John's wheelchair helped him avoid looking at the other patients they passed in the hall. Some of them were drooling, some of them still had nasty leftover food in their teeth.

"Beautiful place, huh?" Big John called out over his shoulder as he rounded a corner.

"Yeah," Henry managed. He followed Big John into a fairly large room with sliding glass doors leading out onto a sunny patio. Away from the pathetic patients, the place looked like a nice hotel room.

Big John zipped toward the bed, then whipped around to face Henry. He patted the edge of the shimmery brown bedspread, gesturing for Henry to have a seat, then waited until Henry sat down before he spoke. He looked very seriously at Henry and said, "I want you to listen to me, Henry. I forgive the old man." Big John glanced down at his missing leg in case Henry didn't know what he was talking about. "I understand why he did it. I could get even with him, but this chain of killings has to stop."

"A chain of killing? Like if you kill the old man then my mom would kill you, then Lynn would kill my mom and then-"

Big John held up his hand. "Enough. You see how terrible it is? I don't care if killing is legal. We, as humans, have to learn to stand up and say that we know what is right and what is wrong. And I've decided to let it start with me."

Henry felt proud of himself. He was beginning to understand how grown-ups spoke. He knew this was serious, so he made a joke like most adults do when things were really serious. "You just have to learn to stand up."

To his delight, Big John smiled.

The evenings shadows grew longer, darkening the room. Big John grabbed the remote and turned the TV on, casting a bluish light into the room. Drum beats boomed through the speakers, announcing the evening news.

The beach-blonde newscaster came on, reading the news with a gleam in her eyes. "Eyewitness News has just received breaking news on the whereabouts of President Pitt."

"My God-" Big John leaned forward in his chair.

Henry's eyes swiveled toward the screen.

"The President's body has been found at the bottom of a cliff in Death Valley."

CHAPTER THIRTY-FOUR

Frank slept off his agony. When he woke up, his hangover pain was gone, but the odd visit from Mr. Wright earlier that morning left him in distress.

Somebody knocked on his door, using an awkward uneven beat that he knew came from Henry. He fought off pangs of hunger and answered the door.

Henry barged in like a freight car plowing through a wheat field.

Frank moved out of his way, shutting the door as he heard the thud of Henry's body hitting the couch.

A cloud hovered over Henry's face, heavy and dark. "I killed that horrible man who killed Mrs. Wright." His troubled face suddenly appeared like a stressed-out adult, the innocence gone.

Anguish descended on Frank. He had no idea what to say to this young man until suddenly a light went on in his head and he did know what to say. In his mind, he saw Mr. Wright's angular bony smile, the arthritic hands gesturing wildly in the air, his cracked lips spouting poetry and clichéd advice. Frank now understood what had happened. He pointed at Henry. "You didn't kill Mike." He pointed toward Mr. Wright's apartment. "That bony old man killed him." Frank remembered how the old man looked transformed today walking into Frank's apartment singing praises to everything and everybody.

"Mr. Wright's too skinny to kill anybody."

Frank laughed. Love fueled his laugh. "You'll understand someday when you find love. You'll understand."

Henry nodded. "I feel better now."

"Good, go home and have a life."

Henry stood, then hovered by the door.

"Yes, Henry?"

"Did you hear that the president was dead?"

"Yeah, I did. We tried to save him, didn't we? We did our best." A small smile formed on Henry's mouth. "I am never going to kill anybody."

"That's quite an announcement, Henry."

"When I thought I'd killed that bad man, I didn't feel good. I felt my insides burning, like all the liquid in my body would just come bursting out."

"Thank you for that report, buddy. That was quite a statement."

Henry nodded. When he looked at Frank, his eyes were piercing. "Do you have any statements for me?"

Frank froze for a minute but he took a deep breath and seemed to be thinking. "As a matter of fact, I have a few. First of all, I'm going to ask Lynn to marry me. And secondly, the two of us are going to live here and look after Mr. Wright. And the final thing is, I'm never going to kill anybody."

"Why?" Henry asked, but this time Frank was ready.

"Because it's the right way to live."

Satisfied, Henry reached his hand out to Frank and the two men shook. Opening the door, Henry stepped out into the sunshine. Far overhead, a plane flew, its nose pointed downward. "I'm going to fly one of those, that's what I'm going to do."

"I hope you have the time of your life."

"I will. I'll be really high." Laughing at his own joke, Henry walked out in the blazing new day.

ABOUT THE AUTHOR

Debbie Prince resides in Las Vegas with her boyfriend, John, and parrot Jinx. She currently works as a Physical Therapist Assistant, treating patients with physical and mental disorders. A member of Tall Club International, Ms. Prince has served on the board as social director and has also run the Miss. Tall International Pageant. She grew up in Southern California, and has a B.A in Journal.ism. Ms. Prince has worked as a nanny in Japan and Germany. She has ridden her bike across Europe and the United States. She believes in the ten commandments and, while she likes Brad Pitt, she would not stalk him.

Made in the USA
San Bernardino, CA
25 April 2016